COLONY LAUNCH

JON DEL ARROZ

RISLANDIA BOOKS

ONE DAY AT A TIME

Earth, San Francisco, CA.

Flashing lights blinked in front of the stage, so many photos being taken by both drone bots and human photographers alike that it would blind someone unaccustomed to such scenes. As governor of North America, Antony Lemkin had vast experience with press conferences, reporters swarming like bees around their hive.

Antony sucked in his bottom lip and glanced at his wife, Bethany. "Are you sure we should go through with this?" he asked.

"We have to take a stand," Bethany said. "This is the best way to get attention and a policy discussion going." She looked as beautiful as ever, wide brown eyes locked on him, seeming as afraid as he was. If only he could provide her solace in this moment, but as soon as he took the podium, their lives would change forever.

Antony tugged on his coat to make sure it didn't bunch and then stepped forward to the microphone. He placed his clammy, sweaty hands on the podium, gripping it so they wouldn't slip. God, he hoped he made the right choice.

"People of North America and of all of the Federated Earth, good evening. I am Governor Antony Lemkin of North America, and I appreciate you taking time this evening to allow me to speak my mind as an elected official and as a citizen." He paused to take a breath. "Last week, Earth's senate took action to remove all Aryshan people—civilian and military—from within our controlled systems. Since then, military conflicts have been escalating with no end in sight. I stand tonight to oppose this action taken by Federated Earth and to condemn acts that would lead our people into a deadly war.

"Without taking a formal vote, our world has proceeded into a constitutional crisis, and further, the senate and president appear complicit in allowing this overreach of power which could cost the lives of millions." Antony blinked, momentarily distracted by a monitor which displayed a holo feed of his speech back to him.

He looked professional as ever, a team of holovid makeup professionals having worked him over prior to the speech. His salt-and-pepper hair slicked back, a light tan complexion of his skin from his half-Pacific Islander and half-European descent, all wrapped in a finely tailored blue suit with a lapel pin of North America's flag.

A news ticker flashed at the bottom of the image. Four dead in an explosion in east-Boston, cause unknown. Stocks down one and a half percent from the day before. The image of Governor Lemkin paused, hesitating. He usually spoke so smoothly, even without a prompter transmitted to his optics. His natural form of speaking had captivated voters for decades.

Antony looked directly into the camera, putting on the hard expression he'd earned from many political battles over the years. This would be his last. "After discussing these matters at length with my advisors and my wife Bethany, I've determined there is no path forward to fight against these policies of endless war. And so I find I can no longer effectively and in good conscience perform the job of Governor of North America." A pause for a heavy breath. "Therefore, effective immediately, I resign my position in protest of Federated Earth's war against the Aryshans."

The reporters broke out into a chaos that Antony had rarely seen, even in hotly contested elections or amidst so many scandals his allies or opponents had been involved in over the years. His stepping-down would be bigger news than all of those scandals combined. For the first time in history, a governor of a full continent would not finish his term of his own free will. Several camera drones flew by to get different close up images of Antony for the holos, becoming part of the image and story themselves. More than a dozen hands rose in the audience, and others simply shouted their questions to try to get the scoop before any of the others.

"I will not be taking questions at this time," Antony said, waving off the reporters. "Please reflect on my actions here and do what it takes as a society to end this cycle of pointless wars. Thank you. It has been an honor serving on behalf of North America. Goodnight."

He turned to step away from the podium, Secret Service following and flanking him so the press couldn't swarm him. One of the drone bots tried to get close, but Antony dodged it and rushed backstage.

Bethany stood, waiting for him. She immediately brought him into a tight embrace, holding him more like a mother than a lover. Antony tried to keep himself from shaking, from falling apart in front of so many others backstage. He had to keep his composure at least until they were in private.

"I can't believe I did it," Antony whispered.

"You did well, my love," Bethany said. "The whole world will be talking about this."

Antony let out a deep sigh. He'd done it. The hardest moment of his life, leaving everything he'd ever fought for or worked toward.

Had he made the wrong choice?

No, he couldn't second-guess himself. They'd talked it over dozens of times, and both he and Bethany concluded they wouldn't be able to do any good from inside the system. The war machine had spun up into full gear so quickly, they'd barely had time to react. And no one would listen, not even Senator Marsh, even though he took Antony's calls and told him platitudes about how he appreciated Antony's service and friendship. A calculated political nicety rather than talking to him as a man.

He hated politics sometimes.

Bethany gripped him by the bicep, leading him out the back of the building to the alleyway where the Secret Service had his motorcade. Hovercars and bots flew above, trying to swoop in and get pictures of the departing governor. Antony kept a stoic face, not willing to give the paparazzi one image of him looking tired or crying. He'd lost so much, but he wouldn't let his sacrifice be in vain by letting those blood-suckers talk about his body language or something equally as trite. He had done all he could to get them to focus on the policy.

It would be up to the people to move.

He slid into the hovercar, with Bethany after him. A Secret Service officer closed the door behind him. Soon, they would be home. A place he'd be spending a lot more time now. He had a lot of time to think.

He'd hoped he would change the world as governor, but instead he became bogged down in bureaucracy, worse than when he'd been in the assembly. Only now, he couldn't write or propose his own bills. Worse, he had been completely helpless while watching this conflict with the Aryshans spiral out of control.

It hadn't been the life he'd dreamed of as a young man. His heart ached with regret, but he had no thought to what he would have done differently.

The real question was, what would he do with his life now?

CRASHING

As QUICKLY AS the Aryshan fighters had descended from the sky like a plague of locusts, they disappeared. Where once stood the city of Vega, there only remained rubble. The attack had started with an EMP burst, knocking out the power grid. Then came a barrage of missiles to ensure the city never came back to life. Pulse beams cleaned up the job, leveling skyscrapers, melting the steel frames like they were candle wax.

Morgan Ezra had been stationed at the edge of the military base on the outskirts of town, in a guard shack in front of the main supply depot. She barely escaped the attack in a flitter, which crashed in the aftermath of one of the pulse beam's shockwaves.

She survived, but her co-pilot lay limp, unmoving in the cockpit. Morgan shook him.

"Dylan! Dylan!" Her companion wouldn't wake. The visor of his helmet had cracked in the impact, and blood stains filled it. He'd hit his head too hard.

Cockpit warning lights flashed. The engine could blow at any moment. She couldn't spend any time to properly mourn him. Remaining in the cockpit could spell her death along with his.

This was not what she anticipated when she signed up for a guard outpost on a distant colony to get away from her family. She shook her head, trying to clear her thoughts. If she wanted to continue to live, she had to stay focused.

Dirt from the impact covered the access hatch, making it impossible to exit through it. Morgan kicked the windshield, which cracked but did not shatter. She kicked again, and this time managed to break an opening large enough to squeeze through. The flitter had crashed in a forest, too dense with trees for the Aryshans to spot targets.

Smoke covered everything in the distance, forming black clouds in the sky. The Aryshans may not have scorched this entire planet, but they did hit civilian targets without fair warning. When the Earth media got wind of this, it would only escalate the war even further.

Morgan crawled out of the cockpit, her body tingling from the force of the crash.

Then, her flitter exploded, blasting bits of metal everywhere. The force of the blast carried Morgan forward, but she managed to keep her footing. She couldn't look back. To do so would bring her far too much pain.

Morgan stumbled over to a tree, her body pulsing. The crash had shaken her—nothing felt quite right. Her spine felt like someone jammed a thousand needles into it. Her heart pounded. Fear gripped her, surpassing all of the problems of flesh. If the Aryshans could destroy planets this easily, would Earth even survive?

She wouldn't let herself fall into dark thoughts. There were others out there, and work to do. After taking a few more moments to collect herself, she ran through fields of tall grass as fast as she could manage in her combat armor. She had to get somewhere—a base, civilization, *anywhere*. The armor shone jet black, drawing in heat from the sun. She'd gotten used to sweating over her last year of this assignment. It would never be comfortable, but she had become accustomed to less-than-ideal living.

After thirty minutes of running, the heavy armor began to take its toll on her. Basic training had prepared her for the burning sensation coursing through her veins. The conditioning also helped her power through all the horrific things she had seen. But sheer weariness crept over her. She couldn't keep going for much longer.

It had only been a few hours since she entered the guard shack for morning duty. Dylan and she relieved the night shift of their duties and talked about their weekend plans. He had hoped to head out in a flitter to take in the beautiful white sands of the southern continent. Now he'd never be able to.

Tears streaked from her eyes. She had to hold it together. Breaking down now wouldn't do her any good. The overlaid GPS display in her visor told her a main road would be in the near vicinity. With luck, she could find someone else from her division, and receive some orders of what she should do from here.

Captain Harper would know what to do. The man had the smoothest, clearest way of delivering orders. It must have been daunting to be responsible for hundreds of people. Morgan only commanded eight. Well, seven, with Dylan dead. She might even have less, depending on how many people were in the depot when the Aryshans struck.

For that matter, had Captain Harper made it out of there alive?

Another dark thought tugged at her chest. Her body had endured so much stress in the last few hours, it didn't want to move. With her armor's radio malfunctioning and all of the destruction around her, it became overwhelming. The road came into her field of vision. *No more negative thinking—run.*

Asphalt stretched wide in either direction. It still had a new feel to it, darker, without much wear. Trucks and transports still traveled by road, but most traffic flew via air-taxi or flitter. It kept congestion down, differentiating Esare from older, ground-bound colonies. She'd been to a few worlds in her time, and most colonies had lofty visions of being different, growing beyond other human settlements.

After the attack, this world might never get a chance to show its potential.

A truck sped over a ridge. From the side of the road, Morgan waved her arms frantically in the air to try to get the driver's attention. They nearly passed by without stopping, but the driver slammed on the breaks. The truck ground to a halt.

Four soldiers in combat armor stood in the back of the truck. One hopped out. "Name, rank?" a man said through a visor filter, while offering a salute.

Morgan returned the gesture. "Morgan Ezra, Second Lieutenant, first guard division of the Vega Supply Depot."

"First Lieutenant Vogt. Engineering division," he said. "We're heading into the city to try to get survivors out of danger. Want to help, Lieutenant?"

"Aye, sir," Morgan said.

Vogt motioned to the truck. "Come with us, then." He climbed into the bed.

Morgan stepped to the truck and lifted herself up. Two of the other soldiers helped her to her feet, and she gripped a handle on the side of the bed.

"I'm Kelly, and this is Robinson," the first soldier said, running a hand along his scruffy jawline.

The driver hauled down the highway. Morgan braced herself on the side of the truck, the high winds causing her armor to flap against her skin.

Every minute could mean the difference between death and survival for someone trapped in rubble. She didn't look forward to seeing more injured people. Seeing Dylan limp and helpless had been enough for a lifetime. She could hardly get the image out of her head.

They soon reached the city. Collapsed buildings, flipped cars, and crowds of people congested the roads. Lieutenant Vogt hopped out of the back of the truck, and the soldiers followed him. Morgan jogged after them.

After weaving through the wreckage, they came to a small encampment of tents. Several soldiers and emergency responders gathered together, meeting, taking notes, helping injured civilians. Everyone appeared to be working hard and to know their place in the relief efforts.

Vogt stepped forward and spoke with another officer. The man pointed him to a larger group of soldiers.

Captain Harper stood amidst the soldiers. He had lived after all. His combat helmet dangled by his arm, propped against his hip, his short, blond hair squished flat from wearing the helmet. He stood on a small supply crate. Everyone gave him their attention. "Okay, people. We're going to split into teams of five. Each team will have a medic brought with them for advice on who can move and who shouldn't. If you see someone who is immobile, call HQ on radio frequency delta-five-oh-four. A trauma team will be brought to the site and relieve you from there. We're going to get through this city as quickly as possible. Objective is to rescue any civilians trapped first. We'll worry about personal property and anything else later, clear?"

"Aye, sir," rang a chorus of several voices.

Vogt motioned for Morgan to join his team. They headed deeper into the wreckage of the city.

Every building around her had collapsed. Windows were smashed out. Every step she took cracked and skidded with broken glass and debris. It was like nothing Morgan had ever seen. Her officer training couldn't have prepared her for this. Humanity hadn't been at war since she'd joined the service. She'd heard stories of the Drenite War from more than a decade ago, but that had been among the alien worlds, not at home.

"Piece of garbage Aryshans, don't respect any life at all," Kelly said under his breath.

Vogt didn't respond to the comment. He held his hand up for his team to stop. They followed his lead as he stood still in the street. He lifted a scanner in his other hand. "Over a hundred bio-signs in that building..." He pointed to their left. "There."

The building had its windows smashed like the others. Originally three stories, the top had collapsed, but the other two bottom floors held their integrity.

Vogt moved ahead, stepping to the door frame. He held his scanner up and pushed the door open. Morgan followed behind. A pile of rubble from drywall blocked what looked to be a small lobby entrance. No sign of a fire or gas leak. "The people are trapped behind here. Let's get them out!"

The team rushed inside to help Vogt, digging through the debris haphazardly. They sifted through books, furniture, and office equipment. Morgan joined them, picking up what she could. Their efforts uncovered a steel beam which had fallen from the ceiling.

"Gonna need all of us to lift this," Morgan said.

Robinson grabbed ahold of the beam and nodded. Everyone took their places.

"One, two, three, go!" Vogt shouted.

Morgan pulled with all her strength. The beam had to have weighed more than a ton. Her legs burned again, a painful reminder she had run several kilometers. It wouldn't take much more to reach the limits of what her body could do after such an exhausting day.

The other soldiers didn't seem to be in as bad shape. Two of the soldiers grunted, but they were able to move the beam a few feet back toward the main entrance before dropping it with a heavy crack onto the tile floor below.

"Almost there. Look, another door," Vogt pointed ahead. His team moved enough of the debris to get to the door, which was jammed closed.

Morgan had to stay back and take a breather. Voices came from the other side of the door. They cried out, first in fear, then in joy as their rescue became clear.

"Stand back!" Robinson shouted before drawing back his knee and kicking hard on the door. The frame cracked and busted inward, revealing a group of weary office workers beyond. Several had small cuts and injuries from the broken glass and fallen debris.

The back of the building had caved in completely. Morgan saw blood on the floor by the wreckage, and a man's arm sticking out the bottom of it, as if grasping for help in his final moments.

A woman shrieked hysterically. She covered her face with her palms, cheeks red and drenched with tears. Blood stained her hands, dirt running down her blouse.

"Joey... not Joey..." she babbled.

Kelly wrapped an arm around her and ushered her out the door.

The rest of the office workers followed.

Seeing the death and destruction only brought back the memory of the flitter crash. It burned in her mind. The world spun into darkness.

* * *

"I'M NOT A PILOT, Dylan. I don't know what I'm doing!" Morgan cried. Her arms shook. They had to get out of here as quickly as possible. The whole base kept getting pelted by missiles and pulse beams.

"The AI will do most of the work. Set the parameters, go!"

"Where do I go?" She couldn't help but yell at him, her fuse short as it could be. It didn't do any good to panic, but tension permeated through her whole body up to her skull. Where was the input control, anyway?

Morgan tapped a button in front of her and to her right. "Drive to Lake Nunca," she commanded the flitter. She didn't know why she thought of there, but it seemed farthest away from any major settlement. The Aryshans would leave them alone there.

The flitter beeped, then took off, rocking Morgan back into her seat. Another wave of pulse beams hit the depot, leaving an explosion trailing behind her.

The blast knocked the shuttle off course. Something chugged and sputtered in the aft of the flitter.

"Shit, engine failure," Dylan said.

Morgan had inadvertently looked back over her shoulder, but by the time she turned to right herself, the ground approached far too quickly.

* * *

MORGAN BLINKED. She found herself on the ground, leaning against one of the office walls. How had she gotten here? The last several moments came up blank.

Vogt crouched in front of her, his helmet cast to the side. He had his hand on her shoulder and shook lightly. "Lieutenant, are you okay?"

"Yeah," Morgan said. The room started to spin. "I'm dizzy. I—"

She couldn't concentrate anymore. The world spun and everything in it faded. The last thing she remembered was her eyes rolling back and the ground fast approaching once more.

3

PYRRHIC VICTORIES

DALTON WARD SPAT blood out the corner of his mouth. He had his fists up, head close to his chest to try to deflect future blows. That last hit would sting for days. At least the iron taste distracted from the foul smell of rotten food rations. Who would have thought an investment broker from the Upper East Side would end up in a place like this?

The ape of a man who had punched him stood in a similar position, circling to try to get an opening. He had a shaved head, a spider tattoo on the back of his cranium, and wore the same red prisoner garb as everyone else on this shithole world. A number of the other prisoners called him simply, "Ogre".

A few other prisoners gathered around them, hooting and hollering about the whole scene. Guards wouldn't be back in the kitchen area for a few minutes at the very least. Not until someone ratted them out.

Ogre took another wild swing at Dalton's head.

This time, Dalton ducked and charged right into him, using his head to ram his opponent's gut. At first, it seemed like a good idea. If he could knock the wind out of him, the fight would end quickly.

Until Ogre laughed, not fazed in the least by Dalton's attack. He lifted Dalton up by the fabric of his prisoner's garb and then delivered a blow to Dalton's gut that had the exact effect Dalton had been hoping for in the other man.

Dalton gasped for air.

Ogre released Dalton, and he fell to the ground. The small crowd gathered, laughing at him as the bigger man circled.

"You see what happens when you fuck with the Spider Clan? This is what happens." Ogre waved his arm across Dalton as if modeling a new flitter or boat. He had a big grin on his face. "And then this happens."

He kicked Dalton hard in the ribs.

They cracked.

Intense pain shot through Dalton's entire body. His breathing became labored. He gasped a few times, but the pain didn't subside. Oh, god. He was going to die. He'd never make it off this shithole of a penal colony. Never meet a wife. Never start a family. What had he done with his life?

Laughter escaped his lips, even louder a sound than the oaf in front of him had made. He cracked up despite the pain each motion brought to his ribs.

Maybe, just maybe, he regretted cracking a joke about the *itsy, bitsy spider* in response to Ogre's recruiting pitch. It might not have been the smartest plan, but what did stupid decisions matter now?

Two years ago, Dalton had been working for a swanky investment firm. He and a few friends had started an exchange tracker to price, account for, and minimize arbitrage between worlds at different ports, all from the comfort of his New York homeland. People bought into an insurance plan that would have protected prices from spiking or dropping depending on various shipments of supplies to different human colonies.

Or so had been the plan.

In reality, the insurance plan ended up being a scam, one that his co-founder, Rodney Vasel, had constructed from day one without telling the others. When government officials raided their office, Dalton got pinched along with everyone else in the company. His title had been Chief Financial Officer. He'd signed off on papers when he hadn't read them, but they did have his very real signature. Vasel went to jail, and so did Dalton. His attorneys couldn't do anything. Even the plea deal failed. There had been too much public outrage.

If he survived this, he vowed to read every last letter on the page before signing papers in the future.

Dalton cackled some more.

"Dude's lost it," one of the other prisoners said.

"You got him good," said another.

Finally, prison guards arrived. They wore full riot gear and pointed their pulse guns at the prisoners.

"Everyone on the floor, now!" one of the guards shouted.

The prisoners were slow to comply, pushing each other to get out of the way. One of the guards fired his pulse gun in the air with a large, electric *thk-aw*. The shot scared the prisoners into going prone on floor.

Dalton winced, clenching his teeth as hard as he could. Breathing still hurt. His mouth still tasted of blood, and it filled with more.

Tears filled his eyes, despite his attempts to maintain a strong appearance. Moisture clouded his vision, but he still managed to see some of the prison guards climbing onto the backs of the prisoners, securing their hands with cuffs. Ogre grunted and complained, but Dalton couldn't make out what he said.

"Save it," the guard said, shoving Ogre forward after having cuffed him. "We know you're up to no good with your ugly tattoo. The Spider Clan is a stupid name, and everyone knows it, too."

Dalton wanted to laugh again, but he hurt too badly. The guard approached him and cocked his head. His helmet and visor obscured his facial expressions. "Little troublemaker, ain'tcha?

Instead of responding, Dalton winced from the pain.

The guard looked up to another. "We're gonna need a medic team.

Some painkillers at least. Don't know what's wrong with him, but Mr. Spider Clan musta broke somethin'.

Dalton couldn't move. The pain made his mind whirl.

"What we gonna do with all these prisoners?" another guard asked as he approached.

"Pick a few to use as an example to the others. We're gonna put Mr. Spider Clan over there and the little troublemaker in solitary. Can't be lettin' fights escalate like this." The guard jutted out a thumb toward Ogre, and guards led him away from the kitchen area.

Dalton didn't move. He couldn't argue with all this blood in his mouth. Even if he could speak, what would he have communicated, anyway? He hadn't wanted this fight, but the idiots starting their "Spider Clan" gang wouldn't take no for an answer. And they were damn persistent. Solitary would be awful, but it might do him some good to be away from them for a while.

A few minutes later, two medics came with a gurney and other supplies. By that point, Dalton had nearly passed out from the throbbing in his chest, the pain exacerbating with each breath. He didn't want to feel anything anymore. Couldn't they let him die?

The medics asked him some questions about the pain, and he told them as best he could. But he would be stuck here with these criminals for years after this. Never able to avoid them.

As they wheeled him away, he could do nothing but lie there and think about his miserable existence.

4

JUNGLE FLAME

Kiyomi shut the greenhouse door behind her, looking out upon her home's sprawling backyard. She stood on a dirt path intersecting grassy areas, the fences on either side lined with *Ixora coccinea*, jasmine plants most gardeners in south Florida called the "jungle flame". Even after spending decades in this backyard, growing up here with her parents—or rather, her father, Fabio, since her mother, Reiko, had passed years ago—she still never grew weary of the sight of her greenery.

The jungle flame jutted in an upside-down bowl shape, the orange-pink petals forming a clover over the fairly robust stems and leaves. They grew effortlessly and were easy to maintain in this climate, which was why so many people used them for color to adorn their yards, Kiyomi's parents included.

The flowers were beautiful, but knowledge of them didn't help her much in her botany master's program. She'd completed her work at the end of the last semester, turning in her final thesis on creating edible flowers from genetic manipulation. The process required too

17

many resources to make for anything profitable for the time being, but as generations of such flowers grew, it would be possible to create an inexpensive, high nutrient food source for humanity's ever-expanding population.

Kiyomi needed more experience before she would start her own company. Entrepreneurship was her goal, but she needed more than theories, lab courses, and toying around in her backyard greenhouse to have a credible enterprise. She had learned from her father's business acumen, if she didn't quite inherit his knack for success.

Her house was huge by anyone's standards, but for only two people living there, it often felt downright excessive. Traditional Spanish-style arches of light brown stucco lined a patio for the windows and doors of various rooms, most of which were never used. She had loved this house growing up, and still did, but it had a dreary emptiness without her mother.

Kiyomi stepped through the glass doors into the kitchen, where Chef Marcus came twice a day to cook her and her father a meal.

Dad sat at the table, scrolling through a datapad of the morning news. His hair had thinned out over the years. Kiyomi remembered when it was black and full of life. Wrinkles above his rosy cheeks and dimples further highlighted his age. He had shunned any rejuvenation treatment, saying he wanted to live a natural lifespan. As much as she respected him for that, Kiyomi didn't want to imagine a life without him.

"What are you frowning about?" He looked up at her, concern in his face.

"Oh, nothing," Kiyomi said, pasting on a bright smile. "Doing some thinking."

"Thinking can be dangerous, you know. The powers-that-be don't want any of that." Dad wagged a finger at her. Even though he had a light-hearted and sarcastic tone, he meant it. He had a streak of the conspiratorial in him. More than a streak, really.

"I don't know why you watch the mainstream newsvids every morning. Every day it's another murder, something horrible going on, another politician doing something that we should be shocked about. Why bother?"

Fabio shrugged. "I need to get the pulse of what's going on."

Kiyomi rolled her eyes. "Why? You're already planning on leaving this place for good."

Dad set the datapad on the kitchen table, glancing up as Marcus brought over two plates of prosciutto panini sandwiches for lunch. A soft cheese had been melted in with Dijon mustard, and it smelled glorious.

Kiyomi took a seat in front of the plate. "Thank you, Marcus."

"Yes, thanks," Dad said, his mouth already half-stuffed with the sandwich. His mind moved at speeds faster than the top-of-the-line FTL drives. Always onto something.

Kiyomi carefully picked up her sandwich, in case it was still hot from the grill, and took a much smaller bite than her father had done.

Dad stared off toward the garden. "We might have to move the timetable up on leaving."

Kiyomi nearly dropped her sandwich. "What do you mean? Your project is set for what, five to ten years? It's not like it's something you can rush."

"There may be no choice," he said, stuffing another bite into his mouth. "I don't know if you heard, but Governor Lemkin stepped down a few days ago."

"Yeah, it's all over the news. Nothing new has come along to break the cycle. I'm not sure what that has to do with you."

"Everything!" Dad's eyes bulged. "He was one of the last honest ones in government. I've spent loads in financing his campaigns." He shook his head. "I need to meet with him and see what he's truly thinking. I know to some degree. Nobody understands these government types like I do. He's scared of this war with the Aryshans. We don't understand their culture at all and don't know what lengths they're willing to go to in order to protect themselves. No, if there's going to be a long, protracted war, I want to be away from here and want our new life to begin immediately."

"You've been saying that human civilization is overdue for a, what did you say, a revolution?" Kiyomi shrugged.

He nodded. "Yes. Every seventy years or so. Three generations. One ascends, one grows complacent, the other causes the fall. It's happened throughout human history. We can track it back to the Revolutionary War here in North America. And then the United States Civil War, World War II, World War III. It goes on and on, even to this Great Death that has the Aryshans so jumpy. Did you know their population was decimated only about three generations ago?"

He'd explained this human social evolutionary cycle before, and it struck her as more than extreme to hold as fact, though she couldn't deny the historical precedents were there for everything he said. At any moment, Dad had warned her often, humankind could enter a new dark age. There'd been fiction written about it before, a long time ago, in a classic novel called *Foundation*. Kiyomi thought the book dry and difficult to read, but her father gleaned new ideas from it.

He wouldn't complain, nor fail to act. Being a wealthy man from his own business endeavors, he'd invested to try to solve the potential collapse of mankind. Again, Kiyomi thought, by pretty extreme measures. It would be no use arguing against one of his manic states. It never did any good. A wildly successful businessman like him hadn't been told "no" in decades, and, with him supporting her and her education, Kiyomi didn't want to rock the boat. "Yes. I know. So, what's this time frame? Is it going to mess with my Ph.D.?"

"I'm afraid so," Dad said with a serious frown.

"Dad, I'm not sure I actually want to go start a life on a distant, secret colony. I'm building a life here. I need to do some corporate internships, maybe work in the Human Exploration Program for a few years."

Dad's forehead wrinkled, an expression followed by a pause and a small sigh. He had never liked confrontation with her. To him, she would always be daddy's little girl. That would never change. He flicked a finger on his datapad, scrolling through more news head-lines. "It's your life, and you're a grown adult. You can make your own decisions."

But I don't have to like it, the unspoken words that lingered in the air afterward.

Kiyomi took a breath and placed a hand on her father's shoulder, giving a soft squeeze. His shoulders were rock hard, naturally that way, perhaps from the amount of stress he'd had over the years in growing his galactic shipping company. "Look, I've got some work to do on my hydroponics. But I'll think about it."

"Hydroponics are exactly what we're going to need," Dad said, his eyes scanning the table in front of him. Kiyomi recognized that look. His wheels were spinning in his mind. "If you could line up what we need to survive as a new colony, what plants would need to be produced from inception, we could make do without you actually being present. It would make a good doctoral thesis project for a botany specialty, like you wanted." He glanced back up and met her eyes.

He tried to connect. This was his way of doing so, even if it appeared a callous desire for his project and not for her. He wanted her to work with him. Work defined his life, just like flowers defined hers.

Kiyomi nodded to him. "Okay, Dad. I'll help. I think it's a great idea."

If anything, Dad laid a great idea for a doctoral thesis right in her lap. One she could produce an interesting beginning to, though if she didn't go with his expedition to start a new colony, a new humanity, she would never know the results of her theories.

No results wouldn't make for a great thesis. She also didn't relish gallivanting off to some corner of the galaxy alone.

His eyes shone at her, and he smiled brightly. "Great. Let's start thinking about this. Whatever we're going to do will have to survive a long journey through space."

Kiyomi bit her lip, considering. "Well, there will certainly be EM spectrum differences that can be accounted for with artificial lighting. You'll need to add those to a prospective hydroponic bay. But you'll need more than storage for the plants. They consume food, too, in their own way. We'll need a wide variety of specimens for maximum impact. Let's sketch out what the bay will look like."

5

WALLS ALL AROUND

Earth, San Francisco, CA

Antony stared at the wall in his house. It wasn't a bad wall, all things considered, but, at a certain point, a wall remained wall. It couldn't hold his interest. If he stared long enough, his eyes lost a small amount of focus, and it gave the illusion that some of the texture spackle started to swirl and move. What tricked the mind into thinking such things happened?

He sighed. It didn't matter. Nothing he thought mattered. Watching newsvids this last week made him want to bang his head straight through the wall.

His grand plan of having the news discuss policy and the repercussions of war had failed. The news only cared for celebrity personality.

"What scandal is Governor Lemkin covering up?" one pundit asked.

"Is this a publicity stunt for the Governor's side business brand? Tonight, at eleven," another broadcaster said.

"Rumors of Governor Lemkin and his wife, Bethany, are splitting. Did the stress of this cause him to resign?"

Idiots. All of them.

He couldn't control it. If he went on any of those networks to defend himself with interview, he would only be ambushed by even more ludicrous questions, and those answers would be taken out of context to spin yet another news cycle of nonsense.

Politics could sap a man's soul, though he signed up in full knowledge of the drawbacks when he first campaigned. Though the political reality taking a toll on him played a large part in his resignation. No one could navigate the current environment for any positive means, even if someone had the IQ of a great scientist and the heart of a saint. Though, truth be told, anyone with those qualities would get chewed up by the system and spit out before they got elected. Earth would still be stuck with a pointless interstellar war.

He slumped over, holding his head up in his hands. There had to be something he could do. Resigning should have made an impact, but instead, it had created a distraction for the public. The war machine kept chugging along.

After the Esare debacle, humanity struck back. Admiral Conley pushed into Aryshan space, taking out dozens of their border defense structures and obliterating one of their shipyards on their colony worlds. The encounters would keep building, getting deadlier. Hadn't anyone learned their lessons from the Drenite War twenty years prior?

Who could say where it had originally spiraled out of control? At this point, it would take an act of God to stop it. Even as the governor of North America, Antony never had enough power to even slow the war down.

These last few days had been torture. Sitting. Doing nothing. With his profile, he couldn't even step outside and go to a restaurant, not that he wanted to anyway. His body ached. Weariness overcame him. If he could exist in some catatonic state until his mental faculty withered away, that would be fine with him.

Or so he lied to himself.

Nothing had been fine as of late. He'd been wallowing in depression—a real sunken state he hadn't felt since his college girlfriend left him in his junior year. He'd been alone then, thinking there would be no way out.

This depression may have been worse, because he didn't only have his own feelings to consider—he had his wife to provide for and protect.

Hell.

Bethany cracked the door open to their bedroom. "Honey, you have to get out of there. It's midday. Have you even showered?"

"No," he said, words barely escaping from his lips.

"What have you been doing?" Her tone didn't hold accusation, but worry. Bethany moved over to sit on the edge of the bed next to him. She stared at the wall as he had been doing for hours.

They sat in silence for a long moment, Antony not having a good answer to the question. Then Bethany cocked her head. "Do you at least want me to bring some artwork and hang it here? Be better to look at."

Antony let out a stifled chuckle. She wanted to cheer him up. "Thanks, but I don't want anything. I don't know what to do anymore."

"I know," Bethany said. She ran her hand up and down his back, her touch gentle, loving.

She didn't deserve to have a husband who acted like this. She didn't deserve the life that he had forced on her. But what could he do? He didn't have the energy or power to do anything.

"I'm sorry," he said.

"It's okay," she said. "I don't expect you to be happy right now. But the news media will calm down, give it time. They forget about everything."

"That only makes it worse." Antony threw his head back onto the bed. His body bounced on the soft mattress. "It means my protest won't be remembered, no one will be discussing changing the policies that are getting people killed!"

Bethany turned to face him. "Do you want to take a trip out to the border colonies? See if we can get a meeting with some of the diplomats? Maybe you can help with their effort with the Aryshans."

He shook his head. "It wouldn't do any good. We'd only be in the way, and it'd be a publicity crisis for the diplomats with me there."

Bethany bit her lip. "You know, you used to tell me it was all about mindset. Winning an election required confidence. The voters had to see that you knew you would win, or they would turn on you, even if you had an uphill battle. In the senate, same thing. Legislation required confidence behind it if you needed to rally fifty percent of the other senators to vote. Everything in life is what you make it. That's what you told me. You're making it hard to bear this last week."

Antony frowned. Making Bethany upset made matters far worse.

Bethany made a face. "Oh, I'm sorry. I didn't mean it like that. I love you, Antony. I truly do."

"No, you're right," he said, shifting to stare up at the ceiling as he had the wall before. "I don't know what to do about it. I feel like I've lost a huge part of me. Like they ripped something out from inside me."

Bethany slapped her hands on her knees and stood up. "That's it."

"That's what?

"We're getting out of here. There's too much to remind you of work. You need a distraction."

Antony scrambled off the bed to stand with her. "What do you mean? We can't go anywhere. Reporters—"

"Will leave us alone or we'll have one of the bodyguards threaten them."

"I don't want to go anywhere."

"Too bad." Bethany crossed her arms. It was to stop arguing. He never won when she held her closed pose.

Antony paused, considering. "Where are we going, then?"

Bethany turned to look toward the window. A skyline of skyscrapers sprawled into a megacity, with hundreds of flying cars going every which way. "Somewhere more peaceful. With nice weather. How about..."

She walked over to the window. "...Florida. We're going to Florida."

6

SHELL SHOCKED

Esare Colony

Morgan stood guard of the makeshift command tents set up outside of the Vega city limits. Mixed teams of military personnel and civilians combed the city trying to sort through the destruction, find survivors, and gather resources. It was a hectic environment. She wished she were back on ship duty, confined in a tin can in space, like she had been on her last assignment. At the time, she'd done all she could to get out of ship duty. It made her more restless than anything else she had done in her life. Until now.

She'd had plenty of experience with planetside guard duty, having spent her days performing that task and managing others doing the same back on the base. Her uneasiness stemmed from the uncertainty of this assignment. They didn't have the resources at their disposal to rebuild. It didn't help that the government building was one of the first buildings vaporized by the Aryshan pulse beams. No one had true authority. Both military and civilian personnel were putting up fronts to try to gain some semblance of control.

Tempers flared throughout the tent encampment.

For Morgan, it meant she had to stand by, along with a few others, waiting, hoping that they wouldn't encounter any riots on the outskirts of Vega.

Captain Harper walked by with his aide, Lieutenant Tanner.

"We're still finding survivors, Captain," Tanner said, "but the rate's slowed. Only small pockets of people per day now. Unless someone lay trapped in a place with food or water, there's not much hope for survival, and it diminishes further every day."

"Keep looking," Captain Harper said, shaking his head. "Bad odds or no, if we save even one life from our efforts we'll have done some good."

"Aye, sir," Tanner said.

Morgan watched them pass, saluting when Captain Harper came close. Perhaps that wasn't necessary anymore, with only a fragment of the military remaining, but Morgan had that action ingrained in her to where it came by instinct.

To her surprise, Harper stopped. Typically, when he passed by in a meeting, he didn't bother with the guards, even to return salutes.

"Go on ahead, Tanner. I have something to discuss with Lieutenant Ezra," he said.

Tanner nodded and went on his way, disappearing into one of the tents down the line.

Harper turned to face Morgan.

Morgan stayed straight, trying not to let the surprise of having his attention show on her face. Though she held similar rank to the men who had walked by, they never involved Morgan in the command discussions. Her shyness had been a part of her distance from the others, not feeling comfortable making decisions on behalf of everyone in the colony. Unlike many of the other officers, she hadn't gone through command schooling, nor ever had to lead more than a guard shack. Her job had been to manage time schedules, make sure her people were at their posts around the base and in compliance with uniform regulations. She didn't have the experience to be able to bring a colony back from the brink like Captain Harper needed from his advisors.

What could he possibly want to talk with her about?

"At ease, Lieutenant," he said.

Morgan relaxed her shoulders.

"How have you been doing these last few days? I know we tried to set you on a similar duty to what you had before, ease you into this whole transition." Harper cocked a brow at her.

"I'm... fine," Morgan said, wishing she had a better answer.

She also wished her words held some semblance of truth. Other than fainting from what the doctors had called "extreme shock and stress", Morgan had barely been able to sleep the last several nights. Whenever she closed her eyes, she saw Dylan, a bloody mess, unmoving in the flitter. She couldn't help but think that she could have done something different, or perhaps taken the other side of the cockpit. If she had, Dylan would have lived.

Restless nights followed from those thoughts. Even when she did sleep, she had horrific nightmares. Aryshans returning, coming to strangle her while she slept. Other nightmares of Captain Harper putting her in front of a firing squad for ineptitude. Yet another of a second attack of the enemy's pulse beams, this time wiping out everything. She couldn't get it out of her head, and the images felt too real, waking her throughout the night.

"Earth to Lieutenant Ezra. Are you with us?" Captain Harper asked, waving a hand in front of her face.

"Oh my, I'm sorry, sir." Her cheeks grew hot. How long had she been lost in her own thoughts?

Disappointment flashed in Harper's eyes. "This is what I wanted to talk to you about. Several of your subordinates have noticed that you've tended to zone out at times over the last few days. Others have reported that you scream in the middle of the night. Are you having night terrors?"

Morgan nodded sheepishly.

"I see." Harper frowned. "I'll be frank with you, Lieutenant. I like you. You have a good work ethic, you turned in your reports back at the base on time, everyone's timecards..." He shook his head. "But after speaking with your physicians and the others in your unit, I think you might have been pressed back into duty a little too soon."

"Sir, I can handle guard duty," Morgan said, her voice coming across all too defensive.

She couldn't have failure at guard duty on her record. It would spell the end of her career. The assignment should have been an easy one compared to many others in the reconstruction efforts. The search parties had a lot more physically demanding jobs, rummaging through the rubble of skyscrapers. For that matter, so did the debris-clearing teams and the reconstruction engineering corps. She could handle guarding supplies.

"How do I put this tactfully? Lieutenant, I don't want to have to order you to undergo a psych exam. That would put too much strain on you as well, from what I'm hearing, but I think you need a break. Likely a long one."

She couldn't deny that there had been some issues since the Aryshan attack. She'd been thinking about them nonstop, and wishing that she could get rid of her nightmares, or the image of Dylan in her head, the tiredness, everything. Morgan glanced down at her shoes. Her boots had the toes scuffed up, covered in dirt. She hadn't bothered to clean or shine them to regs since the attack. No one had called her on it. The captain's shoes didn't look all that clean, either.

"Are you relieving me of duty, sir?"

"I'm afraid I have to. I can't have someone commanding the alert guards who isn't entirely present. I need vigilance. What if the Aryshans were to come back? Or if some desperate people try to raid our command tents? You're our first line of warning. We need everyone to be at a high level of alertness."

Morgan's heart sank. First, she couldn't fly the flitter to safety, now she couldn't even do her job right. God, she was going to get washed out of the military. She couldn't help but frown.

"Nothing bad has to go on your record. You had a highly hazardous situation under your watch, and you'll be taking a paid leave of absence. I've seen to it that the Interplanetary Force will be paying for any psychiatric care or medical expense you might need, as well as an additional shore leave stipend. Take a few months off, see if you really want to go back into this, and we'll see where things are at, okay? But I do need you off these front lines here. You understand?"

She posed a danger to everyone here, in other words. As much as she wanted to argue, Morgan couldn't disagree. But the thought of not working, of spending empty days with nothing to do but to sit and think about her friends dying might throw her into a mental spiral from which she couldn't find her way out. Being alone scared her more than another Aryshan attack.

"I understand, sir." Her voice came as low as a whisper.

Harper appeared relieved at the lack of a fight. "There's a transport shuttle coming in two days' time. It's bringing reconstruction and medical supplies. On its way out, there's going to be room for a few passengers, and I want you to be one of the ones on that shuttle. It'll take you to Toltair where you'll need to check in with the local V.A. psychiatric department, okay? Let's get what's best for you, and then we'll get you back to duty. Sound good?"

"Toltair? Isn't that where DePino Starline Industries is building their Ark Two-Point-Oh or whatever they call it?" She'd heard about it on a local newscast a couple of months ago when she had a late-night shift. She'd pulled up a video presentation of their founder, Fabio DePino giving a speech on an old science fiction novel and a theory of diverging human civilizations without contact in order to ensure species survival. It sounded like eccentric talk at the best, but multi-trillionaires needed hobbies. He did a lot for charity and technology startups, supporting ideas for betterment of mankind, or so she'd read. He couldn't be all that bad.

Lieutenant Tanner popped his head out of the tent, waving for the captain. Captain Harper looked back over his shoulder and motioned for another moment. He returned his attention to Morgan.

"You heard about it too? Suppose there's only so much news on a small colony world. Eh, rich people are strange, aren't they?" Harper shrugged and let out a laugh.

Exactly what Morgan had thought. She had no laughter in her, however.

"I suppose it's as good a place as any," she said, a half-truth. She looked up to see a flitter passing overhead, wondering when the transport would arrive and if she'd see it. Perhaps a trip to Toltair would do her some good. "When does the transport get here again?"

7

BRANDED

Prison Colony 33-X4D

Dalton Ward looked up at the white ceiling of his solitary confinement chamber. The cot creaked. The stains showed they hadn't been washed in a very long time—it probably contained all sorts of bacteria.

The room smelled of the urine and feces of prior prisoners. A bucket lay in the corner for one to relieve oneself, but apparently more than a few had missed, and it looked like no one bothered to do much but hose the floor down. Disgusting.

His ribs still had some soreness to them, but the doctors had used their nanotech to mend his bones, so this would be the best place he could heal, away from any other potential incidents. None of the other wounds hurt anymore.

He'd gone from a rich apartment back in New York, top floor, overlooking a beautiful cityscape, to this. All because of one mistake. Well, a couple mistakes. His brain played tricks on him, forgetting things, jumbling facts after a few days in here. Dalton could only imagine what a month-long visit would be like.

He sat up on the cot, looking across at another white wall. They didn't give someone anything even interesting to look at. True torture. This certainly violated some prisoner treatment convention, but who could complain where they would listen?

One hundred, ninety-nine, ninety-eight, ninety-seven...

Dalton had taken to reciting numbers and the alphabet backward to himself each time he woke. He thought seven days had passed. Hard to tell in here. Mental exercises like that would keep him sharp. He couldn't allow his brain to rot. He already had enough enemies in this place, and he couldn't be considered a prime physical specimen like the ape who had attacked him. There were far too many of those types, angry at the world, ready to beat anyone into submission, and to find someone lesser to pick a fight with.

What number had he stopped at again? *Ninety-six, ninety-five, ninety-four...*

The cell door creaked open. Dalton shaded his eyes from the bright light beyond.

Two armed prison guards came in, pulse guns pointed, armor on. As if Dalton would be a threat to attack them after a week of getting mush fed to him through a slot in the bottom of the door. They were followed by an officer. "Okay, Prisoner One-One-Three-Seven-Five, your solitary confinement period has ended. We expect that we won't have any further incidents by you or it will be met with harsher punishment, is that clear?"

Dalton huffed. "I was attacked. Keep those gangs from shanking me, and there won't be any incidents."

One of the guards stepped forward, adjusting his pulse gun aim right for Dalton's face. "Prisoners don't mouth off to their betters, son."

The officer waved his hand to call the guard off, also stepping forward toward Dalton. "I've reviewed the vids. I know what happened. Everything in here is monitored, prisoner. There's only so much we can control. There's an old saying. If you can't beat 'em, join 'em. I recommend that course of action—it's the only advice I'll give you. Now scram." He pointed toward the door.

Dalton stood slowly, his legs tired and tight from several days of doing absolutely nothing. He supposed he should have spent more time doing jumping jacks or other workouts to stop his body from deteriorating, but stuck in solitary, mustering up the will to better oneself proved challenging.

The two guards with guns circled behind him, one pushed him in the back with the side of his gun. He winced at the metal stabbing into his back and stumbled forward.

They walked out of the isolation room, into a hallway of several of them, and out to a courtyard that led to several dormitories of single-room residencies. Twin suns shone down heavy on the world. Those that were here indefinitely moved out into the rough terrain of 33-X4D, trying to make a life for themselves in any way they could, but those who had shorter sentences stayed close by, waiting for a drop ship to come down from the station above and recirculate them back into regular life within society.

One of those ships dropped in the distance, by the well-guarded landing pad. From what he understood, the guards took shifts, here and up on the station above, so that they wouldn't burn out. Must be nice.

Several people lounged outside the dormitories, some playing cards made from whatever makeshift materials they could find, some chewing on the stem of a plant that grew on this world. Several watched Dalton walk by, sneers on their faces. Either they were hardened themselves, or they knew something about him.

The guards peeled off from Dalton at some point, without word, letting him ease his way back into the population. After several months there, he hadn't made friends, but instead tried to stick to himself, read what he could, and learn. Unfortunately, he'd been noticed anyway.

A couple of men walked by, adorned by the same spider tattoo that Ogre had had on his head. He considered what the officer had said: if you can't beat 'em, join 'em.

Getting caught up in a gang couldn't be considered one of Dalton's top priorities, but those words held a kernel of sense. He needed some form of protection if he were to survive. The longer he stayed, the more aloof he had become, the more others wanted to pry into his business or injure him.

Dalton adjusted his course, following the path of the two Spider Clan men in front of him. Not too closely, as he didn't want to provoke another fight. They passed a couple of dormitories and a work center where inmates performed mundane hard labor, until they finally came to another residence. This had more of the same men with shaved heads and spider tattoos. *Not creepy in the least.* Dalton shuddered.

The men went in, and Dalton stopped in front of the ones he presumed were standing guard. "Who's the head of your clan, anyway?" Dalton asked, trying to sound casual.

"You gettin' smart with me, boy?" One of the guards sneered at him.

Dalton held up his hands in surrender. "No, not me. I'm dumb. Can't keep myself out of solitary, you know? My own fault. I wanted to see about joining up."

The guard smirked, turning to his friend. "Little bitch wants to see about joining up. Ain't that funny, Beats?"

"Sure, is funny. Why don't you scram," the other guy said motioning his head in another direction. "I'm sick of lookin' at yer ugly mug."

"Yeah, scram," the first guard said.

"Hold up, hear me out," Dalton said. He should have spent more time thinking about this before approaching these pea-brained bruisers. The sales pitch had been his forte in his past life, however. He'd sold investors after nights of binge drinking, not preparing at all. These guys couldn't be that difficult to persuade. "You know why I'm in here?"

"Don't know, don't care."

"Well you might, and your boss might too. What's his name?"

"Call him the Tarantula."

What was with these idiotic arachnid names? He bit his lip, trying not to roll his eyes. "Right, I know. I'm in for business fraud. I'm not your average felon here." He pointed to his head. "I've got smarts. Maybe your boss can use that to the Spider Clan's benefit, you know? Make a nice little enterprise on this world."

"Enter prize? We don't have a prize for entering."

Hoo boy.

"Never mind. Tell... the Tarantula... that there's someone here to make him a business proposition. Get him more territory and followers, maybe figure out a way to get some nice things for the clan. Money, you know?"

The second guard had a curious expression. "Red, he seems pretty smart. Might not be full of shit."

Red stared hard at Dalton. "Quiet, Beats. I'm thinkin'. Boss won't be happy if we bring in anyone from out here. Waste his time."

"Look," Dalton said. "If I waste his time, he'll take me out, right? What can it hurt?" In a normal business presentation, his inclination would be to smile, to try to persuade the person across from him to associate him with happiness, something that felt good. This time, he held his face as expressionless as possible.

Red squinted and then stepped aside.

"Thank you, you won't regret this," Dalton said, ascending the steps and not looking back.

"I'd better not," Red said.

Inside the building, it looked like any other. A hallway, stretching out on either end with a row of dormitory rooms, with a restroom facility at one end and a laundry facility at the other. No fire by which to cook, nothing that could be used as a weapon. It occurred to him he didn't know which room would be the Tarantula's, but he decided to head to the left, toward the end. Not a bad place to start.

The door to the last dormitory room hung open, and Dalton looked inside. Someone had blown out the walls between a couple of the rooms here for a much bigger one. A couple of the cots were pushed together, and a nicer mattress adorned the bed in the corner. It had blankets, real ones, not just the thin, scratchy sheets that came standard issue. A chair and desk rested against the opposite wall, a holovid display on its desk. Dalton wondered idly how these items had gotten here. Guards didn't let this kind of stuff through on processing.

"Why're you looking in my room?" a deep voice asked from behind Dalton.

Dalton turned around to see a tall man, more thoughtful-looking than he expected in this place. He wore the same red prisoner garb that Dalton did and had the shaved head and tattoo that many of the other Spiders had scrawled into their heads.

"I was looking for..." he paused. Could this man be the Tarantula that the others mentioned? "The Spider Clan leader. I have a proposition."

The man inclined his head, appearing to be sizing Dalton up. "I know you. You're the guy that Ogre beat the shit out of."

Ogre? Tarantula? Beats? Red? Did everyone get an absurd nickname in their little club? He hadn't been too off in calling the guy a big ape, now that he thought about it. He'd have to remember to be amused about that later.

"That'd be me," Dalton said, trying to sound as confident as possible, but it was hard to come across that way with the question at hand.

"You have some balls coming in here after that," the man said. He brushed past Dalton's shoulders and made his way into the open room. "You coming in or what?" He didn't stop, but headed over to a roughly built bar area in the room, something unusual for one of these dormitories. He reached behind and pulled out an old bottle.

Dalton stepped inside. This was a dumb idea. Too dangerous. Also, too late to make any other decisions about it now. If he took off running, that may well be the end of his life in earnest. Instead, he took slow and deliberate steps, keeping a decent enough distance from the man.

"By now, I'm sure you've figured out that I'm the one they call the Tarantula. Prisoner One-Oh-Nine-Eight-Two, the guards call me."

"One-One-Three-Seven-Five." Dalton gave a nod. There had to be some common ground between them, a way to prime them for the sale.

The Tarantula swigged directly from his bottle before letting it clank back down on the bar. If he were trying to make a show of his power here, it didn't impress Dalton. Having come from the real business world, seen how the real sharks acted, anything on this prison planet felt like a pale reflection in comparison. Anyone who ended up here was already—by definition—a failure. The Tarantula may not have considered that in the way he wiped his lips with the sleeve of his jumpsuit. "What's your offer then? I am a busy man."

Dalton breathed in slowly to collect himself. How would he present this? "I assume a lot of the Spider Clan are here for crimes that would keep them here a long time…"

The Tarantula gave Dalton a look that said don't waste my time.

"What I'm trying to say is, there's only so much you're going to accomplish here through brute force, and that's because there's only so much people are willing to work and build. There's a decent-sized planet here, yet the vast majority of us are congregated right around where the drop ships come in. I know most of us are ready to leave and want to be on those shuttles day-one when our time is served, but we can make this planet a lot nicer. There's a lot to explore, a lot to build. You already have people working together for your clan, so why not take the next step to really improve quality of life?"

The Tarantula stared at him for a long second, then snorted. "Oh, you're funny."

"I'm being serious."

"I'm sure you are, which is what makes it funnier. Don't you know who the people are here? What're you in for? Are you even guilty of your crimes?"

"Theft and fraud. Yes," Dalton said, forced to look away as he stated his guilt.

"I'm here for inciting a riot on Ryjesta colony. That went too far, and I found myself having to take out some of the law enforcement coming after me." He held his gaze firm on Dalton, as if to test him. "Lotta others in the clan are in for the same or worse."

Dalton studied him. "What you're saying is that the people here won't have an interest in building, even if it's for their own comfort."

"You do have a brain." The Tarantula grinned.

"Doesn't mean we can't make it work."

"What's this 'we' you're talking about?"

Dalton stepped forward, locking eyes with the Tarantula. "If you weren't interested, I wouldn't still be here talking to you."

The Tarantula picked up the bottle again and took a swig. "Maybe I find you amusing."

"Doubt it. You're a busy man, as you said."

They both stared at each other another long moment. The Tarantula cracked a smile. "Boys! Initiation!"

Footsteps pounded as if a stampede were imminent. Dalton turned back to the door to see Red, Beats, and a couple of other men with shaved heads and spider tattoos with them. They pounced atop Dalton before he could move, two holding his arms back.

Dalton squirmed.

The Tarantula stepped out from behind the bar with a razor in his hand, grinning all the while.

"What the hell are you doing? Are you crazy?" Dalton spat.

Another one of the Spiders held Dalton's legs. He couldn't move. For the second time in as many weeks, Dalton considered his pending mortality.

The Tarantula brought the razor close, sadistically running the flat along Dalton's chin and then up to his skull.

A small cut grew on his head from the sharpness of the blade. He clamped his teeth together but didn't move so he wouldn't make it worse.

Once more, the Tarantula brought the blade back, and Dalton closed his eyes. The Spiders started laughing. Then, Dalton felt the blade run long his scalp.

But he didn't get scalped as he had thought.

Dalton let one eye open to see hair floating off the top of his head and down to the floor in front of him. The crazy bastard shaved his skull.

The fourth Spider who had entered the room had an open flame from a lighter on a needle.

He wasn't going to die today. Judging from the looks of the others, he'd soon have a spider tattoo and he would be one of their own. He would be branded for the rest of his life.

8

DESIRES

EARTH, JUPITER, FL

KIYOMI SAT at a table under an umbrella at the outside seating of Little Comfort's, a quaint place to have lunch along the coast. She looked out onto the beach, which held a packed crowd for a weekday, waves hitting the Florida coastline and a gentle breeze making the summer heat bearable. She had a salad in front of her and picked at it while she had a conversation with Jim Singhal, one of her father's favorite contractors.

Jim had handsome features, dark skin, black hair, a charming smile. He had really nice teeth, Kiyomi had always thought. When she asked him if he'd ever had braces in one of their earlier conversations, he'd said no. She wasn't sure why that stuck in her head now, but, to be honest, she found it hard to listen to the conversation about construction.

"We've built three new skyrises in the last two weeks," Jim continued in between bites of his fish tacos. "I mean, it's crazy. You'd think by this point we'd've run out of land, but there's always something to redevelop. How's your dad hanging? Sad to be retired?"

"Well, he still has his hands in a lot of investments and projects," Kiyomi said.

"Oh yeah. He told me about that project, made me do a pretty crazy bid on some construction in space that he said he'd have shipped out to one of the outer world colonies. I have no idea why he'd want two dozen prefabricated buildings or how he's planning on transporting them."

Here we go, thought Kiyomi. "I'm sure you've heard about his colonization project."

"Start a bold, new mankind!" Jim said in a dramatic tone, mimicking the news conference where Dad had spoken a few months prior.

Kiyomi couldn't help but roll her eyes. It wasn't as if she thought her father's plans were stupid, they were... eccentric. Something one might expect from a man who's somewhat out of touch, worth trillions of credits. "That's the one. If something's fabricated in space, it's not like there's any friction or weight restriction that would change anything about the transport."

"It's still a crazy idea," Jim said. "But I like it. I might want to go myself, to assemble whatever project it is when I get there. Could be easier. You going to be going on this one-way cruise?" He cocked his head at her, a thin attempt to be cute.

Kiyomi shrugged. "I don't know. I've got a lot of work to do for my Ph.D., and I'm not sure I want to commit to leaving this world behind for real."

"Even if I'm there?" Jim leaned closer to her.

And here Jim presented his one problem—his pushiness. He'd wanted to get with her for far too long.

He reeked of cologne—a floral scent, obviously chosen to try to impress her. What flower created the smell? Familiar, yet distracting. She leaned back and laughed as if he had amused her, not wanting to upset him. "Might keep me from going completely. I don't know. This is my father's dream, it's not mine. But, I know that he'd need my help if he were going to make this work. He has such lofty ideas, but sometimes forgets some of the practical details."

"Don't I know it," Jim said, smiling all the while. "That's why I think we make such a good team, Kiyomi. The two of us could really change his empire from a bunch of crazy side-projects into something real."

And here came the pushing. As of late, Jim had stopped by the house more often to say hello, even if he didn't have a construction job for DePino Industries going at the time. He'd linger around the kitchen counter by their chef, and try to strike up conversation with Kiyomi.

She didn't mind talking. Jim was a nice enough guy. By the same token, she didn't have a spark for him. They could never be together. The way he looked at her now made her want to run away, but she wouldn't. He had solid business acumen, was a good man, and her father needed him.

But she also needed to be clear.

"Jim," Kiyomi said finally.

"Yes?"

"I'm not on the market, okay? I'm focused on getting my Ph.D. I don't know if I'm going on my father's expedition, or even if he'll see it through. You know how his projects go, he never knows. But we're not a team beyond friends, you understand?" She didn't waver, meeting his eyes.

Jim flinched. Then forced a smile. "Yeah, of course. That's exactly what I was saying. I'm trying to say that if we do go to this planet off in the distance, there won't be many people there. We'll have to work together. On projects."

Kiyomi didn't need to know what he had in mind in terms of projects. "So, you're fully committed to this venture?"

"Yeah, actually." Jim shifted. His chair creaked on the stone surface of the patio. "I think it'd be a lot of fun. I don't have anything here. I mean, I'm not close with my parents like you are. Separating from them wouldn't be as big of a deal. And my brothers would manage." He shrugged.

Separating wouldn't be a big deal. Those words rang in her head. Kiyomi didn't want to think too hard on separation from her father, as much as she wanted to stay focused on her own goals. She loved him, and as years went by without Mom, he came to rely on her. No matter what happened, it would be a hard decision. That's why part of her hoped that her father would change his mind and move onto his next idea.

"Let's talk about something else?" Kiyomi took another sip of her iced tea.

9

VISITORS

EARTH, JUPITER, FL

ANTONY GAZED out from the yacht. The boat had automated driving, so Bethany and he could maintain a nice view of the water and the Florida sun. Wind rushed over his face. Both his and Bethany's hair went wild. They wore sunglasses to deflect from the glare of the ocean.

Few boats sailed the waters today, a weekday—the best time to vacation, in Antony's estimation. He hated crowds. They'd left a few more paparazzi behind on the shore, along with reporters. A couple of drone cameras came close, but the yacht's navigation lost them with ease.

This was one of his favorite places to relax. Bethany and he had taken this trip several times, allowed the use of one of his best donor's yachts. One of his staffers once asked, "You're from Hawaii, why do you bother going to Florida? Isn't that a long flight for the same atmosphere?"

"Because it feels like home but without any of the pressure," Antony had said.

For whatever reason, this vacation hadn't instilled him with the peace he usually found here. A nagging sensation kept ticking in the back of his skull. When he returned home, he wouldn't have work to do. With a couple of weeks having passed since Antony went through with the decision to step down, it became clear he'd made a mistake. He'd conceded a battle. In many ways, this course had been worse than banging his head against the wall and trying to fight the machine.

Bethany stood from her place across from him on the boat's bow. She wore a black, one-piece bathing suit, something that Antony had in the past voiced as his favorite. Though she had a slender figure, the bathing suit accentuated her curves in all the right places. Especially when she contorted herself to look behind her as she did now. The sight made his heart race, even decades into their relationship.

"Oh," Bethany said, picking up Antony's earpiece, which she had tucked in the cushion under her. "It vibrated."

"In a good way?"

"Stop it, you dirty old man," Bethany said, smacking him in the chest with her free hand. She offered him the earpiece. "You have a call."

"Probably one of the reporters having figured out my comm number. We can ignore it."

Bethany tapped one of the panels below the bow's railing. "No, it looks like it's Fabio DePino. He hasn't called since your reelection. What do you think he wants?"

Antony narrowed his eyes, looking out across the skyline to that place where the water met the sea in spectacular fashion. What did Fabio DePino want? He was one of the few donors who didn't seem to have any strings attached, no "you scratch my back, I'll scratch yours" quid quo pro for helping him with the election. Fabio had merely wanted a quiet phone call and liked meeting after each election, but beyond that, he'd never asked Antony for anything.

That's not to say the man didn't have projects that interacted with the government. He had a startup, "Skyway AI", which air traffic thought would be a solid application to free the air of hovercar congestion and truly use all three dimensions to advantage for speed's sake. His clean the ocean project, extracting sludge and grime from the industrial age out of the sea, had good intentions. It didn't last very long after the logistics of the scope of the project became unbearable. Antony had heard that he wanted to colonize some area out in the vast reaches of space somewhere, create a second humanity away from this one and attempt to start anew. But Antony wouldn't even be able to help authorize the launch of a project so large, though DePino might not have needed authorization under Federated Earth law. There hadn't been any precedent for such a venture.

He shook his head to himself. "He still trying to call?"

Bethany smiled, warmth radiating from her. "He's a persistent one."

"Alright, let's see what he has to say," Antony said.

He scooted by Bethany to make his way around the center cockpit and back into the rear of the boat so he could go into the lower cabin where he'd have less wind noise. Bethany nearly blocked him, a mischievous grin crossing her face as she forced him to brush against her body. Not that Antony minded. He mimed a kiss back her direction for her efforts before making his way around and heading down below.

The cabin had an odd smell to it. Old, dusty, even though the vessel had only been through ten years of sailing. Time flew. He shook his head. "Comm on. Answer call."

Antony turned back around in the room, its layout comprised of two benches in front of portals to the side and a table that could fold up into the wall. It had some light cooking amenities, a bedroom, and a lavatory beyond. The comm screen rested on the back wall.

The face of Fabio DePino flickered on the screen. He looked much older than Antony remembered him, not having spoken to the man in several years.

"Hello, Governor, or should I say ex-Governor," Fabio said.

Antony gave a phony politician's smile to that. "Either would be acceptable."

Fabio waved at him to stop. "Don't give me that, I can read through the B.S. even through a comm line. Some stunt you pulled. I'm glad you did, though. Someone had to stand up and speak on the behalf of the rest of us. Sometimes, it feels like the galaxy goes round and round, and there's nothing we can do to stop the juggernaut."

"Sometimes that's true," Antony said, seating himself on one of the bay benches. "But you didn't call me to congratulate me for knocking myself out of power."

"Right you are," DePino said. "Always knew you were a smart one. That's why I liked you."

"It wasn't a particularly difficult observation," Antony said.

DePino laughed. "No, I suppose it wasn't. Tell me, Governor, do you have time to meet? I heard through the net tabloids that you were vacationing not too far from my humble abode."

By humble abode, DePino meant mansion compound. "I'm not too far, but I was taking the time to relax with Bethany..."

"This won't take too long. And I'll have Marcus cook you up a hot meal and make you some nice cocktails. He's got a great mixer from this hybrid pomegranate strain with a native plant of the Cestus colony called gradates. Mixes fantastic with vodka. Trust me. I want to talk about things, but it'd be better in person."

Those words usually meant someone wanted to sell something. Antony had heard the phrase far too many times over the years. In politics, it spelled corruption and not wanting the potential of a recorded line. His instinct was to flee from such meetings in person, but those instincts weren't useful anymore. Even if DePino wanted something, it couldn't be something involving improper use of his power now. He had no power.

"Why not. Let me talk to Bethany and make sure it's okay."

"You got it. Be here for a four o'clock happy hour. We'll meet out on the back deck past our greenhouse. I'll send out a bot with a raft to the buoy. You have my coordinates?"

Antony looked at the bottom corner of the screen, which did list his location on the GPS. It would be less than a fifteen-minute boat ride to arrive. "Got it."

"See you soon." DePino's image winked out.

Bethany and Antony continued to zip around the ocean for

another several hours, admiring the scenery of the coast, pointing out every time a fish or dolphin jumped in the water, having a few laughs and listening to music. They found that they still had some time to kill before they had to meet with DePino. Antony took her by the hand, led her back around to the cabin. Watching her in her swimwear all day made him famished for her. Even after all these years, he still held every ounce of passion that he remembered from those early days. He spun her around somewhat aggressively, pressing her up against the back wall of the cabin and kissing her hard.

She responded by running her hands wildly along his back, pressing her body against his. He could feel her curves, her breasts against him. It took everything in Antony not to rip the swimsuit off of her body. Then he wouldn't get to see her in it again, and that would be a shame. He hooked a thumb over the strap around her shoulder and pried it down over her arm, signaling for her to assist and work around with the rest.

It was the first time he had been in the mood since his announcement, since his depression had taken all of his fight and spirit out of him. Having a purpose gave him such a rush. It turned him on nearly as much as the sight of Bethany.

Antony pushed her up onto the table and made love to her.

When both felt satisfied, Antony nuzzled against her for a long while. At least he had Bethany—that much could never be taken away from him.

"It's time, dear," Bethany said, brushing past him in her full naked glory, reaching for her swimsuit by his foot.

Antony gave her a pat on the behind when she bent down, grinning all the while. "Never be on time to a party. You know that. It's best to be fashionable." He made a faux-thoughtful look. "Perhaps I should go like this."

Bethany chuckled. "I'm not sure that's the latest fashion, but I wouldn't protest."

He laughed along with her, keenly aware that he hadn't laughed in a couple of weeks. Did this mean his funk had disappeared? Perhaps the vacation helped after all, as much as he hadn't liked the idea when

Bethany posed it. Or perhaps DePino's invitation meant something more to him, let him know he still held importance to someone in the world.

They dressed, and the boat's autopilot pulled to a buoy offshore from DePino's estate. A drone guided a raft out to the boat to retrieve the Lemkins and brought them back to the sandy beach in front of DePino's deck. The old man DePino spotted them, waving from behind a translucent railing on his deck. Antony saw the big green-house behind it. The structure felt out of place in the otherwise lavish, resort-style property. The main residence looped in a horseshoe shape toward the shore, two ends meeting at the deck where he stood. But the greenhouse didn't fit the rest of the modern architecture, a boxy, translucent structure right in the middle, where a nice open yard might have been. Along its walls grew colorful flowers, which, though they were well maintained, weren't as clean and organized as the rest of the place.

Antony wouldn't criticize the tastes of his host. He hopped out of the raft, feet kissing the cool ocean waves as they washed over them and the hot sand. He helped Bethany from the raft soon after, and they trudged up through the sand to the small set of stairs by the deck. DePino opened the gate to greet them.

"No butler to lead us in?" Antony asked, his tone teasing.

"Not for my friends I've been waiting all day for. Come in, come in. Glass of wine? White or red?" DePino wore a flower-patterned silk shirt and seersucker pants. A gold necklace and a tuft of his chest hair protruded from where his top shirt buttoned. He sauntered over to an open-air bar where he had several bottles of alcohol from which to choose.

"I'll take a chardonnay," Bethany said.

Antony scanned the wine bottles until he found one he recognized. Bigglestone Vineyards. "The zin is good by me," he said.

DePino reached into a cabinet under the bar and grabbed them glasses, pouring white and red respectively. "Lovely day out today. You must have had a great time boating."

Antony smirked at Bethany mischievously, but she gave him a look that said he'd best not say how much fun. "Yes. Wonderful day."

A man came out from the house with a tray of cut cheeses, cured meats, grapes, and some crackers. He nodded to Antony and left them on the bar.

"Please, help yourselves," DePino said, handing the wine glasses to them. "How are things going since your big announcement? Shocked the world, I think. I lost a lot on the markets that day. No one knew what to make of it."

"Mm, sorry about that," Antony said, taking a sip of his wine. A deep zinfandel, more complex than most, which is why he liked it. "I'm doing okay. Living day to day now."

DePino nodded, scrutinizing Antony. He reached over for a glass filled with ice and some cocktail. "I don't buy that, politician."

Bethany stepped forward, her defensive instinct kicking in from years in the public eye. "We've had a great vacation, thank you," she said somewhat icily, reaching over to pick up a slice of cheese and a cracker, no meat.

Antony touched her arm but maintained focus on DePino. "No, it's okay. Fabio here reads people well. Likes to test it from time to time."

He remembered when he first met the man, when he lacked experience in politics, looking for any leg up in donations he could for campaigning. DePino had stood in his office, behind his desk pacing, making Antony nervous. He told Antony to tell him everything he believed about his platform and everything he didn't. And not to lie because he didn't tolerate lies. Antony nearly shook from the pressure at the time, and there were talking points he didn't necessarily believe. He gambled with the truth rather than giving his stump, and DePino had respected him for that ever since.

"Just like old times," DePino said with the small inclination of his chin.

"Alright, I've been miserable. I won't lie. I don't know what to do with my life anymore. And I'm frustrated as all get out that I didn't seem to make as big a difference as I wanted to. Hell, I don't think I made any difference."

"That's not true," Bethany frowned between bites of the cheese and cracker.

"It's a matter of perspective. People noticed. People are talking. Actually moving a populace..." DePino shrugged, then sipped his drink. "That's what I want to talk to you about."

"Enacting real change?" Antony canted his head, hopeful. If he had the backing of someone wealthy, perhaps they could find a way to work the system to back off of the escalating interstellar war.

DePino snorted. "No, of course not. You know a well as I do how the pulse of the voters goes. If it doesn't directly impact them, or if there's no scandal, you've got no chance. He motioned skyward. "What happens out there is an abstract."

"What do you propose?" Bethany asked.

"I told you. Actually moving the populace."

"I thought you might mention that. You still working on the ark project or whatever it was?"

DePino nodded. "The ship is coming along as planned. Crystal drive secured. Hull is in good shape. It's about filling in what we need to. Obviously cold sleep chambers with some backup power to make sure there's no issue. Hydroponics is a big deal, my daughter's working on that." He set his drink down and looked back to the house. "She's not here at the moment. Seminar on genetic splicing going on at Miami University. She may be by later." His attention drifted back toward Antony, but past him, more like he gazed into the ocean. "Where was I? Oh yes. What to fill the ark with. Two of every kind, right?" He laughed.

Antony joined him with a courtesy laugh. It was a crazy idea, and he couldn't be certain which parts of the eccentric rich man's schemes were real. "What can I do for you? Are you looking for a lobbyist for government permission? I know much better ones than I would be. I'm not exactly the most popular person right now with them."

"You'd be fine," Bethany said.

Antony gave her a smile to say he appreciated the support.

She winked at him.

"Okay, love birds, settle down," DePino teased. "Yes, actually. I do want you to work on that behalf. No one's actively working on stopping me now, but that's because the project doesn't feel real to them yet. Once I'm taking people away, they'll see it as taking their power, slapping their power in the face. The senate will vote to do something about it at that time, and the President might even make a stink. I don't want that to happen."

Antony took a sip of his wine, glancing at Bethany out the corner of his eye to see if she had any cue he could take from her. She seemed to be giving him the same look back. It wasn't the first time he'd been asked to lobby on behalf of a project—and certainly if Antony liked the person or if he thought the cause had merit, Antony had taken up those offers before, or had Bethany do so when it would have been inappropriate for him to—but none of those ideas had been quite as ridiculous as this.

Loading people into a big ark and starting a colony off in the middle of space. Even if there had been surveys from afar, one had to trust the ship to run, the cold sleep to work, no power failures, and then hoping that the environment would support human life upon arrival. Even with a one percent chance of failure, it could result in death, and at the cost of leaving all family, friends and loved ones behind. Who would go on such a crazy adventure aside from this eccentric rich man in front of him?

But he hadn't asked Antony to recruit for the voyage. He'd asked to talk to the senate and make sure it would be smooth as the voyage came closer. They would probably think it as preposterous and not give it serious consideration. If it did look like a success, they would begin to worry that there would be other copycats, full corporations packing up and using their resources to start new worlds too far from contact with Earth proper. It would be a threat to the government's power, and the prospect of losing some good workers and minds—if those types signed up for the voyage—would bother them even more. Of course, money would be the solution, like in most situations. What would happen with the credits left behind by the people on the voyage? Their houses? Their personal property? So many details to consider, and knowing DePino, the man probably hadn't considered them at all.

"I'm not sure, Fabio," Antony said after a pause for consideration. "Seems to me there's a lot that could go wrong with this. I'm not sure I support it."

"I can show you all of my documents, everything we're doing to line this up and make sure that we've got a good plan. We do. You know I hire the best people, and my daughter Kiyomi is working very hard on the sustainable elements like crop growth and modifying plants to cope with an alien environment."

"Have you picked a world?" Bethany asked.

DePino looked at her, blinked, and then raised a finger. "Of course, let me show you. Lisila," he said, speaking to the home AI program, "display star map sector three-three-zero-two by four-eight-seven-one-three, vertical axis point seven-oh-one."

The wall behind DePino's outdoor patio countertop shimmered out of existence, and a holographic display appeared, showing thousands of stars in the blackness of space.

DePino pointed toward an area on the right upper end of the quadrant, leaning closer to it to show Antony. "Right here. Lisila, highlight planet nine-nine-two-three-one."

The display drew a perfect red circle around one spot on the map. Antony narrowed his eyes but couldn't see much about it other than the star.

"We identified this particular place for a couple reasons. One, because it's at current speeds, nearly one hundred years travel to get there. No one would ever be able to catch us in time, hassle us, even contact us. And the better part is, if they tried, there's some strange EM radiation that blocks comm signals. Nothing in, nothing out. Pure silence for a place that has a very temperate climate."

"How can you tell the climate if communications can't get through?" Bethany asked.

Antony smiled to himself, wishing he'd thought of the question.

"An astute observer as your husband is! Are you sure your background is politics and not science?" DePino laughed. "Zoom in on the sector." The map complied, showing a fuzzier picture, an asteroid belt with a planet. Even with the hazy view, the planet appeared to have water regions, mountains, a green belt. It looked from here like it did support life, even at first glance. "We have several deep-space probes out into the galaxy. Have done so ever since we came across the Xy space and had the incident with them. Better to have a probe have such an incident and get blown out of the sky than some people. This direction, we found nothing. No intelligent species, no one traveling in space along with us. It appears to be a completely free sector of the galaxy."

"And that doesn't completely answer my question."

"No, but I've had some astrophysicists and xenobiologists through here. I've shown them, and they've assured me that this world would be one they could put in a definite category."

"You said you had a report, I can read it later," Antony said.

"Good man," DePino said. "Refill your wine glass?"

"Probably best to take it slow for now. You'll use my drunkenness against me to get me to agree to something otherwise."

DePino place his hand over his chest and made a face to feign offense.

Bethany laughed at that. "You couldn't have expected us to be so easy. We never allowed bills passed without a thorough reading from the governor's desk. It bothered lobbyists and legislators alike, but we never missed any small print."

"No, we didn't," Antony said, smiling fondly at his wife. They made a hell of a team. "What do you want us to do anyway? It seems like you've got this all under control."

"I do, except for convincing the senate. Even though you're no longer governor, I know you have good contacts among them." DePino smiled. "Politics is all about who you know."

Antony side-glanced at Bethany, not sure what to say.

"Of course, I don't expect you to commit to anything without reading my full proposal. You'll do your due diligence, and I can promise you, you'll find that we've done ours."

The amount of passion in DePino's voice made Antony begin to suspect the man had thought his plan out far more than posing an eccentric idea. DePino actually cared about this project, and was willing to put his money where his mouth was.

"Send it over to us. We'll read it and think about it," Bethany said.

Antony looked at her, perplexed. Bethany smiled.

EVALUATING

Toltair

Morgan sat in an uncomfortable chair in a lifeless room. It didn't help that she'd been here for more than an hour, even though her appointment had been set for 1100. Why must she suffer through the indignity of waiting for something she didn't want to go to?

People like her filled the ward. She'd never been big on vibes or feelings, but the grief and pain in the ward made the wait unbearable. She briefly glanced at a man who had a scar across his face, unable to help but keep looking over at him.

He met her eyes with an expression that told her she would be in for a lot worse than what he suffered if she continued to stare.

She lowered her gaze to the black and white checkered tile floor at her feet. Other people had datapads. They surfed through news or played games, but Morgan had no will for idle tasks. Her energy had been at an all-time low since leaving Esare.

The colony had never been a home for her. She hadn't been assigned there long enough. But it had gone better than most of her other assignments. On guard duty, one would be surprised at how poor the company could be. For the most part, if people were intelligent or well-trained enough to have better job options, they didn't often get assigned to standing and watching, with the sole purpose of looking intimidating with weapons. Most of her people had been as dumb as bricks. Dylan had been the rare exception. He made those late shifts tolerable, and she found she actually liked him.

But he was dead. Dead, dead, dead. Nothing would bring him back.

Her hand started to shake. Morgan gripped the fabric of her pant to stop herself. She couldn't lose it here. She had to come out of this cleanly, show the shrink she could do her job and do it well. Then, she could return to duty. If not to Esare, then somewhere similar. What else did she have?

"Lieutenant Morgan Ezra?" a female's voice called.

Morgan looked up to see a woman standing at the door with a datapad in hand, scanning the room. She met Morgan's eyes a moment later, giving a cordial nod.

Morgan stood, heading over to the door.

"I'm Dr. Carol Resin, happy to meet you. Please, my office is down the hall." The woman motioned for Morgan to come through the waiting room door, into a room of hallways beyond the counter where she had registered. Morgan followed her back to her office.

The office smelled of cinnamon, the scent coming from small candles lit on a shelf at the back. The woman had a shelf with a couple of intricate vases and some odd, shiny sculptures.

"Like the art, do you? I have some friends who are on the cutting edge of capturing chemical reactions within a field, then sealing them. It creates some interesting colors."

"Yeah. They seem nice," Morgan said politely. A long couch rested in the middle of the room. She moved over to it and seated herself.

"Can I get you tea or anything?"

Morgan shook her head.

Dr. Resin sat not quite opposite of her, but at a ninety-degree

angle in a leather chair. "Art is interesting. It has therapeutic proper-
ties, that much is certain. Do you do anything artistic? Even for fun?"

Morgan tensed, shifting and then leaning back into the couch to
try to hide the body language. Even the innocent question had potential repercussions to her evaluation. Sneaky. "No, don't have much
talent."

The doctor took a note on her datapad then looked back over to
Morgan. "We all have our own talents in our own way. What are you
passionate about, then? I see you've moved around assignments. Does
traveling appeal to you?"

"Not really. I don't know. I do what I'm told."

"Both ship and planetary duty. That's unusual, as they usually
make a person specialize. Some people can't get their ship legs," the
doctor said.

Morgan shrugged.

"You want to tell me about your time on the *Hellfire?*"

Morgan glanced back toward the shelf of art. Neither the questions nor the demeanor of the doctor bothered her much. She didn't
want to talk, didn't want to be here. She had to remind herself that
this woman had a job, like she used to have herself. "Not much
happened. Ship had a standard patrol duty of several colonies and
stations close to the Drenites. It's not like they were going to attack us
after the ceasefire."

"No, I suppose they wouldn't. They hold to their word. An interesting species they are. Did you hope to meet any non-human sentient
with your service?"

"I did what I was told."

"I see," Dr. Morgan said.

What did she see, though? Morgan started to worry.

Dr. Resin scooted to the edge of her chair to face Morgan, forcing
Morgan to look her in the eyes. "This must be difficult for you, with
the colony attack so recent. I'm not here to judge you or take your
career away from you."

The doctor's job literally entailed judging her, but Morgan didn't want to fight. She wanted everything to go back to normal. For the pain to be able to go away. To be able to sleep again.

"Is there anything I can do for you, Lieutenant Ezra?"

"No," Morgan said.

"I know this is difficult. Trust me, I do. I work with patients like you on a regular basis. And it may be too early to want to work through the details of what happened and figure out exactly how you feel about the situation. Yeah?"

Morgan nodded. Tears welled up in her eyes, but she wouldn't let them out. Not here. Not in front of a stranger who could take away her career.

"I want what's best for you, and I want to work with you to help you figure out what that is, as well. This isn't about what I think you should be doing." Dr. Resin leaned back into her chair. "Do you have any family or friends on Toltair?"

Morgan shook her head. "I'm here temporarily. Fastest place they could get me off-world."

"Sensible, that your commander would want to make sure you were out of the area that reminds you of pain."

Sensible, yes, but Morgan resented that decision all the same.

Dr. Resin tapped a few more notes on her datapad. "How about other worlds? If you like, I could make sure you're transferred to somewhere you have a better support network."

Morgan's family hated her. They'd fought tooth and nail against her desire to go into the military. She hadn't spoken to them in years. Her college classmates hadn't kept in touch, no one on her assignments so far had really bonded with her. Should she mention that? It made her sound callous or psychologically unstable if she didn't have any friends. "No, here is fine."

"Well, if you're going to stay here. Let's make it some R&R, does that sound good?"

She would have preferred going back to work, but from Dr. Resin's tone of voice, that sounded out of the realm of possibility. The decision had been made. "It's fine."

"It will do you some good. I've spoken with the commodore here on Toltair, and we've agreed that as part of the coverage, you'll be allocated some additional discretionary funds for entertainment and recreation. I'm not sure what you're passionate about, but we have some good sporting events, a baseball league that rivals Earth's from what I understand, and it's in season. I can recommend some good restaurants, night life, virtual gaming groups."

A stipend for her to vacation? Morgan found that rather strange. "Whatever you think is best," she agreed.

"This is about what *you* think is best, Lieutenant Ezra."

"I... don't do much outside of work, to be honest. I take overtime shifts when I can. Read. It's not that people don't like me... I rarely connect with anyone." Morgan regretted the words as soon as they came out of her mouth.

"I'm sorry."

Morgan felt like she shriveled before this woman.

"Don't be sorry. I'm not. I'm fine. I want to go back to work." Her voice cracked.

The doctor looked at her impassively. "I know. We're going to work together so we can get you working as soon as we can, okay? For now... how about an assignment? Why don't you meet someone, see if you can connect? In situations like yours, it's better to have someone there for you. You understand?"

Morgan nodded. Easier said than done, though.

"I'd like you to go out and make a friend. See what you can do. There's a group of military folk that meet nightly at 1900 at the Gastro Lounge if you want to try there. I can recommend Zanzo's Bar on Fourth Street, otherwise. Very friendly local crowd." Her eyes lit up some with the mention of that place. "Or anything I mentioned before. I'll send over a full recreation guide to your database, as well as my personal comm codes. You can call any time, after hours, anything. If I don't answer, it's because I'm in a session, and that's the only reason. We have emergency hotlines as well, in case of that."

Morgan sighed. She still didn't want to fight the woman. Even with what she said, Dr. Resin had far too much data on her. And if she saw the potential tears or the shaking in the waiting room on any video footage, Morgan wouldn't be back in an assignment any time soon. She had to play along for now. "Okay. Thank you, Doctor."

"My pleasure," Dr. Resin said. "Our time is up. Let's meet again in three days, same time, and we'll see how you're doing."

Great, Morgan thought.

SPINNING A WEB

Prison Colony 33-X4D

Dalton hadn't been this busy in a long time. It reminded him of operating a startup company. He had catalogued all of the Spider Clan's resources, all of the personnel, and started interviewing them for their strengths and weaknesses. They had a lot of strength, in the physical, expected sense of the word. The Tarantula had gathered a lot of folk around who could protect him and each other from rival gangs on the colony.

The colony had a program for those wishing education. They had AI installed and classrooms that taught every day of the week. One could go to the classes and obtain any remedial education they needed, as well as higher education. Dalton had toyed with the idea to shore up his credentials, but he had always found hands-on experience to be the best way to learn.

Most of the Spider Clan felt the same way about the classes, but for another reason—they didn't seem interested in learning at all. Dalton wanted to enact change there. Knowledge would do wonders here. If they found a team of engineers or geologists, they could find natural resources to exploit and at least make the colony nicer through hard work.

His first attempts to recommend studies were met with derision. It earned him his nickname among the clan, *Smarts*. With the little success he'd had in trying to cultivate learning, he certainly didn't feel *smarts*.

Without education, Dalton needed another plan. Unfortunately, he hadn't been the best at being the idea guy. He could execute a plan, sell it to people, raise capital for the job, and turn the idea into a reality. But what could a bunch of prisoners do here? They could use some of the goods-printers to make machinery or other items for luxuries, but they only had basic necessities stipends, which made it hard. It meant that they did need to cultivate resources themselves somehow.

"Smarts." The voice of the Tarantula came from down the hall. He had Beats at his side. And he didn't look too pleased. "What's going on here? You told me you were going to make the gang better."

"I did. It's only been a couple of weeks. I'm working on it. But it's like I keep telling you, we need to get educated first before we're going to come up with an effective plan for that."

"Not good enough. We need something now." He motioned for Beats, who stepped close to his desk and loomed over him.

Dalton looked up at the monstrosity. *Oh, no.*

Beats picked him up by the collar. Dalton kicked and squirmed. "What the hell? This isn't a way to get me to come up with better ideas! I want to help! This isn't helping anything."

"Motivation."

Beats delivered a quick punch to Dalton's kidney.

Pain shot through him. He exhaled hard and found it even more difficult to find a breath again. If Beats didn't hold him up, he would have fallen over.

"Guys are getting restless. There's talk of formin' another gang because we let in pussies like you. I don't want to regret doin' this. Everyone's watching, wondering what you're up to." The Tarantula inclined his head to Beats again.

"No, no!" Dalton mouthed, unable to find actual breath still.

Beats socked him in the gut again.

"So I'ma give you 'til tomorrow. Or the next day if I'm feeling really generous. But you need to come up with something to make the clan better, or else. You hear me?"

Dalton nodded. His body hurt so much. Please let it be over.

Beats dropped him right onto his knee, knocking him in the gut for the third time. This one sent Dalton rolling off his knee and onto the floor.

He *smacked*, face first, into the floor.

If he had been able to think before, plan, he hurt far too much for any ideas now.

"Thank you Beats. Let's go get our lunch mush and leave Smarts here to do some brain work," the Tarantula said.

Dalton could watch both of their legs exit the room, not even a goodbye, no ideas of their own on how to do good work for the clan. They were bullies who wanted everything done for them.

Dalton had known that going in. For now, he simply lay there on the floor, doubled over in tremendous amounts of pain. He rocked back and forth, unable to keep still. He needed to recompose himself and act fast. Something. Anything.

Another one of the Spider Clan came in—at least, Dalton saw someone's shoes from his vantage. That person snorted and laughed at Dalton on the ground.

"Smarts, why are you so stupid sometimes?" he chuckled.

Dalton grunted from his place on the floor. He slowly pushed himself back up onto his knees, taking it one breath at a time. The pain still debilitated him. Beats hit hard, imagine that.

He forced his face upward to look the man at the door. Red prisoner garb, a big man, shaved head, spider tattoo. He could have been any of the Spider Clan. This particular man had greyish-green eyes that were feminine, though. Hard to mistake.

The other inmates, of course, called him Pretty.

Dalton and Pretty had talked a few times since Dalton's head-shaving experience, about the Spiders, their purpose, the Tarantula's motives, and getting out of here. Both of them had in common that their sentences would only last them a couple more years. Both wanted to make more of their lives and not fall into the same prison trap forever. Pretty didn't quite have the wherewithal to do well with some of the academic courses that the prison had to offer, however.

Pretty bent down and grabbed Dalton by the arm, helping him back up to his feet. "They gotcha good, eh?"

Dalton huffed. "I don't know how they expect me to think of some business ideas when under threat all the time."

"It's how the Spider Clan works, you know that."

"Yeah, I do. Sleep in the bed I made, right?"

Pretty blinked at him. "You that hurt? You need to lie down?"

Right. Metaphors weren't going to be the best idea. "No, I'm fine. Hurts like hell, but it's mostly pride. At least, they didn't get my rib again."

"Ah yeah, that was you in the courtyard a few weeks ago, huh?" Pretty smiled.

"Yeah, I'm trying not to relive that one."

"You spooked some of the others real good. No one laughs like that 'cept a crazy man."

"I might be crazy. This idea might have been crazier." Dalton paced around the Tarantula's office. "I have to come up with an idea to better everyone's lives before they kill me."

"Good behavior might get you back into space and out of here."

Dalton shook his head. "It'll take too long for the guard to notice any good behavior, especially since I've already got a bad rep." Space. Not like the stars, but distance. "Wow, you might have come up with something good, Pretty."

"What's that?"

"Space. Everyone's at odds because of proximity, but we have a big world. If we all had our own homes instead of these dormitories, tempers might flare less."

"So you're gonna build stuff?"

"We are. The Spider Clan."

Pretty laughed a deep guffaw. "You think they'll work?"

"They will if it's for them. We'll be exclusive at that point. It'll be prestigious for clan membership and would keep us all occupied. It's a start. I have to work out electricity and plumbing... but with the hard labor plant we should be able to fabricate some piping, maybe even wiring. I'll have to study up on engineering, but it won't be that hard to build small residences."

"What about the guards? Will they let us?"

"Do they bother us about anything else?" Dalton shrugged. "I love it. Let's go take a walk and survey some property. Give the Tarantula a prime lot." He stopped in his tracks. "Oh, wait. We'll need lumber. That will require cutting. We'll need saws, blades."

Pretty smirked. "Spider Clan got plenty of those."

"You do? I thought all weapons were confiscated."

"You don't know how this works very well, do you? For Smarts, you sure can be stupid."

Dalton shook his head. Perhaps his plan would be enough to satiate The Tarantula. It'd buy him some time, at the very least.

PACING AND LEADING

Earth, Jupiter, FL

Kiyomi made her way through the grandiose double doors into the banquet room. People gathered around the bar, even more sat at white tables with cloths and hors d'oeuvres. She recognized some reporters from the Sol, the Terra Chronicle, BuzzBeats Today, and more. A lot of these beat reporters had covered her father many a time in their business sections, or personal interest columns, for some of his more eccentric ventures.

This should make both, or perhaps even the front page of some of these rags.

There'd been some rumblings in tabloids about his plan to reboot the human race on a different planet far from here. It sounded like a crazy idea. No expedition had ever left without the full cooperation and support of the government and sponsoring corporations. No one had ever ventured so far that it would take more than a human lifetime to get there. People couldn't believe it.

Kiyomi wasn't sure why he asked her to announce the project. Perhaps he wanted to market her to build her own brand. Perhaps because she had youthful features, a more energetic voice that could generate more excitement. She hadn't had a ton of experience public speaking, but the prospect didn't bother her either.

Her heart beat faster than normal, though. Once announced, this project would steamroll like never before. People across the Earth Confederation would latch onto the idea and flood them with ideas, applications, probably death threats as well. She would have to remind her father to up security around their house.

Kiyomi stepped through the sea of reporters, many of whom waved to her and called her over, but she didn't have time. Her whole presence might be an ambush to them. Her father had a flare for theatrics. She still hadn't decided whether she believed in the project or even wanted to go herself yet. How could she deliver this speech and not be a fraud?

Deep down, she understood she had no real choice. She would never abandon Dad or his dreams. He'd worked too hard for her to do that, and her own weren't too far off from his. She would be able to integrate a whole planet's species of fauna with another's. How many scientists or any people got to say they could accomplish something of that magnitude in their lifetimes?

Plenty of time to think about the hypotheticals later. For now, she had to deliver a speech. She stepped around the temporary stage set up, ascended a couple of steps and made her way to the podium.

The crowd vacated the bar and quieted. Several drones and cameras turned to her, snapping pictures and recordings. The reporters at the tables hushed each other, and people turned to face her, eyes eager for their next news cycle's story.

Kiyomi composed herself, taking a moment to look around the room. Showtime. She smiled. "Good evening everyone. My name is Kiyomi DePino, Fabio DePino's daughter. Ever since my father started his venture, DePino Starline Industries, I've watched as he transported millions of people across the stars, making their travel dreams come true.

"Everything my father touches seems to turn to gold. He's been named *CrossTime* Man of the Year three times and owned a majority stake in over five hundred business—not including his vast real estate investments. Truly, my father is a remarkable man, and with his remarkable talent has come passion for new adventures that make all previous endeavors pale beyond comparison."

Kiyomi turned around, and the lights dimmed with her. A holographic image of her father's ark shone behind her, rotating in three dimensions. People muttered behind her.

"This is the ark. The concept is a high-tech world in space, meant to be able to transport both plant and animal life, along with humans and supplies, in a deep cold sleep to a new world destination.

"Conceptually, it will be like the stories of old. Through advanced cryogenic chambers that will be integrated throughout the entire vessel, it will preserve anyone and anything inside from decay for a near hundred-year journey to its destination, Planet 99231, as it is dubbed by current researchers."

She motioned to the ark as appropriate, along is dimensions. The ship had a big, boxy shape with contoured angles meant to cram in as much life and supplies as possible, with a big hatch at the back where it sealed it all in. When she motioned, it zoomed to the inside to show both macro cryochamber rooms as well as individual cold sleep pods for human passengers.

"The ship will be piloted completely by an artificial intelligence, programmed with the top-of-the-line piloting skills that DePino Starline Industries are known for."

Kiyomi turned back to the audience who gaped, lost, as her father had intended with the speech. Soon it would be time to hit them with something that would knock them out of their chairs. "We plan to launch this program in six months' time, and through our network, we are taking applications from all over Federated Earth for crew and colonists for this historic journey to planet 99231. Specifics will be available to read online."

That got the reporters out of their seats like she thought. They were clamoring for questions. The camera drones hovered for a close up of her. People waved their hands around like mad. She couldn't quite make out what any of them were saying individually.

Kiyomi pointed to one. "David," she said to a reporter from the *Boston Times*.

"Thank you. Why are you making this announcement and not Mr. DePino?"

"My father is currently hard at work on the project and wanted me to act as spokesperson. Next question."

"Six months? How will you find suitable subjects for this crazy idea?"

"We have algorithms in place to process applications. DePino and its subsidiaries have had hiring practices in place for a long time. There will be in depth psychological as well as intellectual evaluations."

She said it all as if it were easy, but it would be anything but a simple task. In truth, she had reservations. It would be difficult to find volunteers to leave all of Earth and humanity behind in such a short time span. A big idea without the details executed, like her father typically did. She could piece together those details for him, bless his heart.

Kiyomi inclined her head. "Besides, there's been plenty of colonies established already. The only difference here will be that this will be so far away it is out of Federated Earth's jurisdiction or potential interference."

"Or any help humanity could provide you if something goes wrong. Speaking of which, will the ship be able to return?" another reporter asked.

"No, the ship is specifically designed so its parts can be used for the construction of buildings and infrastructure for the first city, including the use of its crystal power reactor which will be converted for dirtside use. We have a team of contractors from many fields already working on that."

"Will you have more of the plan released soon?"

"All the information is available online for you to read. We've thought out every contingency." Kiyomi smiled again. "Alright, enough questions. I have to get back to my father and work. Thank you very much for your time. There are refreshments free for everyone, please enjoy!"

The reporters again clamored together, trying to get that one last question in. "Is your father crazy?" "What is possessing him to do this?" "Is this treason?"

The negative questions flooded in. She'd been to press conferences before, even worked on ones for DePino in public relations, mostly in a charity capacity, as she wanted to focus on her own studies. "Always end the conference on your own terms," her father had told her when she gave her first one. "Never answer a final question. No matter what."

That advice held firm, as reporters tried to get more aggressive. Kiyomi slipped off the stage as fast as she could. Security held reporters off of her as she exited through a well-placed side door to a service hallway where none of the guests would have access.

"You did well," Dad said. He leaned against a wall, a long coat covering him and a hat with a large, round brim obscuring and concealing his face.

"You look ridiculous," Kiyomi said, turning toward him.

Dad looked up and grinned at her. "Only the best."

"If anyone sees you, you know, it destroys the credibility of my story that you're hard at work on the logistics of the ark."

Dad shrugged. "I have teams who are working on it. And I'm not a micro-manager. Never get anything accomplished that way. The application will go up soon enough, and with the press present, and if the net vlogs spiral the way I anticipate them to, we should have people filling out every portion of our new dwelling in no time. Civil engineers, crystal drive specialists, farmers, hunting sportsmen, all sorts."

Kiyomi shook her head, at amusement of her father's strong confidence in his success, if anything. "Did you find a new biologist yet?"

"I'm hoping that our original offer will be accepted." Dad smiled at her.

"Dad..." Kiyomi said.

He held up a finger to his lips. "Not now, Kiyomi. This is a celebratory day. I know you're still thinking about it and that you have reasons both to go and not to. I'm not going to pressure you."

Except you already are pressuring me, Kiyomi thought. She wouldn't say it though. This whole exercise may have actually been something to pace and lead her into accepting the offer. The thought infuriated her, but she had to calm down. When Dad got excited for these projects, he definitely manipulated, but didn't do it consciously.

"We're on track now. The technology element is pretty much done. All we need are the people." Dad rubbed his hands together in excitement. "Shall we head in and get some refreshments?"

"You're busy working, remember?"

"Oh, I finished up early and had to stop by." He moved toward the door.

Kiyomi rolled her eyes. His presence would create a media uproar inside. Dad played them like a fiddle.

Dad held the door for her, motioning inside. "M'lady," he said.

"Thank you."

They entered, and sure enough, the reporters caught wind, cameras turning on them, though no one approached. They knew better than to harass the DePinos during family time. Dad smiled and waved. "No questions, remember. Keep it casual."

"Of course."

"I'll meet you at the bar." He stroked his chin. "I wish the Lemkins would get back to me. I can already tell by our reception here we're going to need their help smoothing things over politically. If they reach out, let me know," Dad said.

Before Kiyomi could answer that she hadn't heard anything and ask him why would he expect she had, he took to socializing with members of the press. Kiyomi took a deep breath. *Here we go again.*

13

DECISION POINTS

Earth, San Francisco, CA

Antony watched as the movers set furniture into the living room of his upscale apartment in one of the tallest skyrises in the city. It had a great view of the bay—when there wasn't fog down below—but rose above that skyline for an equally stunning view of beyond.

It had a beautiful and elegant architectural design, was made for safety rather than luxury. As much as the governor's mansion over the last six years had been pleasant, he preferred the feel and views here. This building also had top-of-the-line security features with retinal scan access and stun-shock systems on the first-floor walls for potential intruders. He hoped it would make up for his former security detail.

Despite their powerful position, they didn't have incredible wealth. Antony had done well enough in government, been careful with his investments over the years, and Bethany had landed some pretty lucrative legal contracts from some of the biggest firms in North America, but they couldn't build starliners like Fabio DePino.

They had modest belongings, which Antony noted when the

movers set up the furniture: a comfortable sofa, a couple of chairs, and a nice holographic entertainment system would adorn this room. He had some art commissioned by a friend of his years ago, a nice landscape piece. He watched as the artist hung a rendition of inland Maui, where Antony grew up, on the wall. Though slightly impressionistic, the painting created a feel of home.

It relaxed him.

Bethany came out of their master bedroom, her hair unkempt and face shining from sweat. "Are you just going to stand there?"

Antony smiled at her.

She wore a casual attire of loose pants and a shirt meant for functional working, and even though she hadn't done up her makeup, her beauty stilled his heart.

Her cheeks flushed as she noticed him staring at her.

"I'm... supervising. There's a lot to set up in here, you know," Antony said, motioning to the men hanging the painting. "I don't want this to be crooked, would throw off the whole room."

Bethany made a tsk. "For that, I'm going to make you unload double the boxes. Glad to see you're in a better mood, though."

Antony shrugged. "I'm glad we moved from the mansion. We've got new space and can start a new life."

"I think it's the new job that does it for you, for real."

"This isn't a job, just some politicking." One of the movers carried a big box marked "office" and Antony motioned for him to take it in the proper direction. "You're making it seem much bigger than it is. We're just going to have to talk to Senator Marsh and a few of the others, get them to deal with approvals."

"I know you. You've been reading up on the colony every night, late, even when I ask to you to go to bed—which I highly recommend you do tonight, by the way. Or I might get upset."

"I wouldn't want that." Antony placed his hand over his heart.

"As long as we're on the same page."

Antony watched the movers work, thinking about what she said. Bethany moved back into the bedroom, where he could see her opening up a box of their clothing. He followed over.

"Maybe you're right about this plan. I want to get more involved than simply politicking. Maybe I'll end up drafting the bill which allows the colony launch. I'm craving something to do. Something that will help people and make a difference."

"I'm always right about you. How long have I lived with you?" Bethany chuckled.

"It's a purpose. I'm not even really sure I'm on board with it—"

"You are."

"What do you mean?"

"I mean you are. Go on."

Antony shook his head, watching her take clothes and place them on hangers. "I like the idea of lobbying this, though. He might meet with some resistance, because it's a bad public relations look to have people seceding and starting their own colony."

"That's why he wants you. You know your way around the senate better than anyone. And knowing DePino, he wants more help than a meet and greet."

"I am pretty familiar with a lot of the senators," Antony said. He moved over to the bed and leaned against it. "I think I'm going to help him."

"Of course, you are." Bethany held up a dress against herself. "Am I too fat for this now?"

Only one way to answer that. Antony waved his hands. "No, no. Not at all. I think you'd look amazing."

"Hmm..." Bethany said. She didn't want a real answer to that question, of course, and probably had already made up her mind. Not that Antony would have answered any differently for real. Few women maintained as good a shape as she had.

"No, I think I'll send it to Goodwill." She placed it in another pile.

"It's all about spin, really. I think we have to present this as some exploratory committee, not as a complete separation from Federated Earth."

"That's going to be hard to do with the way that the DePinos are already blitzing the press."

"We'll have to get him to shut up somehow," Antony said with a laugh.

"And we'll tell the bull in a china shop to ignore the red fabric everywhere and lie down quietly."

"You getting negative on me? We've had tougher situations before and gotten the senate to pass things. Remember the Midwest Agriculture Reform bill?"

"Yes, but we had something to offer them afterward. What are we going to offer the senate now, when we're telling them that the people who can do the offering will be gone and can't give them anything afterward?"

Antony considered. "I don't know. That's something to think about." He reached over and grabbed the fabric of her shirt, tugging gently.

"Antony... the movers are here."

"Don't care." He tugged on her harder, and she pretended to stumble into his lap. Her face came suddenly very close to his, her breath hot on his face. Antony gave her a small kiss.

"You should probably try Patty Carter in the defense committee. She'll be your best inroad in making sure that the more military-minded folk don't see this as a rebellion to shoot out of space."

Antony nuzzled against her. "You're right, of course."

"That's why you have me."

"No, I have you because you're nice to look at... and touch, for that matter. This is a bonus."

Bethany poked him in the ribs. "That's all you think of me?" She pulled back, faking a pout. "Well then you're going to have to settle until tonight." She slid off his lap, softly brushing her legs, hips and rear against him in a slow, teasing motion before standing. Then she pointed across the room at a large box. "There's your clothes, now put them away. I don't want to have to tell you twice."

"Yes ma'am," Antony said, feigning remorse, and moved to get to work.

14

VACATIONING

Toltair, Nuevo Ciudad del Rio

Morgan sat, legs crossed, feet dangling over a long chair in front of a small round table at the Night Moves Bar and Dance Hall. The bar had a transparency to it, changing color to the beat of music playing in the background. She had never had the luxury of sitting around drinking and listening to music. Never once in her life. Guard duty didn't lend itself toward loud anything. Some guards listened to music in earbuds, but Morgan wanted to be alert, never adding more distractions to her duty.

Life had been simple for her then. Eight-hour duty shifts. Grocery shopping. Going home and curling up with a good book. Even then, Morgan never had the most robust of social lives. Why had she listened to her doctor in coming to this busy place?

She shifted. The chair was made of some metallic compound—designed more for its looks than for comfort.

People packed into the club. A bartender shook some mixed drink, people cluttering before the bar. Bartending had a nice appeal as a job. It sure beat the night shift security duty of a military supply depot in terms of keeping busy. Though she enjoyed the quiet her old post offered.

Morgan closed her eyes and saw flashes of the bullet-shaped Aryshan fighters descending on the base. The blasts hit so close by. The screams of her companions and friends. Whenever she closed her eyes, she relieved the attack. It wouldn't go away.

She opened her eyes. A man stood in front of her.

"I close my eyes and listen to the music sometimes, too," he said. "It helps me feel it better. I think it amplifies my hearing abilities to turn off one of my senses." He smiled at her. He stood tall and had dark stubble on his face. Deep, dark skin and smooth contours to his cheeks. He couldn't have been more wrong about what she'd been experiencing.

Morgan tried not to panic. She wanted to get out of the loud music and crowded atmosphere, find somewhere to be by herself. Even if that was an alleyway out in the cold, she didn't care. This whole situation overwhelmed her.

Breathe, she told herself. And she did that. Inhale through nose, exhale through mouth. Slow, deliberate, and focused.

The man cocked his head at her with curious intensity.

She couldn't force a smile right now, it'd be too unnatural. He probably already thought her to be crazy, or disinterested, or both. A pang of guilt shot through her. He clearly wanted to talk to her. It would be rude to run away.

"Yeah," Morgan lied as best she could. "Helps you focus, right?"

"Exactly," the man said. He motioned to the chair across from her. "Join you for a bit?"

"Sure," Morgan said.

She couldn't look him in the eye for very long, not with his intensity. Not with how she felt so vulnerable right now. She eyed the dance floor instead, kids going crazy to the beat, rubbing up against each other like there would be no world tomorrow, trying to feel pleasure. They could be right. If the Aryshans came here, this would be the end. The thought made her shiver.

"You cold?" the man asked. He observed her with accuracy. "The bartender makes this drink he calls 'the fires of heaven' with a liqueur, I don't remember exactly what. It tastes really good though. Will heat you right up?"

Morgan swallowed, despite her dry mouth.

"Yeah, that sounds good," she managed to say.

The man stood and moved to the bar, giving Morgan a much needed respite from his advances. Not that they were unwelcome, a glance at him from behind definitely showed some attractive features. He had a very nice behind indeed. But he had the worst timing. She tried the breathing exercise once more. That would help. Hopefully, she had at least a few minutes to herself to calm down. Then she could try again.

It'd been two days since she'd seen Dr. Resin at the veteran's hospital. She'd see the psychiatrist again tomorrow. So far, Morgan hadn't gone out at all, sat in her room and read books, played light holo-games, ignored the world around her in procrastination. She didn't want to go out and see the sites in Nuevo Ciudad. She had no intention of lingering on Toltair longer than she needed to. So what good would it do to go out and make friends? But she didn't want to report that she hadn't tried, at the same time.

The bartender moved through the patrons with expert efficiency before making it to the man. He ordered two drinks, pointing back at Morgan. She waved to the bartender, who started mixing some red and orange alcohols with some clear stuff. The bartender carefully poured a topper and then flicked his wrist. It gave the illusion of fire coming from his fingertips, lighting the top of the drinks aflame. "Oohs" and "ahhs" came from the bar around the man Morgan had met. The bartender took a bow and the flames flickered out.

Must have had some nanotechnology or some device to use as a lighter. Morgan had been around the block too many times to be impressed by parlor tricks.

The man, however, seemed to be very impressed. He laughed on his way back to her. "That was fun! Bartender's great. Has the whole room captivated even though there's loud music and dancing going on!"

He slid the drink to her. Morgan looked at it skeptically. She could smell the potency of the alcohol without leaning in toward the glass.

What did she have to lose? She'd be taking anti-anxiety sleep meds later regardless. This might do the trick so she wouldn't have to. Morgan took the drink into both hands and brought it to her lips. The cool liquid had a bite and burn to it, and a pleasant cinnamon aftertaste. "Hmm."

The man's eyes lit up. "You like it?"

"A little strong, but maybe I could use that," Morgan said.

He drank his own fire of heaven much more casually. "I love it. Never gets old. Just the right amount of complication, I think. What's your name?"

"Morgan."

"Ah. I'm Zechariah, nice to meet you. You can call me Zee."

Morgan gave a half-hearted wave. "Nice to meet you, Zee. Thanks for the drink, by the way."

"Think nothing of it," Zee said, helping himself to another swig. When he set it down he'd already swallowed nearly a third of the concoction. "So what brings you here? Meeting some girlfriends and showed up early? Can't help but notice you look a bit distracted."

"No." Morgan shook her head. She looked down at her cup, the liquids not exactly mixing well within as darker hues swirled toward the top. She rotated her cup in front of her. "I'm actually new to Toltair. Don't really know anyone here."

Except for Dr. Resin. But she didn't need to mention her psychiatric therapy to someone she had just met. Perhaps she didn't have the best social skills in the world, but she could maintain a conversation without scaring someone off.

"Welcome, then," Zee said, all smiles. "What brings you here, to Toltair that is? If I'm not prying too much?"

"No, not at all." What would be her excuse then if she couldn't tell him the real reason and still appear to be sane? "I'm... vacationing."

"Solo?" He tilted his head in that cute manner like he had when he first approached, eyes hopeful.

Morgan shrugged. "Yeah. Needed some time to think. Figure out what I'm gonna do next."

Zee guzzled the rest of his drink before setting it down hard as if he had accomplished something. "Maybe some of the locals could convince you to stay here."

Morgan laughed lightly. "I'm not sure about that. I can't envision this planet feeling like home, if that makes sense. Uh, no offense to you."

"None taken. Well, there's always the ark project." Zee pointed skyward as he spoke, his tone holding light sarcasm.

"What do you mean?"

"You haven't heard of it? Where've you been the last few months? I mean, I know not here, if you're vacationing, but it's been all over the news cross-galaxy."

Unfortunately, that made Morgan start thinking of Esare colony all over again. She didn't want to remember that place, not now, not when the very word flooded her with darkness. She shivered. Then took a big gulp of the fires of heaven. Liquid courage, they called it. Didn't they?

"Busy. I work a lot, don't really watch news holos or anything like that," Morgan managed to get out.

Zee didn't seem to understand, but then, he couldn't. She hadn't given him anything for him to even get an idea about regarding her experiences. He wiggled out of his thin, black coat and held it up to her. "Don't see how you're cold in here, but would you like it?"

"No, thank you," Morgan said. What a sweet man. It hurt down to the pit of her stomach to act so cold. She didn't intend it, but it came out that way. Yet here Zee smiled at her, radiating kindness. Better he kept talking. "So tell me about this ark project."

"Ah, do you know who Fabio DePino is?"

"The starliner guy?"

"Yeah, him." Zee set his coat across the back of another chair at the table. "He's had this crazy idea he's been going off on the last few months, building a giant ship with everything humans could need for a new colony and heading off into space to start fresh. Apparently, he's got some planet a hundred years away at top FTL speeds to go to. Got computer modeled images only. They're building the ship above us." He motioned upward again.

"At the shipyards orbiting Toltair?" What an interesting story.

"Yup. They've got ads all over holos and the nets trying to recruit people to come to the colony. I think they're pretty desperate to fill the slots."

"Huh." Morgan said. She couldn't imagine herself cutting off all contact to humanity. The concept intrigued her all the same. She'd have to look into it. In all likelihood, the military would never let her come back into service, she had to be honest with herself. And though she did have officer qualifications, her tangible experience didn't offer much besides manning a guard shack. "I wonder if they need security."

"Probably. I hear they're trying for ten thousand residents, which is what they think they'd need for a long-term survival plan. With that kind of population, you have to have at least some police. Right?"

"I'd imagine so." There were probably already hundreds of applicants more qualified than she was. And they would probably ask for access to her psych exams for such a venture. Morgan didn't know why she even considered the idea. Could she commit to something so *final*? No turning back. A fresh start sounded about as appealing as anything else, though. What did she have to lose?

"You're seriously thinking about applying, aren't you?"

"Yeah," Morgan admitted. "I mean, the guy knows how to run things, at least. That starliner company is the biggest there is, isn't it?"

"Yeah, it is. Apparently, he's got a lot of real estate developments back Earthside, too. A real mogul. Makes you wonder what skeletons he's hiding that he'd want to leave all that, though."

Skeletons. Like the ones in her head. "Yeah."

"Hey, I didn't mean anything bad about you."

"I know."

Zee looked off toward the dance floor then back at her. "I gotta admit, I thought about it once or twice, too. I think I like Toltair too much to go for real." He hooked a thumb toward the dance floor. "But enough about this. Let's have some fun for your vacation, hmm? Dance?"

Morgan averted her eyes. She'd look like an idiot dancing. Definitely not her thing. Going into a dance club had been a bad choice, but the concierge at her hotel had insisted she would love one of, what he called, "the prime hot spots of Nuevo Ciudad". The liquor hit her like a brick, and her whole body loosened. *You only live once, Morgan. Suck it up.* And she hadn't been doing much living at all lately. She looked back up at him and forced another smile. "Sure. Let's do it."

A fresh start it would be, then. One way or another.

15

A HITCH IN THE PLAN

Kiyomi waved to a couple of her girlfriends in the hovertaxi as they ascended back into the night sky. She'd had a great night at an equally great restaurant, a much-needed night out after days of wall-to-wall barrages from reporters. Fortunately, none had followed her after she had given them a thorough rebuking upon leaving the house this evening.

She pressed her thumb into the front door's security panel slot. The locking mechanism accepted her credential and popped the door ajar, which she pushed fully open. In contrast to the darkness outside, the lights shone bright from the kitchen.

"Hello," Kiyomi said in a sing-song tone.

Marco popped his head out of the pantry, the older Latin man grinning with his chubby cheeks protruding. "Hey there, Kiyomi. Enjoy your evening of cheating on me?"

Kiyomi laughed. "I can't eat here for every meal."

Marco gave a mock frown, fully exiting the walk-in pantry with a box of flour in his hands. "Sure you can. It's what I'm here for."

Kiyomi walked up to the marble countertop where he put down the cornmeal, got to her tiptoes to give him a kiss on the cheeks. "No, you're here because you're family. I do need to have a social life sometimes, you know. It's not often I get to go out, with all the studying I have to do, or tending to my garden."

"Which I appreciate. I have some fresh chives and parsley for pancakes tomorrow morning because of it."

"Sounds savory," Kiyomi said, scooting her bottom up onto the countertop. "Where's dad at?"

"Been quiet in his study since dinner. I didn't want to disturb him in case he's going over the applications. He's been fretting about those quite a bit."

"I told him he needs to pick the top-level positions and leave the rest to his various department leads. I'll go snap him out of it."

Kiyomi slid right off the countertop as fast as she had seated herself there and rounded the bend to the hall that led to her father's study. Her heels clicked on the tile floor, echoing in the large house despite the hallway being lined with old family photos of her father, her mother, and her.

"Dad?" Kiyomi asked. The antique wood door remained closed. She reached for the knob but held back and decided to knock first.

No answer.

Kiyomi waited a few more moments and knocked again. "Dad?" she asked, louder. She turned her head toward the kitchen and yelled, "Marco, you sure he's in there?"

"One hundred percent. Went in, hasn't come back out. I've been here!" he called back.

Kiyomi scrunched her face. The quiet perplexed her. No, on second thought, it *scared* her. She knocked even harder. "Dad!" she near screamed.

Still nothing on the other side.

Kiyomi gave up and went for the handle, jiggling the old brass knob. She opened the door to her father's study, filled with old books, the smell of leather and old dust overwhelming anything else. He had a single desk and a computer there, along with a couple of pieces of artwork on the wall. He lay slumped in his chair, bent over his keyboard. Had he fallen asleep?

"Dad?" Kiyomi asked yet again. She rushed over to him and swiveled his chair some to try to wake him. Then, she shook him.

He didn't move.

"Oh my god," Kiyomi shrieked. She shook him harder. "Dad! Dad! No. No. No. Come on."

She flipped him back up to where he sat in an upright position, but his limp body fell over onto her. The sight of his face horrified her.

His eyes had rolled back into his head. Drool trickled down the side of his mouth. His complexion had turned his normally vibrant dark skin into a pasty mask. He breathed, but his head bobbed in a rapid convulsion.

"Marco! Call an ambulance!" Kiyomi screamed. She tried to prop him up, but failed again as he slid back like he would fall off the chair. This time, Kiyomi grabbed him under each armpit, dragging him from the chair. His weight proved far too heavy for her to carry, but she managed to lay him on the carpet floor.

He convulsed, but then he stopped.

Kiyomi cried while she waited for the paramedics to arrive.

WAITING

Earth: Jupiter, FL

Kiyomi paced the hospital waiting room. The place reeked of whatever sterilizing cleaning agent they wiped the place with. Bots circled the flooring for that very purpose. A few other tired and haggard people sat in chairs across from the room, but Kiyomi couldn't sit still. She had to move. Had to do something. Holotainment games or movies did nothing for her right now, couldn't distract her from the single focus on her father. She wasn't the most religious, but she prayed that if a God could hear her, He would listen this once.

A nurse came through the door. "Ms. DePino?" the short, plump woman asked.

"Yes?" Kiyomi asked, afraid to hear any news.

"Your father is awake now."

Kiyomi rushed forward.

The nurse stopped her with a gentle touch to her shoulder. "Hold on. He's very weak right now. He suffered a stroke, and we don't want to overstimulate him. He has asked to see you, and I can let that happen, but I want you to remain as calm as you can for now, and this will have to be a short visit to let him rest. Okay?"

Kiyomi nodded. She tried to moisten her lips but dryness lingered in her mouth. "Okay."

The nurse led her back through the waiting room, giving her a wristband for access before leading her through hospital corridors. Doctors, patients, guests, and orderlies wheeling gurneys carrying sick people clogged the halls. It seemed like a lot of people for so late in the night—or early morning. The plump nurse stopped in front of a room that said 422-B and held the door for Kiyomi. "He's inside. I'll be by in fifteen minutes to check on him. His vitals are hooked up to our machines for monitoring."

Cautious as she could be, Kiyomi stepped inside.

The room constricted around her, far too small, seeming even more so as doctors had cluttered her father's resting area with wires and tubes protruding from his arm, his nose, his mouth. Machines blinked and beeped by his bedside, and he lay propped up at an angle on his cot.

"Kiyomi," he said, voice so weak that she could barely make out the word.

Kiyomi stepped to his bed and knelt beside it. "Dad. Hi."

"Don't be afraid. Okay now," he said. It took him a long moment to turn his head toward her, in which he appeared supremely frustrated. "Muscles not working right. Getting old is a bitch."

Kiyomi couldn't help but laugh. "That's your takeaway here? What happened?"

"I was working on the project when my body froze. Right arm tingled. Could barely move. I beat on my chest with my other arm." He tried to mimic the motion but barely could raise his hand into a fist. "Thought heart attack. Even worse. Strokes mess with your brain."

Kiyomi reached for his hand and squeezed it. "You seem okay. Talking a little short."

"Hard."

Kiyomi nodded to that, trying to look as understanding as possible. She wanted to project love. But she couldn't hold back tears. Wetness dripped down her cheeks. "I was so scared."

"I know." A weak squeeze to her fingertips.

"So now what?"

"Doctors say lucky. Should fully recover."

"That's good news, at least." Kiyomi smiled despite herself, wiping away her tears with her free arm. "Mascara's going to run."

"Beautiful anyway."

Seeing her father like this tortured her. One of the most brilliant minds she had ever seen reduced to quick bursts of words. If the doctors said he would fully recover, then she had to trust that, but she hoped that he would return to form soon. It must have been far worse for him than her vantage as a bystander.

"They're not going to allow me much time. You need to rest up and get back on your feet, okay? Marcus is waiting to cook us meals in the morning."

Her father wheezed a laugh. "Marcus good. Keep ark project going." Of that last line, he sounded as adamant as she could remember him ever being.

"Your health's what's important to focus on, dad."

"No. The project. Promise."

Kiyomi saw her own stubbornness in his eyes. The very stubbornness that her teachers all the way from elementary school to her master's degree told her that she had. She was his daughter, after all. They were the same. She couldn't win this fight, and truth be told, she didn't want to.

"Okay. I'll go through your files and start working."

"Thank you," her father said. He closed his eyes, as if it were a strain to keep them open any longer.

"You're welcome. Now sleep. I'll come by in the morning to see how you're doing. Okay?" Kiyomi squeezed his hand one more time. Then she turned toward the door. She gave one glance back at him and stepped outside, where the plump nurse rounded the corner.

The nurse waved. "Visiting hours are over. He's had enough excitement for the evening. He'll be stable. We'll call you if anything changes." She bit her lip.

"Something's wrong," Kiyomi observed.

"It's not my place. Word should come from one of the doctors, but I know your father has been involved in this ark project that's all over the news. I saw you and liked your news conference."

"Thanks."

"After a stroke, muscles can get pretty weak. That includes the heart. I've read through his charts, and I wouldn't recommend him going off-planet any time soon, or perhaps ever."

Kiyomi blinked at that. Ever? This news would crush him. She couldn't deliver it to him while he lay in a weakened condition.

"Don't say a word, please."

"I won't. We wouldn't jeopardize a patient like that. I thought you should know, though."

"Damn," Kiyomi said under her breath. She put on her best professional face. "Thank you for informing me. We'll have to monitor this and see what this means for future plans."

He couldn't go. His whole dream, everything he'd spent billions of credits on in the last year down the drain. Kiyomi's heart sank on his behalf. Would he still want her working on the project, knowing that? So many chips had been set into motion that could hardly be abandoned now. But if a creator lost passion for a project, what chance did it have?

Kiyomi would follow her father's wishes for now. And she'd have a long talk with him when he stabilized.

For now, she'd head home. She doubted she would be able to sleep while her father remained in the hospital. Instead, she'd work on his dream, as she'd promised him.

17

LOBBYING

ANTONY'S SKYCAR arrived at the capitol building, the rotunda which had been used in the past for the United States of America, prior to the transition of the United Nations to the Federated Earth government. Now it housed the senate representing all of humanity. The skycar driver parked at the area in front of the rotunda steps, having received clearance to descend. When he looked out the tinted window of the black car, his eyes widened in surprise.

"Bethany," he said, patting her on the leg then pointing out the window.

Outside stood dozens of protestors, holding up signs, riled up and shouting. He read one of the signs. "Don't let traitors leave!" Another said "Lemkin Loser". Yet another had a picture of Fabio DePino with the words "Greedy Corporate" and the word "Colony" crossed out with a big red slash.

"I'm surprised they mobilized people this quickly," Bethany said, sounding completely unfazed.

Antony chuckled. "Nothing rattles you, does it?"

"We've seen protestors before. Some are paid by interests; some are people following their hearts. All of them don't have the inside information required to actually make decisions on policies. You'd think they'd want to protest the war, though. That is what will send their sons and daughters, their friends, their neighbors off to potentially die."

As the car descended, the protestors started to chant something that Antony couldn't hear through soundproofing. Police on the ground pressed forward, pushing the protestors back to give Antony's car a berth. They had riot gear on, in case. Antony wouldn't worry. Protestors had always been a normal part of government. He wished he could engage them, spend a few minutes with them to address their concerns, real or fabricated as they may be. But it never did any good. It might have a reverse impact of creating media footage to make him look foolish. Better to stay professional, walk inside, and not even look toward the crowd. He glanced back at Bethany, noting her black dress. It'd been an expensive purchase, but well worth it.

"Are you looking me over again, Mr. Lemkin?" Bethany's eyes twinkled at him.

"Always and forever. You ready?"

She nodded.

"Let's go." Antony motioned to the driver in the front of the cab. The man opened his door and then Antony's, shielding the side from the protestors to create another wall if someone slipped past the police.

Antony stepped out, clasping the button of his suit coat. He took a deep breath and put on his trained, expressionless face. Bethany followed, and he helped her out of the car with a hand.

"Thank you."

"Always." Antony turned, the direction opposite of the protestors, so as to not accidentally engage them with eye-contact, then proceeded up the steps.

The majesty of the capitol building stirred him, filling him with a sense of pride in humanity. Lawmakers and dignitaries had graced its hallways and the chamber inside for generations. The ancient building had been retrofitted and refurbished during his youth. He remembered watching news stories about it on television and dreaming of being here one day. The columns and art on the inside ceiling had an air of unparalleled statesmanship, which worked as well for Federated Earth's business as it had for The United States of America before.

Protestors shouted. Antony didn't listen. He couldn't. He had to keep focused on the task at hand, making sure the lawmakers inside understood his points on the ark project and didn't hold similar feelings to those outside. At least, someone inside did, because they had to organize it.

It might have been Senator Cristina Reyes from New Mexico. She'd never particularly gotten along with Antony, and made a big fuss on the news networks when he had stepped down. Alternatively, Jeff Shaner from Ohio had a strong patriotic streak. He might be opposed to the project on the grounds of what in his mind would be treason. He would be an important one to convince of the validity of this project, and that it wouldn't interfere with Federated Earth Operations or cause a string of copycats for a mass exodus.

Bethany's comm buzzed, and she pulled the device out, typing reverently into it as she walked. Antony thought of asking what could have been so important to message about in this situation, but knew his wife wouldn't be responding if it weren't an emergency.

They continued up the steps until they reached the door. Security opened it, ushering them in through the private entrance and not the direction the tourist public took. They had a quick scan for weapons, even people of their stature having to go through the security routines. One couldn't take a chance with the level of people involved inside.

Antony and Bethany were taken down a long hallway. "What do you think the mood will be inside?" he asked.

"I'm not sure. You received a lot of calls when you stepped down to make sure you were all right. Even people who fought our agenda hard were gracious. Perhaps some of that goodwill carried over?"

"Possibly, but I doubt it. With stepping down, it means we have less to offer them, doesn't it?"

They passed two large double doors to the main chambers area, where they were met by one of Senate President Justin Marsh's aides. Marsh served from Nova Scotia, which didn't have the population to make him one of the more prominent senators, but his general congeniality had earned him the slot. He'd been a fixture in the senate for years.

After rounding a corner, they arrived at a private office chamber, where they were ushered inside the Federated Earth capital building. A dozen senators sat at a long conference table, most of whom Antony recognized. Reyes, Shaner, and Marsh were there as expected, along with the six who made up the armed services committee leadership, California's two senators and Hawaii's lone senator, Koa Foley. The west coast representatives would be his allies. They owed him a lot over the years when he'd campaigned for them. Antony gave Koa a nod, which she returned.

"Mr. and Mrs. Lemkin. I'd half expected never to see you again," Marsh said from the long end of the table. He stood and motioned to the chairs at the opposite end for Antony and Bethany. "Please, both of you, have seats."

"Hello, Justin," Bethany said, her tone warm. She smoothed down her dress and seated herself in the chair to the right.

Antony moved around Bethany's chair and sat beside her.

"How have you been holding up?" Marsh asked.

"Oh, you know. Enjoying retirement. As much as I can with a galactic war going on."

Marsh frowned. "We probably should avoid too much talk of foreign policy."

"Agreed," Antony said.

"My office received the message that you're working on this project with Mr. DePino, so my first question for you is what you expect from us?" Marsh focused his eyes on Antony, intense as any hearing he'd ever presided upon.

"The project is underway. We're about half-staffed for the journey and want to make sure we're not going to meet with any unpredicted entanglements from the government. I wouldn't imagine there would be any, but..." Antony shrugged, letting that be the conclusion of his thought.

"I have a team researching the legality of this move, Mr. Lemkin," Reyes said, folding her hands over the table. She watched him like a shark moving in for the kill. "As you are aware, this is unprecedented, and to take so many vital roles out of our system in the middle of this crisis we have with the Aryshans..." She shook her head, a hint of mocking Antony in the way she didn't complete her sentence while pausing. "It's a bad look."

"The war is a bad look, Senator Reyes," Bethany said flatly.

A cool silence hovered in the room. Antony looked at Bethany. They'd discussed not making too many splashes before the appearance, but that had ended.

Bethany didn't return the glance but stayed fixed on Reyes. "Another bad look is hiring protestors to get the media cycle on this topic when we're having a private discussion."

"Nonsense!" Reyes glowered at Bethany

"Pardon, is there any evidence of this, or are you basing this on conjecture, Mrs. Lemkin?" One of the armed services committee members asked.

Bethany produced her comm unit and slid it across the table. "A job posting for the protestors outside. Traced and originated from Miguel Estrada's office, who is Senator Reyes's chief of staff."

Antony blinked in amazement. How had she procured that information so quickly? Her resourcefulness always amazed him.

Three senators hovered over to inspect the evidence on her comm, frowning.

Marsh shook his head. "Senator Reyes, you may want to recuse yourself from this meeting. I'm frankly disappointed that you'd stage such a publicity stunt to try to undercut Mr. Lemkin. He's no longer in office, nor a threat to you."

"I'm going to stay right here because I want to hear what they think they can accomplish with this absurd plan," Reyes said. She crossed her arms angrily, not backing down or appearing the least bit remorseful from the call-out. She would try to hurt them at every turn now, though she likely would have done so anyway. "My constituents are liable to be hurt by an exodus of some of the best and brightest in the galaxy, and moreover, we have to consider the morale hit to our troops that this will cause in our battle against these alien invaders."

Antony wanted to argue about the invaders. This Aryshan war started over an Earth vessel crossing into their space. Getting into the argument of the lack of a just cause on the Earth side of the conflict wouldn't be fruitful, however. Not with so much of the armed services committee here. They may have had other objectives with the war, and all arguing about it would do would be to waste time he needed to convince them the project wouldn't cause harm.

"That's enough, Senator Reyes," Marsh said. "You can stay, but I don't want outbursts. We have business to discuss."

Tanya Martinez, junior senator from California sucked in her bottom lip. "Are you intending to go with this expedition, Mr. Lemkin?"

Antony gave her a smile, sensing her nervousness. A lot of her political cache came from him and Bethany, and so she would be rightly nervous in losing that. "No. Bethany and I have our place in San Francisco. We want to do what we can to help change things from the outside. I can assure you though, we plan on staying here. Earth is our home."

"Hmm," Senator Shaner said. He had slicked-back salt-and-pepper hair and small, peering eyes. The others turned toward him. He often listened more than he spoke, which tended to make people listen far more intently to him than they did to others. "If you don't believe in the project enough to go, why should we consider giving blessing, even if that blessing is largely symbolic? I haven't discovered any laws on the books that would preclude Mr. DePino from doing whatever he damn wishes."

"Because it would make things easier. As stated by Senator Reyes, we don't want the public to panic or the troops to lose morale,"

Bethany said, gesturing toward Senator Reyes but never looking at her.

Senator Reyes turned red, fuming at her statements being reversed on her.

Antony swelled with pride for his wife. She was brilliant. Much better at debate than he ever had been.

"It's a valid point," Koa said. "If we act like the plan had our blessing all along, it would do wonders for appearances."

A couple of members of the armed services committee whispered together, then nodded. One looked to Senator Marsh. "We agree."

Not as hostile as Antony had expected. He relaxed his shoulders some as the tension in the room seemed to evaporate as well. "Would it be possible for the senate to then approve a non-binding resolution in support of Project Ark?"

The faces at the table stared at him, most looking contemplative. Reyes narrowed her eyes at him, anger seething from her. Marsh shook his head. "I'm not certain. As much as Mrs. Lemkin's point about the morale is a good one, Ms. Reyes also had a good point about taking some of the best and brightest and removing them from our ecosystem. While Senator Shaner is further correct that there is no law on the books precluding such an exodus, it is also against our best interests to endorse it. The question falls on you, Mr. Lemkin, why should we?"

Antony scanned Bethany from the corner of his eye. She gave him nod as if to tell him "you got this." He focused back on Marsh. "I haven't discussed this with my client yet, but it's my understanding that Mr. DePino is intending to take his daughter on the mission with him. She stands to inherit the entire DePino empire. We could, in theory, have those assets, or at least the value thereof assigned to the government. It's my understanding that he's accumulated enough wealth that it would create a budget surplus. You could do a lot of good with his resources, and the public relations gain would be huge."

Marsh considered "I don't buy the public relations gain. We're going to have hard enough time if we do endorse the project. But those assets are good."

"Also a one-time thing," one of the defense committee members said.

"There is also that," Marsh agreed.

Shaner leaned toward the table. "How about I propose something more tangible and lasting?"

A few of the others at the table whispered amongst themselves.

"I'm all ears," Antony said.

Shaner didn't waste time with nonsense. Something Antony could respect. One never could tell what side he'd fall upon on an issue. He seemed to have his own internal weighing mechanisms that were beyond normal partisan influences or even lobbyist influences. That's why his constituents loved him so much.

"We have a problem," Shaner said. "Are you aware of Prison Colony 33-X4D?"

Antony had heard of the place, but never dealt with it beyond a cursory glance of the news. "It's my understanding that many of the worst criminals are shipped out there so that they're away from regular society."

Shaner nodded in his usual deliberate manner. "That's right. My committee provides budget and oversight for the colony, and we've noticed an uptick in guard hazard cost as of late. This made me look more deeply into the problem. It seems a recent influx of prisoners has created a population bubble at the prison itself. Now, there is a full continent they can explore and spread out, but the amenities, food dispensaries, and the like are all centrally located. This is for our guards' safety as much as it is for theirs."

Antony listened, not sure where Shaner was going with this explanation, but he also had nothing to add.

"The result is an overcrowding in close quarters, from which violence follows. We can't have this, and so I have a solution that would benefit both of us."

"The funding we proposed from DePino could help build more infrastructure," Bethany said. "That's not a problem."

Shaner waved her off. "No, I mean a much more permanent situation to alleviate the problems. If you took, say, ten percent of the prison population with you on this venture, it leaves us time to fix the infrastructure, as you mentioned. Right now, it's a powder keg waiting for a single match. We can't have that."

Antony considered. The creation of a new humanity would be DePino's objective for the expedition. A humanity away from violence and strife, one with the greatest minds assembled to work together for a fresh start. If they had to take thousands of prisoners, it could be disastrous. "I'm not sure that's in the cards, senator."

"It's going to be my condition on supporting such a resolution," Shaner said.

"I agree with him," one of the armed services committee members said. The others voiced their assents as well.

"Seems like this would be a good condition. You proposed a creative solution to what could be a dangerous problem. It would assist to alleviate tension, which would help remaining prisoners who reintegrate back into society, and give the government incentive to allow the ark project to go forward," Marsh said.

"The ark concept is not one that lends itself to a violent prison population," Antony said. This might kill the whole thing. He didn't have a good answer. DePino would never agree to it, would he?

This was exactly why Antony dropped out of the government. All the bureaucrats only considered their own problems and how to shuffle them onto someone else. His face became hot, and he clenched his fist. Even the "good" senators had one-track minds when it came to politics.

Bethany placed a hand on his wrist. "We'll talk it over with our client. Perhaps we can work out a compromise such as non-violent prisoners going," she said, all smiles. "Senator Shaner, do you have dinner plans this evening? I haven't been to the Brazilian steak house here in over a year, and I find myself craving it. And some good company, of course."

Shaner considered and then nodded. "I'd be happy to join you."

"Good. This is a good starting point," Bethany said, releasing Antony's arm. "I'm sure there's more details that we can all transmit through our aides, but this has been very productive." She gave a nod to Reyes specifically. "Thank you all."

"Yes, thank you." Antony maintained his stoic face while Bethany took over. He watched her stand. DePino wouldn't like this one bit. Even his assets were supposed to be a down-the-line negotiation point, but Antony figured that amount of credits and assets would sway them more than anything.

Antony didn't much want to go to dinner with Shaner after he'd pulled a fast one on him like this, but he had to play along. At least he had Bethany to calm him down.

18

NIGHT TERRORS

TOLTAIR, NUEVO CIUDAD DEL RIO

MORGAN LAUGHED. She laughed so hard she couldn't remember having laughed like this in years. What had kept her from being this happy before?

Wine glasses clinked at the end of the table. So many happy faces were with her. Her mom, her dad, her sister, several of her girlfriends from high school—they all sat at the table. They laughed. A joyous occasion for celebration. What were they celebrating? Morgan seemed to remember being estranged from them, but it didn't seem to be the case here.

The table had a white cloth with ornate gold trim around the edges. Candles lit the whole length of it. Severs prepared a full banquet. Wine, lots of wine everywhere. Morgan couldn't remember a happier time. She belonged here.

One of her girlfriends grabbed her arm. Morgan looked down at the grip on her. Tense, white knuckled.

"What's the matter?" Morgan asked.

She glanced up to her friend, and saw a face she didn't recognize. Dark eyes, a silver hue to the skin, pale. Strange ridges protruded from the head like a crown adorning her skull. An Aryshan replaced her friend. A spy. What would one of those be doing here?

The alien smiled, but it didn't seem like something happy at all. No, it bared its teeth.

Morgan recoiled, pushing her chair backward to try to scramble away, but she couldn't get out of the Aryshan's grip. "Help!" she shouted.

Another glance around the table revealed everyone there to be one of those strange aliens. Her family had disappeared. Her friends as well. Aryshans surrounded her, and they all stared at her like predators ready for a feast.

The sound of sharpening knives came from a seat to the right of her at the table. Steel on steel, a cringe-worthy noise. The Aryshan repeated the motion.

"Please, stop! I'm not your enemy. I don't know why you're doing this, but you have the wrong person, I swear!" Morgan protested.

Laughter ensued from around the table, not at all like the type she had heard moments prior.

The Aryshans moved with incredible speed, much faster than any human could have mustered. They came for her, holding her down, squeezing her more and more tightly.

* * *

Morgan tossed and turned. Her sheets constricted around her. Her sweat dampened the bed, and despite being wrapped up like a cocoon, a chill ran through her spine.

She squirmed until she broke free of the sheet's clutches, sitting up against one of her pillows and pulling her knees toward her. Then she wrapped her arms around her legs, using her thighs to prop her head.

It was a dream. That's all. No Aryshans would be coming to get her. Toltair was far from the border. She had Zee here, too.

With that last thought, she turned her head to her left, noting her new friend, lover—whatever people called these things these days— lying next to her. He slept soundly, his chest rising and falling with each small breath, head tilted to the side.

Morgan wondered what he dreamed about, and if those dreams shook him like hers did her. Likely not. She had problems. Despite a couple of weeks together now, she hadn't made him aware of those very same issues. Maybe tomorrow. That's what she told herself every night when she woke like this, unable to get any rest.

Since moving to Toltair, each day had become more of a grind to get through. Staying awake became challenging. She yawned during conversations with Zee. He questioned her on whether she felt distant, and she lied and told him not to worry. Everything he did held such selflessness. He didn't deserve to be treated the way she treated him. Perhaps she should break it off...

But then what would she have? She couldn't leave here, remaining on a forced vacation as her shrink had told her to. Those meetings hadn't been a success, either. More questions, more note taking, and very little in the way of answers. Dr. Resin wanted Morgan to "de-stress" herself. She had homework to look herself in the mirror and say positive things aloud to try to affirm her way to normalcy. The idea had been a stupid one, and she'd stopped doing it after the first couple of days, though she told Dr. Resin it helped her.

Now what would she do?

Morgan pivoted, sending her legs dangling over the side of the bed. Zee's apartment didn't allow for much privacy. It had one bedroom that overlooked Nueva Ciudad from a few stories up. Other skyrises blocked most of the view, but it still had some charm. He had a small living area and kitchen past the bedroom. It had a couch and a nice holotainment center for her to peruse when she couldn't sleep.

Morgan tiptoed away from the bed and out to the living area, plopping herself down on the couch. She turned the lights to low and stared at a chrono over in the kitchenette that read "0300". Hours yet before Zee would wake and go to work, leaving her alone for the day. No more alone than now, in reality.

She should tell him about her nightmares. Why did she have so much trouble with it? Truth came out eventually. One of her prior boyfriends had cheated on her for more than a full year before she caught him on his comm. It faded into distant memory now. Her anger had faded, but it had sent her reeling at the time.

A boyfriend cheating on her could hardly be compared to the

death and destruction she'd witnessed. She overthought everything and internalized the pain of her trauma—again.

She picked up a privacy visor to turn on the holotainment system, placing it over her eyes, and the earbud speakers in her ears. Instead of using the usual voice command, she motioned in the air in front of her to turn the system on, a useful feature for trying to keep quiet. She'd never had such a thing in her life. Her mother wanted to keep her away from too much entertainment so she'd be focused on the real world. As an adult, Morgan kept with those lessons for the most part. She'd never gone too far into the entertainment world. Now she wished she'd had more interest in it. To turn off her brain and relax sounded like heaven.

Oddly, she found herself drawn to news vids. A news anchor had a couple other guests projected on either side of him. A political discussion show, no doubt. Morgan hated those, a big waste of time. But before she could flip the channel, an image of a large ship in drydock appeared over the host.

"Welcome to Talk at Lightspeed with Marlin Scott. Today I'm joined by Joanna Goodnow of Io Free Press and Ola Erickson of EGH Consulting group. News of the day is former North American Governor Antony Lemkin met with the president to discuss eccentric trillionaire Fabio DePino's ark project. Joanna, what do you think the mood was in the meeting today?"

The woman to his right inclined her head. "Thanks for having me, Marlin. It was a tense meeting. It's no secret that Governor Lemkin is no fan of President Ely's foreign policy, after his shocking resignation several weeks ago. From my understanding, he's got some members of the senate who feel betrayed by the action, and they relayed their concerns to the president. It's also odd that DePino hasn't been present at these meetings. He's usually very hands-on with his projects."

Marlin nodded. "I agree, but DePino's spokeswoman gave no comment on his whereabouts. As far as the former governor, I can't imagine what Lemkin is thinking. Perhaps the tabloids have some truth about his subsequent mental breakdown. Ola?"

The man to Marlin's right shook his head. "All of these reports are unsubstantiated and, no offense to Joanna, but she exemplifies the inherent media bias to the situation."

"There's no bias. We report on what we see, and this entire idea of picking up a bunch of people in six months and starting a colony is crazy," Joanna said.

Ola laughed. "You forget we're dealing with shrewd businessmen and politicians here. Everything is calculated before they even make a move. It's no secret that people are tepid about the Aryshan war. I mean, if you look out to the colonies—they're probably as angry about it as Governor Lemkin is."

Anger welled inside Morgan as she watched. These people had no idea how people felt out in the colonies. How their lives were upended by this alien force. The Aryshans showed no mercy, and she, for one, wanted revenge for that.

She tried to calm herself and turned off the program with the motion of her hand. News only upset her, as she thought it would. But then, everything upset her.

Even though Governor Lemkin's thoughts on the Aryshan war didn't appeal to her, the ark project did. It had lingered as a thought in the back of her mind since Zee had mentioned it the first time they'd met.

"Function, search," Morgan said softly, still not wanting to wake Zee. A display of a search bar appeared in front of her visor. "Ark Project job postings."

The network took a moment to respond, and then pulled up the DePino Industries official page. The big ship rotated on the holo, a majestic display. A sun rose behind it.

"Welcome to the DePino Industries Ark Project job registry. There are still more than fifteen hundred postings available, and you might qualify for the work. This promises to be a fresh new start for everyone involved and for humanity itself! Please inquire, and the DePino Host AI will answer all questions."

Morgan watched the polished graphic. These people sure knew how to make slick marketing brochures. But was this a crazy idea like the pundit had said? It couldn't be any crazier than working for the military on border worlds. She'd nearly lost her life already.

As much as Dr. Resin wanted her to continue her relaxation program, Morgan shifted with antsy energy, wanting to get back to work. Sitting around doing nothing made matters worse, not better. She had more to think on, more to reflect on. The relaxation was meant to purge these thoughts from her system as she evaluated them, but Morgan wanted a distraction that would take a substantial amount of hours. Real work, not games and recreation.

"DePino Host AI," Morgan said, a friendly bleep returning her words as an acknowledgement. "Are there any security postings available for the colony?"

Without a delay, the AI responded, "There are seven security postings currently available. Chief of colony security. Power plant watch. Night patrol officer..."

"Pause. Tell me more about chief of colony security."

"Military service preferred, five years of security related experience as a minimum. The chief would interact with all six other colony security posts to maintain order and ensure the laws of the colony are obeyed."

Much beyond her experience. She'd managed people in security postings before, though... Even so, she would probably never get the job.

Morgan bit her lip as she considered. She could always apply, worst they could do would be to say no. And if they said yes, she didn't have to commit to going. She could always back out. It's not like they'd be around to make her life harder about the process. Why not try it? "Send relevant bio and work experience to DePino Host AI."

The network complied, and an hourglass appeared, rotating as it processed. Another bleep. "Application received," the AI said. "Your experience and qualifications appear to be on par for the task at hand, and DePino representatives will be reviewing and contacting you shortly."

Morgan yawned, her body telling her she'd had enough excitement for the morning and that she hadn't gotten nearly enough sleep to make it through the day. She disconnected the headset, placing it down on the table. She'd made it past AI screenings, but as soon as a live person reviewed her experience, she would probably be out of the running.

She stood and tiptoed back into the room where Zee still slept soundly.

19

COMPROMISES

EARTH, SAN FRANCISCO, CA

KIYOMI SAT across from both of the Lemkins, who casually leaned back on their sofa. They were an adorable couple, even for their age. In fact, they looked much younger than their stated ages on their profile.

Kiyomi had met them before, once, but only in passing when she studied for her bachelor's degree. A handshake and a smile at a dinner, like most of the people who her father dealt with. Now, she found herself in the apartment of a former governor. Most people her age would look up to her and think she had incredible talent for being able to attain such a high-profile meeting, but Kiyomi had work to do. She wouldn't congratulate herself until she accomplished what her father wanted.

She crossed her legs and picked up the cup of tea that Mrs. Lemkin had poured for her.

"On our end, positions are filling up fast," Kiyomi said. "We finally found a good applicant for security chief with a military background and a good service record. A woman who lives on Toltair, which is perfect, since that's where the ark will be launching from. We're progressing on schedule and close to budget."

"Good for you," Mrs. Lemkin said with a warm but very political smile. She ran finger through her hair to push strands back behind her ear. "We've met with some success as well in getting government approval."

"That's good news."

"There's a caveat to that," Mr. Lemkin said, glancing at his wife and then back to Kiyomi.

Kiyomi raised a brow. "What's that?"

"The senate committee laid out some conditions for their support. I've been trying to get them to back off it, but you know how political types can be once they have their mind set on something. It turns out that the promise of a portion of DePino Industries' wealth as a donation isn't enough to satiate them. They do like the one-time boost, but they don't see it as a long term assistance after they resell the assets, and the government has no interest in taking on operations."

"We could always appoint an advisory board to run the industry. The companies run themselves at this point, to be honest," Kiyomi said."

Antony waved her off. "I tried mentioning similar when I spoke with the president. The senate got to him and convinced him that he should ask for more."

Kiyomi considered for a long moment. "Asking for more means they didn't say no. Unless I'm missing something?

"You're not wrong," Mrs. Lemkin said. "But what they ask for, they're firm on."

"You're not wanting to tell me something. Come on," Kiyomi said. Politicians annoyed her. They were far too good at saying nothing and making it sound like they had said everything.

Mr. Lemkin looked her in the eye, unfaltering, as he had been trained to do. "The president and senate wish us to take a number of prisoners from Colony 33-X4D with us on our journey."

Kiyomi laughed. "A few prisoners? That's not a big deal. I think we can handle them... isn't that the violent crimes prison planet, though? Are we talking murderers?"

Mrs. Lemkin shook her head. "We've negotiated that murderers are not a risk we can take because of the small group of colonists we will have. They agreed that would be an undue burden."

"The number, however," Mr. Lemkin said, "is far more than a few. They want us to take two thousand."

Kiyomi couldn't believe the number, and laughed. "That's more than the open job postings we have left."

"The government is not open to negotiation on this front. You'd better make room," Antony said.

Kiyomi set her tea cup down, considering it. Two thousand prisoners? That would overwhelm the colony. There's no way that would work. It would undo everything her father had set out to accomplish in the first place. Her father's vision required the crew to be the best and the brightest, a new humanity that could shed off some of their worse basic instincts. With so many criminals, it would never work. "We can't do it. This would ruin Project Ark."

"That's what I tried to tell them," Mr. Lemkin said.

"And they didn't listen? You were supposed to be our ace-in-the-hole lobbyist. People respect you."

"Far less than they did before. I tried to tell your father that," Mr. Lemkin said.

"We did what we could," Mrs. Lemkin said.

"I don't even know that my father will want to go through the project with this news. But... I suppose, if we can get psych profiles on the prisoners we take... Did the government specify any requirements?"

Mr. Lemkin shook his head. "No. They seem more concerned about removing quantity than anything else. We could likely have our pick."

Kiyomi stood and paced toward the window. She liked to move around when she thought. Sitting kept the blood from flowing. She looked out onto the San Francisco skyline. Could this work with a pick of who they wanted? Resigning colonists to mixing with prisoners required gambling with people's lives. They would need to shore up their security measures. The seven that they had planned for the ten-thousand strong population wouldn't work if such a high percentage of those were convicted prisoners.

"I'll talk to my dad about it. I think it's possible it can work, depending." Kiyomi paused. "I don't know. Maybe I'm wrong. I'll have to bring this to him and see what he thinks. This is a really big change to the plan."

"I know," Mrs. Lemkin said. "Trust us, we did everything we could to try to say no to this during both of our meetings. They wouldn't budge once they had the idea in their heads."

Mr. Lemkin stood and joined her by the window. "Kiyomi, there's been something I've been meaning to ask you about, if you don't mind."

Kiyomi looked at him, somewhat taller than she was, handsome, wearing a very fine suit that added to his professional credibility. She could anticipate the question, something she'd avoided answering. "Yeah?"

"Where is your father? It's strange that we haven't heard from him at all these last couple weeks. He lit up my comm with calls before."

Kiyomi betrayed her hesitation by looking away from him. A trained politician would have to see her reluctance. She'd seen enough of her father's negotiations to understand the importance of body language.

"If I tell you the truth, this doesn't leave this room. Okay?" She met Mr. Lemkin's eyes.

Mrs. Lemkin slowly raised herself from the couch and maneuvered over to them. She stayed unobtrusive, as if intentionally not trying to spook Kiyomi.

"Of course. You're our clients. We would never betray any confidences," Mr. Lemkin said.

Kiyomi let out a long breath. "Okay. My father had a stroke. He's in the hospital recovering, and we've actually managed to not have the media track it for once, thank god. As far as anyone knows, he's being reclusive and strange in his home. We have an actor as a body double there to pop into windows occasionally to keep up the illusion. With all the press as it is, we didn't want to stir up any more concerns during the job application process. It's already tough enough to get people to sign up for this venture."

Silence filled the room, broken by Mrs. Lemkin, "Smart thinking. I'm sorry to hear about your father."

"Likewise," Mr. Lemkin said. "When is he going to be fully recovered? By launch time?"

Kiyomi frowned. "The doctors don't know. They are advising against him going on this trip at all. They're not sure his body can take exit velocity from the atmosphere without severe issues, and so they're telling him he has to remain Earthside."

"As in, he wouldn't go on Project Ark at all?" Mrs. Lemkin asked, shock in her voice.

Kiyomi looked over to her. "Yes, that's what I'm saying. I've talked it over with him a few times, and he's insistent that he wants this to go on... and that he wants me to go."

"Are you going to?" Mr. Lemkin asked.

"To be honest. I don't know. This is his project, but I at least have to see it to the finish line." Kiyomi heard the regret in her own voice. If she didn't project that she believed in this, how could she convince others to sign up? She probably said too much to these politicians, even if they were working for her father.

"Thank you for letting us know, Kiyomi," Mrs. Lemkin said. "I'm sure this is a heavy burden for you. But don't worry, we'll still work on this."

"Agreed. Your father's always been there for us. He believed in me before I had a name to myself in politics, and I am a loyal person. We're not going to do anything to hurt him or his project, especially when he's in a condition like you said. Send him my best?"

Kiyomi nodded. Perhaps she'd been too harsh on these two, calling them politicians in her mind. From the looks in their eyes, they at least believed they were being genuine with her. She found she respected these two.

"I will. I should go talk to my father about these changes you mentioned. I'm sure he'll want to know."

Mr. Lemkin moved toward the door to open it for her. He turned the knob and held the door. "Thank you for coming, Kiyomi. Let us know what else we can do to help."

"Thank you both," Kiyomi said.

She couldn't bring herself to force a smile, and so she departed without one. Her father would fume. Hopefully, he'd have some ideas on how to mitigate the problem of prisoners. Kiyomi couldn't honestly say she would feel safe on the expedition, with hardened criminals aboard. If word of this got out, a number of others would bail on the project.

She shook her head and wondered to herself how she went from being the expert in botany and ensuring the food production of the colony would be suitable, to being full time public relations damage control.

20

OPPORTUNITY

SOMEONE RAPPED their knuckles on the top of Dalton's hard hat. He recoiled, despite no actual danger to himself. Too many times on the prison colony, someone sneaking up behind him or even coming at him openly had led to him getting his ass kicked. He developed quite the nervous tic, but staying wary meant staying alive, so he didn't mind looking foolish from time to time.

Beats, the Spider Clan member who pranked him, doubled over laughing. "Gets you every time, Smarts!"

"You're a funny guy," Dalton said, trying to take a conciliatory tone even though he dripped with sarcasm.

Before them stood Dalton's first construction project. "Stood" might have been a loose term, as several Spider Clan members worked to push the recently constructed wood framing of the building to make it square with the opposite side.

It had taken some time. They had to secure lumber, which meant cutting tools. The prison guards didn't like letting those out, but finally agreed to it with their supervision. Dalton had sold the guards on the idea that building and spreading out the prisoners would eventually lead to less work for their team.

He'd had quite the run of success in selling his ideas as of late. The Tarantula bought into his plan, the guards had, and now the majority of the Spider Clan appeared willing to work for him. But even with his good sales track record, no string of luck ever lasted that long in his experience. Something had to give.

The opposite side frame came crashing down, clanking hard on the ground. A couple of Spider Clan members dodged out of the way of the fallen frame, barely escaping broken bones.

"You have to secure that before letting it go!" Dalton shouted, rushing toward the construction crew.

The Spider in charge shrugged. "I ain't never done this before! Neither have you. You didn't tell us."

Dalton wasn't an architect or a contractor. He learned what he could from the prison enrichment and education holosystem. The prison had some deep hypnosis speed training, but that only went so far when one had no practical experience. He may have missed a step here or there.

Dalton surveyed the frame, motioning for a couple others to lift it up. They did so, and he inspected the wood. The nails held. Nothing appeared to be cracked. They had gotten lucky. "We're okay," Dalton said, projecting calm as best he could. "Let's try it again. This time have someone hold this frame in place so we can get the other up and attach some beams."

The Spider Clan men grunted, never happy about additional work, but they complied. They pushed each frame up again, and people didn't move from their posts this time, holding the frame secure. Beats went to get a ladder and with the assistance of another, raised one of the beams.

Perhaps he'd underestimated some of the prison population in thinking that they were irredeemably dumb. They didn't have book smarts, but they did learn quickly, even if for mostly manual labor tasks.

Dalton stepped back again to survey the whole job.

"I am pleased," a voice said behind him, causing Dalton to jump again.

He spun, and in front of him stood the Tarantula. The leader of their little prison gang didn't come out into the open too much, which made sense, because he could be a walking target, even with so much of his crew around. It also added an air of mystery to him which made him seem more important than he might actually be. Some of his psychological manipulation of the other prisoners inspired Dalton. A business tactic to remember for the future, if he ever managed to leave this place.

"Yeah, we're about to have the skeleton of our first building up. Best thing that's ever been done here, yeah?"

The Tarantula peered beyond Dalton, narrowing his eyes on the scene of gang turned workers. "Yes. I agree. You know, several of the clan wanted me to make an example of you for being so 'smart', Smarts. I thought about it for a few minutes." The Tarantula patted him on the side of the arm, more of a smack that burned. He grinned. "You could have been flayed and displayed on a post outside the office."

By office, the Tarantula meant their co-opted dormitory. Dalton didn't want to appear rattled, though. Strength and confidence went a long way with these people. "How nice of you not to."

The Tarantula laughed a deep belly laugh. "You're funny, Smarts. Keep it up. Amusing me is good. I think I'll reward you by making an example of your detractors instead." He walked forward to the construction scene, ignoring any potential response Dalton may have had.

Dalton's mouth fell agape. He didn't want anyone dead. This had been a mistake to get involved with the Spider Clan on a few levels, but if he had ended up alone, or with a weaker, smaller gang, odds were he wouldn't have survived.

"Good work! Good work!" The Tarantula bellowed. "All of you will be the first to get your own rooms. You won't have to share and cuddle anymore. Though Wrecks may miss that."

Wrecks flushed a combination of angry and embarrassed red,

holding the frame, and nearly shaking to do so, leaving him unable to respond. The other Spider members laughed.

Beats banged his hammer into a nail and beam, securing the frame so it would stay this time.

The Tarantula looked like he was about to give more of a speech, when a flare shot up into the sky, followed by a loud blast like a firework.

A bright red laser message wrote itself into the sky, large enough to be seen from anywhere on the small continent.

ALL PRISONERS TO MAIN COURTYARD.
REQUIRED.
REPEAT: ALL PRISONERS TO MAIN COURTYARD.
REQUIRED.
PRISON MEETING TO COMMENCE IN 20 MINUTES.
REQUIRED.

FOUR MORE RUMBLING blasts sounded in the sky. No one could have missed this message.

Odd. Dalton had never heard of an all-prison meeting in his time here. He wondered what it could be about.

"Beats, finish up securing that and then let's go," Dalton called over to him.

Beats held up his hammer to affirm he'd heard and then started pounding again. He turned and moved to get the other side of the frame, securing it with several nails as well before making his way down the ladder.

The men holding the frame stepped aside. Dalton watched, praying it would hold. And it did.

Two large beginnings of walls hung up by a single beam. It would be the basis of this building. They would have additional shelter before too long, and it'd only taken a few days' work.

"Let's go," The Tarantula said, motioning to his men to lead the way. They complied without delay.

Their construction site had been way off into a clearing through a forest that surrounded the main prison encampment. They wanted to keep it far enough from the other prisoners as to not be disturbed, but close enough that they'd still have access to the thrice daily meal drops. It took a few minutes to walk through the forest and arrive back in at the compound, the path leading directly to the Spider Clan's office and further into the other dormitories and prison square.

Thousands of other prisoners had gathered there already. It wasn't like many of them had reason to travel far beyond their place in the complex, though a few who had gone off exploring wouldn't make the meeting.

More guards surrounded the square than Dalton had seen in one place before. Was this a round up and execution? It worried him. Something seemed wrong about this whole set-up.

The crowd had a tension to it, people rumbling loudly between them as Dalton made his way with the rest of the clan into the sea of people in red jumpsuits.

A giant hologram appeared in front of the counseling and processing building, a man over twenty-five feet tall, Dalton could tell from its relative length against the third-story building windows. He had narrow eyes, thinning black hair and a pointed chin. He wore a suit, someone professional.

"I am Warden Park. Many of you have not met me before. This prison is my domain, run from the station up above." The hologram man motioned toward the sky. "We've had a relatively peaceful prison, and we aim to keep it that way.

"You'll note that the last several weeks, there have been some crowding issues with our buildings. People have become restless, and this is due to proximity as much as anything else. I have petitioned the Earth Senate to do something about this crowding before it becomes a crisis.

"My first recommendation was to create a second prison colony, but they have decided to take another route.

"There is going to be an expedition of colonists leaving Earth, going on a journey to a new planet more than a hundred years' travel away. These brave souls are looking for a new home, and, with that, came an opportunity. Two thousand of our current prison population will be going on this mission with them. You will never return back to Earth, but you will no longer be considered a prisoner on this new world. You will be able to start anew." The man paused, as if to cast his gaze around the courtyard.

"The counseling office will first be taking volunteers for this expedition, and if the number isn't met adequately, we will be making determinations based on psych profiles and life sentences. We will also be excluding known murders and rapists. Please think on this matter, and, if you would like to volunteer, approach the office within the next two days' time. Thank you."

The warden's image blinked out. That created even more of a rumble from the prisoners. Pushing and shoving happened. And then punches were thrown.

Dalton couldn't escape. In the sea of prisoners, he became a fish trying to swim away from the stream, but he had already gotten too far into the crowd by the time the message ended. Moving around the courtyard proved impossible. He bumped into someone, who turned around, blood rage in his eyes.

This wasn't good. Dalton tried to put his hands up in a surrendering gesture. The man would have none of that. He cocked his arm back, balling his fist, and then punched right for Dalton's nose.

Dalton closed his eyes, ready to absorb the hit.

But the blow never came.

He opened his eyes again to find the Tarantula standing between him and the other prisoner, holding the man's fist in his bare hands. "No one messes with Smarts. He is under our protection. Bad move."

The Tarantula squeezed on the fist, and Dalton heard a crack. The man had an expression of immense pain on his face, but the Tarantula kept squeezing until the man dropped to his knees.

"Please... it hurts! I won't hurt him! I won't hurt him!" the man said.

The Tarantula didn't release and delivered a kick to the man's gut. The man went pale.

Prisoners formed a berth around them, as people watched the scene unfold.

The Tarantula kicked him again. And again. Soon enough the man collapsed to the ground, balling into a fetal position. The Tarantula moved to stomp him on the head.

Dalton didn't want to cause anyone's death. He clasped the Tarantula on the shoulder. "Enough. He gets it."

The Tarantula turned his head to Dalton, rage in his eyes like Dalton had never seen. "Are you telling me what to do?"

Dalton hadn't encountered many men as sick as the Tarantula. The gang boss's eyes held a lust for creating pain in someone else. He enjoyed beating someone to death. It wasn't some play for power. Dalton knew he had to back off, or he might be the next one on the ground.

"No, Tarantula. I'm not telling you what to do. Do what you want. We've got something good here though, and I want to be smart..." he pointed to his own head. "Keep you out of solitary, you know?"

The Tarantula considered, and Dalton was sure the man would attack him, but then the Tarantula turned back to the prisoner on the ground. He cleared his throat and then spat something nasty on the man's face. "You don't want to make enemies of the Spider Clan."

"Guards coming!" one of the prisoners surrounding them shouted.

"Let's go," The Tarantula said.

He grabbed Dalton by the jumpsuit fabric and dragged him through the crowd, leaving the man there. People parted for them, fear radiating in the area. With so many prisoners, they lost themselves in the sea of prisoners soon after.

As soon as he could, Dalton would sign up for the expedition to get away from these madmen.

21

PARALYZED

TOLTAIR, NUEVO CIUDAD DEL RIO

THE TWIN SUNS SET, leaving a pale red glow over the city. Morgan overlooked the busy city streets from her apartment balcony. It was pretty here, a place where she could feel safe and comfortable, but Toltair would never be her home.

Perhaps the city had too much traffic, or the accents the people talked in didn't quite sound natural to her. Her appointments with Dr. Resin had improved since their first meeting. She'd developed a rapport with the doctor after trying everything the woman suggested from exercise classes, to going out more, and even to further pursuing her relationships with Zee.

Still, though, nothing quite clicked. She couldn't blame Zee. A woman couldn't ask for a man to be more attentive, and he gave her good conversation. He cleaned up pretty well for dates and even smelled nice. But a sinking feeling nagged at the back of her skull. Morgan found herself feeling smothered by him every time he touched her, instead of aroused like she should have been. She'd needed at least a few days off and told him such last time they went out for dinner. The disappointment in his eyes had been heartbreaking, but he didn't fight it at all; he gave her the space she asked for.

Until today.

He'd called her three times so far: first, to chat, the second to "make sure you're okay," and the third he went into some desperate rambling. He had become attached to her, far more than she could reciprocate. It wasn't fair of her to do this to him, by any means.

Morgan hadn't answered any of those calls, but let each go to voicemail. She'd listened to each a couple of times now, trying to think about what she could possibly say back to him. Any words of meaning escaped her. She didn't want to deal with it. No matter what she tried to come up with to shut him out politely, it sounded terrible when she said it aloud to herself.

Besides, what if she snapped out of this funk? What if, in a few days, she changed her mind? She could have a life with Zee. Didn't she owe him some time to consider?

Odds were, he'd get sick of waiting for her and move on. The poor guy didn't deserve a broken woman around anymore than he deserved the treatment he received from her now.

Six stories down below, a hovercar honked at another, the sound echoing throughout the streets. The city darkened, a shadow from taller buildings falling over Morgan's apartment. Wind picked up, and goosebumps formed on her arms. She shivered.

She turned around and headed back inside, where it would be warm and temperature controlled. Modern amenities and everything she needed, provided by Earth and her former military service, as phony as everything else set up on this colony.

That might have been the real problem. The colony felt so manufactured, for lack of a better word. It was as if the buildings here were stamped in, copies of greater versions back on Earth, to create a similar atmosphere for a budding metropolis. People worked, did commerce, went back home again, all unaffected by the perils that the border worlds with the Aryshans faced. Outside of the colonized area, Toltair had beautiful forests with unique fauna, but Morgan had never found a good way to venture out that far. No one here, not even Zee, seemed to want to leave the place created for them by Earth corporations.

The holovid news had been left on in her apartment since she went outside a couple of hours ago to stare off into the traffic. Another Aryshan attack, this time an explosion that took out a supply depot at the Cestus colony. How the Aryshans infiltrated the dome there, no one could be sure. The government vowed proportionate and swift response, ensuring the cycle would continue.

The news switched again to a report on Fabio DePino and his Ark Project. Apparently, the ship had been signed off on by his internal engineers, and they began to supply it with retrofitted coldsleep tubes, as well as full warehouse-sized rooms to carry different food crops and domestic animals. Building materials for the colony would be stored in another hold, along with a retrofitted crystal stardrive that would double for the colony's power output when the ship descended upon its new world. "If any unforeseen issues with the planet were to occur," the newscaster said, "the ark itself would be a sustainable habitat so that a human colony will be able to thrive for generations."

Since she had sent in her information for the security job posting for the Ark Project, Morgan kept seeing information about it everywhere. The news picked up more stories regarding it, which made sense since the huge ovoid ship loomed right above their heads beyond the atmosphere. But she'd received no more word of whether her application had been accepted. She tried not to dwell on it.

Morgan hovered her hand to click through for more information on the ark. The ship doubled as somewhere to live and could maintain food crops indefinitely through its robust farming technological systems, including bots and drones to man it. Beyond that, however, the colony promised a simpler form of life than most people had.

The more Morgan thought about it, the more this Ark Project appealed to her. Getting away from everything and starting completely anew sounded wonderful. A simpler life could have benefits, one away from busy city streets that seemed to close in on her. Away from the war. But would she be okay away from psychiatrists who were trained to deal with her stresses?

But maybe it didn't matter. So far, all of Dr. Resin's work hadn't helped her. She still had terrible dreams nearly every night. She still felt like she was a ghost walking in this world, somehow dissociated from reality. Could a good cold sleep and fresh air from an unknown world be what she needed? Exploration sounded appealing as well, being the first person to step on dirt. It all had a romantic appeal that returning to work as a security guard somewhere, if they even would let her do that, didn't quite compare to.

If the DePinos did reply to her and offer her a job, and if she did accept such a position, her choice would be irrevocable. The prospect scared Morgan. She'd liked her assignments so far, that all seemed fairly simple, something she could quit as soon as her tour of duty ended, or she could re-up if she decided she liked her assignment. Options wouldn't be possible on a colony a hundred years from here. Though she didn't have anyone keeping her here or anywhere else in Earth's territories.

Except Zee.

Morgan wrinkled her nose. She couldn't say she lived for Zee. Nothing she'd done so far gave any indication of a long-term future with him. She had to admit to both him and herself that it wasn't going to work, no matter how much he tried. She closed her eyes and let out a breath. "Dammit," she muttered to herself. She didn't want to do that at all.

Her comm chimed, alerting her to a new message.

FROM: *Kiyomi DePino*

RE: *Ark Project Application – Security Chief*

DEAR MS. EZRA,

. . .

I AM PLEASED to inform you that your application to the Ark Project has been accepted, pending a formal interview. Please meet with our representative on Toltair, Evelyn Tellmann, at the DePino Shipyards Wednesday at 1100 local time.

IF YOU HAVE ANY QUESTIONS, you can contact our office via this remittance.

Kiyomi DePino
  Managing Director – Ark Project
  DePino Industries

MORGAN PURSED her lips and whistled. She hadn't expected a reply this quickly, or even one at all. She'd job interviewed enough before joining up with the military. Out of the hundreds she had sent out, only a few ever sent a response back—most of those had been negative. This had come quickly, which signaled to her that this project had fewer applicants than they'd hoped.

As much as she had been excited a moment prior, her fears about the expedition got the better of her. What if this group were incompetent, and the colony died out? She'd read about the first colonies from Earth to other solar systems and how more than ninety percent of the people died within two years of colonizing a new world. Lack of supplies, conditions they hadn't accounted for, unknown viruses. There were far too many variables that could go wrong with a colony, without proper supervision. Any new world that the Earth settled nowadays had robust infrastructure ready to go. Toltair made for a prime example.

It was also a prime example of where Morgan felt uncomfortable. She waffled on whether she could make the move. This would be the hardest decision of her life.

Should she stay or should she go?

Her comm chimed again, this time with a call. Only one person would be calling her, and Morgan could tell who without looking—Zee. Her chest tightened as she considered answering, but thought better.

She had to decide what to do with her life before dealing with him, but how would she go about making that decision in earnest?

Morgan flopped down onto the sofa in the apartment and stared back outside at the city lights from the tall buildings across from her apartment.

22

MOVING FORWARD

EARTH, JUPITER, FL

KIYOMI KNOCKED on the door of her father's study. "Dad?"

"Come in," he replied weakly. Even though he'd been moved from the hospital to an in-home care set up, he still spent most of his days resting. A full-time nurse had been brought to the house to assist with his medical matters, make sure he could get up and walk to the bathroom without slipping and falling, as well as work on physical therapy for his recovery. The study itself had been converted into a makeshift hospital room, with a reclining bed. He already had his workstation and a holotainment system inside.

Kiyomi turned the doorknob then stepped inside. The room still had that old-book smell to it, something her father would find comforting as he recovered. He sat propped up on his bed by several fluffy down pillows, a large holographic display in front of him with a flow chart for the Ark Project supply shipments.

Most of the construction materials were produced at subcontracted factories on Toltair, but a number of goods couldn't be sourced directly from the colony where they were planning to launch. The livestock proved a particularly tricky item to handle—not that Kiyomi considered the animals mere items. But bringing them compounded the complicated process of planning. Large quantities of cattle, horses, pigs, and chickens required a substantive amount of work before being allowed through different port customs. Ensuring the animals would survive their trips between worlds required much more oversight than one would have thought. Fortunately, Kiyomi had been able to delegate the task.

Her eyes drifted to the part of the screen where it detailed the crops, fauna, and other plants that the expedition would be bringing along to the new world. Along with that were dozens of micro-drones that mimicked the pollination habits of bees. Those had to be replicable on-world in case of breakdown or if more were needed from the colony's natural expansion. The botany garden also contained sizable space for the jungle flame flowers. She couldn't help but smile at the plan.

Kiyomi approached her father's bedside and pointed to the area of the flowchart that held her flowers. "These are for me."

"Of course. I want you to have everything you love at the colony." Dad tilted his head toward her.

"We still need to talk about that." Kiyomi met her father's eyes and took his hand with a soft squeeze. "In earnest, hash all of the details out."

"I suppose we do." The smallest trace of a faltering appeared in Dad's eyes. Not many people would have noticed it. He'd been on camera for far too much of his life to let his guard down that much, but Kiyomi had seen it before. His self-confidence in his ideas that he portrayed had roots to them from his prior success, and rarely did he show any sign of anything but surety.

"You know this project isn't exactly the dream I had for my life. It does offer me the opportunity to work in my field in a way very few can, setting up an ecosystem, learning about a new one, combining them and integrating..." Kiyomi shook her head. "I'm getting distracted. It's actually exciting for me. This prisoner demand though, it changes things. I don't even know that I feel comfortable in a situation of a colony where criminals make up a substantive part of the population. It doesn't match with your vision for a fresh new humanity, either."

"You're presuming they can't be rehabilitated or that there's something amiss with them beyond social situations that forced them there."

"I've studied enough biosciences to understand there's both genetic predispositions and societal causes. You know better than to guilt me for that."

Dad gave her hand another soft squeeze. "I do. But it doesn't mean that in a new environment where they have a real stake in their survival, that they would repeat their errors. In fact, that change in stimulus may be exactly what they need to start a better life."

Kiyomi pulled back her hand. "Dad, this isn't some sociological experiment. Your plan was to move some of the best and brightest so we could chart out a new evolutionary course that kept us out of conflict. Remember?"

Dad shrugged. "That's still the intention, and we still have many of those people signed up to go."

"Until this prison deal gets announced to the public!"

The words silenced her father. He turned back to the display in front of him, the series of flowcharts that had held there. One of the cells turned from red to green as several tons of lumber had been procured and the status bar changed to "ready to transport."

Dad had fixated on the location. A deep wrinkle appeared in his forehead, where he often had one during his deep contemplations. "Australia. The British sent hundreds of thousands of their prisoners to the continent to resettle. The experiment is very similar to what we're proposing now. "

Kiyomi thought back to history. He had a point, but as usual left out important details. "A lot of people died of starvation. They had a lot of problem with crime in those early years, didn't they?"

"Initially. But for the long term, Australia became one of the most

peaceful and productive countries on Earth before the world govern-
ments formed. It's not a bad model. And we won't have such a high
rate of prisoners compared to them. We have scientists and brilliant
thinkers in every field to guide them. Think of it more as a trainable
labor pool."

Kiyomi crossed her arms. "Yeah, I'm not buying that."

Dad shrugged. "Believe what you will. As I understand, the
Lemkins did negotiate that the prisoners will be of the non-violent
sort, because of the very fears of what a large number of them would
do to the population pool. We have some control over who we bring.
Perhaps they'll end up resourceful?" He narrowed his eyes on the
screen. "We do have to plan for many generations down the line.
Speaking of which, do the livestock we've secured have enough biodi-
versity?"

"You're changing the subject." Kiyomi waved her hand in front of
her father's face to direct his attention toward her. "You always do
that when you want to avoid hard topics."

Dad frowned. His age showed heavily in his face when he did. It
pulled on Kiyomi's heart strings. As much as she pressed him about
the viability of his project, she didn't want to lose him. She couldn't
lose him.

She found herself worrying about her father then. After his stroke,
she'd had no time to process his near-death experience. Work on his
projects had consumed her, but she'd let that happen. If she were
honest with herself, she had intentionally buried herself in work
because she didn't want to slow down and deal with reality.

Kiyomi scooted herself onto the bed and leaned her head back into
her father's shoulder, resting there like she had as a child. He had the
smell of someone who'd been infirmed and in one place for too long, a
mixture of body odor and sterilized medical components, but it didn't
bother her. She felt her father's hand reach up and stroke through her
hair. It comforted her.

"Yomi," Dad said, shortening her name in a way that didn't quite
make sense in the original language, but sounded as endearing as any
other cute word she could think of. "As much as I believe in the ark,

this isn't like the news says. It's not my attempt at playing god or thinking that I have all the answers. I do believe there's merit in those old science fiction groups that talk about diversifying humanity, fewer eggs in one basket, and that we are close enough to a possible fall into another dark ages that it's better to be away from the epicenter, here on Earth.

"The Aryshans are a powerful enemy. They may not seem overwhelmingly so from the vantage of the senate on Earth, but they've weathered far more than humanity has during the course of their evolution. We don't know their full capabilities. If they unleash on us..."

Kiyomi felt him move, and looked up to see him shaking his head. "I know. I worry about it, too."

She'd lived with him long enough to understand his instincts on important events. They usually ended up being right. Eerily so. His warnings held great weight with her.

"Even before my health problems, I've been an old man. And don't tell me otherwise. I hate disingenuous compliments!" He chuckled, his chest reverberating against her head. "Even though I may have made it to the colony before, I would only last a few years there at best. It'd be nice to see my dream in reality, but knowing that I accomplished it is enough for me."

"Dad, don't talk like that..."

"Shh. It's reality. I'm not going to live in some fantasy world pretending I'm fine. I know my time is limited. I do fear for you here, though. You'd be able to take over the business or pursue whatever dreams you had if you decided to sell it, but what about the long-term here on Earth? That's what this Ark Project is all about. I don't want to see you swallowed up with the rest of my legacy."

Those words didn't hold any new information Kiyomi didn't already understand, but she'd never had to face them like this before. It pained her to think about her father leaving her like her mother had all those years ago. She would be all alone, and that prospect scared her half to death. Her mouth felt dry, and she tried to swallow but it led to more discomfort.

"I don't want you to die," she whispered.

"I know." Her father placed his arm around her shoulder and squeezed her closer to him. "I don't want to either, it sounds horrible. But like I said—"

"It's reality," Kiyomi finished for him.

"That's right. Now, I can't force you to go to this new world, I wouldn't do that to you even if I had some power over you, but I do have to implore you that it's the right choice."

Kiyomi breathed in deeply, holding the air before exhaling again. She had thought about this at length and still hadn't come to a decision. If she left, there'd be no coming back, but if she stayed, she would miss the chance to be on this journey of a lifetime. Both ideas had merit, both had drawbacks.

At the same time, she had held off on pursuing her doctorate. The deadline to sign up for this semester had passed a week ago, and Kiyomi hadn't slowed down on working on the Ark Project even to ensure her enrollment. If it were anyone else, she would have chalked it up to error or being caught up in work. Kiyomi knew herself too well for that. It may have been subconscious, but she had missed the deadline intentionally.

This meant deep down, she had made up her mind, even if she didn't want to admit it to herself.

She closed her eyes, felt her father's warmth and his heart beating.

Lying there reminded her of those trips they took to Utah in the wintertime to go skiing in her youth. Her parents had rented a car and driver once they arrived in Utah. Kiyomi would sit in the back, nestled between the two of them, leaning on her father, so she could fall asleep on the drive. The very act made her weary from muscle memory, but it also brought a sense of comfort.

They both lay there in silence for a long moment, while the hum of the holotainment system buzzed in the background.

"Okay, Dad. I'll go." A newfound resolve welled inside of her. This project would be her father's legacy and her own. A far more ambitious project than studying flowers in her backyard greenhouse by the beach.

He squeezed her around her shoulders. "Thank you." He shifted, which allowed Kiyomi to raise her head off of him. The display in front of him changed with the motion of his hand, revealing a blank brainstorming template. "Let's talk about how we can change the perception of having prisoners at the colony so that it's more palatable to those joining on. I have some thoughts."

TRAPPED

Prison Colony 33-X4D

For the first time in years, Dalton felt free. He left the counseling office, descending the long concrete steps back into the prison colony courtyard. Several prisoners moved about like any day at the colony, their bright red jumpsuits standing out against the backdrop of shoddily constructed buildings. The simplistic boxes of the colony had been rushed into place, both from the conceptual side and the labor aspects.

Hopefully, he wouldn't have to be here much longer. Thousands of prisoners stood in line for the colony relocation sign-up, but Dalton had arrived early, and his name should be on the top of the list. After how intense the Tarantula had been at the announcement of the volunteer program to head on an expedition to a faraway world, Dalton worried that the man could turn on him at any moment. His "protection" now could make for troubles later, when the Tarantula decided that Dalton caused his problems. He couldn't trust that the Spider Clan leader would remain rational.

He shook his head and continued along the path to his office, or, at least, the office he had been handed by the Tarantula for the time being. The two Spider Clan guards stood outside as usual posts outside the main entrance door, boredly staring off toward the main courtyard and the other dormitories in that direction.

When Dalton looked up at the second story of the Spider Clan's building, he wanted to retch.

A man, or what used to be a man, dangled limply from what appeared to be his own intestines. His features had turned pale, and his torso had been filleted. Dried blood darkened areas of his bright red jumpsuit, streaking down his leg. His eyes held unfocused, lifeless.

Dalton nearly stumbled into Beats, the leftmost guard of the building today. "What the hell?"

Beats looked up, unfazed by the horrific display above him. "Oh, yeah. Looks like someone wanted to send a message."

The blood drained from Dalton's face, but he tried to hold as stoic of an expression as he could. He couldn't portray weakness, not now. "What kind of message?"

Beats shrugged. "How'm I supposed to know? I didn't do it."

Of course not. That would have been too convenient, not that Beats would have owned up to it anyway. The scene reminded Dalton all too much of the first time he had come into the Spider Clan's lair, ready to join, and having those scissors pointed his direction. They'd scared the living daylights out of him but ended with shaving his head and giving him an all-too-painful tattoo on his skull.

He had been staring at that horrific display for long enough. It had to come down, if anything because such a display would reflect terribly upon the Spider Clan in the middle of their construction project. If the guards came by and implicated any or all of the Spiders, that could lead to solitary isolation, a complete halt of the project, perhaps a breakup of the clan itself. What were these people thinking?

He stepped inside, heading into the hallway and down toward the back room where the Tarantula made his office. The door hung open, allowing Dalton entry.

The Tarantula sat, drinking a hazy brown liquid out of a glass, laughing at something that Red had said beside him. Red had his scissors holstered in his belt like a pistol, feet up on the desk table and crossed. His shears dangled when he swiveled in his chair. Enough stubble had grown on his face to produce an oily look from a lack of washing.

Dalton thought he could make out dried blood on them. Danger signs surrounded him.

The Tarantula dropped his laugh, but his lips still curled into a smile. "Smarts. Good of you to join us. Looks like your little dollhouse is proceeding under budget and ahead of schedule. I am pleased!"

The concept of under budget would have been funny, since all of the resources came from the labor of other prisoners or from what could be extracted from the guards, but Dalton didn't feel like laughing. These men had murdered someone in cold blood.

"I'm glad it's working out."

"I believe I am to be rewarded with one of the new rooms. A room to myself?" Red asked, his head canted toward the Tarantula.

The Tarantula waved him off. "Of course, you'll get one of the rooms. And perhaps our grand architect Smarts will, as well..." He paused mid thought, making a smacking sound of his lips. Then he narrowed his eyes, all of the levity disappearing from his face as if into a black hole. "That is, if he is staying."

The look, the phrasing, they were meant to rattle Dalton. He couldn't let it happen. He had to stay firm.

"I applied for the relocation program," Dalton said. There wouldn't be any use in lying. That would make the Tarantula angry, and if Red had gutted and hung the man up on the roof, Dalton didn't want to test that anger today. He stood as tall as he could, not shifting his weight. He couldn't afford to display weakness. "Doesn't mean I'll be accepted. They have some stringent requirements and a lot of people are applying."

Silence held in the room before the Tarantula burst out laughing again, throwing his head back into the soft headrest of his own chair.

"You're so tense all the time. I love to watch you squirm." He slapped his thigh. "No, no. You don't seem the type to settle down, even in the buildings that you are having us build."

Red raised a brow at the Tarantula. He didn't agree with letting Dalton leave with the program—anger was written all over his face.

Dalton shrugged, trying to look casual, but he couldn't manage to relax all the tension from his shoulders. "I wanted to check on the project, make sure you were satisfied."

He thought about the man hanging from the roof again. Should he bring it up? Would that be wise to get the Tarantula thinking on that track?

"Did you see your present when you walked in?" The Tarantula asked, eyes shining with maliciousness and amusement.

Dalton nearly choked. Present? The Tarantula could be referring to something else, but Dalton hadn't seen anything other than the hanging man when he'd walked in.

"I... I'm not sure what you're talking about."

"The man I flayed and left for all to see," Red said. Quiet. Controlled. Like a complete sociopath.

"Yes," the Tarantula said. He took a swig of his drink. From the brief grimace he had after consuming the liquid, it had to be alcoholic. "That was Twinkle Toes. He walks—walked—on his toes," the Tarantula said. "Surprisingly fast though. Good for delivering messages." Those last words were spoken with some regret. "He spoke about how all of us were working for no pay, and that it was a scam of yours. Tried to rally some of the other Spider Clan members to give you a good beating, or worse."

So that's why the Tarantula had summoned him. Many members of the Spider Clan didn't like him. There'd been enough fights over bringing him in, and then more over his project. The name Smarts didn't come to him because people respected his brain. It mocked him, like any of the other names that the Spider Clan members seemed to have–except the Tarantula. He'd half expected more active attempts to hurt him, but he didn't want this to be the result of it. It made his own situation all too dangerous.

"People who undermine my authority are dangerous to the clan. They must be sent a clear message." The Tarantula nodded.

Dalton's stomach turned over. He wanted to retch. Someone had been murdered, and in a horrific way, because of him. But what could he do? He couldn't question the Tarantula like the others had, the result of that hung as clear as day from the exterior of this very building. He tried to think of arguments that wouldn't sound combative, but none came to mind.

The Tarantula raised a brow toward Dalton. "Is there a problem?"

"No, no problem." Dalton said. "I'm hoping that the guards, uh, don't see the hanging body and rescind some of the help they've given us for the construction projects."

Red paced to one side of the room, which caused Dalton to tense, hoping that the man wouldn't come close to him with those scissors or needles again. He didn't, but passed to a cabinet where he grabbed another bottle of whatever the Tarantula and he were drinking.

"That's no problem," The Tarantula said casually. "I have someone on the roof spotting for guards. It will be hidden if someone comes by."

"If other prisoners start complaining, I'm not sure the guards won't search here. And if you have other contraband?" Dalton motioned toward Red and the bottle he held.

"Hmm," The Tarantula said. "Your point is valid. Red, go ensure our little display is removed and buried somewhere that can't be connected to us."

Red huffed what sounded like a grunt of agreement, then brushed past Dalton toward the door. The room became quiet, as if the Tarantula were waiting for him to leave.

"I want you to know I considered your defection to this new colony carefully," The Tarantula said. "At first, I thought it was offensive, that you might be betraying me personally after all that I've done for you." He clicked his tongue. "But then I realized it's opportunity, like everything else you've presented."

Dalton didn't want to commit to too much, finding it easier to let the Tarantula say what he would, and then work around those parameters as best he could when the man didn't have his eyes on him. "Oh?"

"Yes, that's why I've decided to sign up for the new colony, as well.

I'm going to have my most loyal men come along, too. We'll have to convince some of the other prisoners it's a bad idea to ensure we all make the list, but I doubt there will be a problem with that." He grinned, his crooked teeth showing in full, like a predator ready to bite. "This demonstration," he motioned toward the roof, where the man hung, "will serve two purposes in that regard. Some of my men now are spreading rumors as to what happens to those who sign up without the Spider Clan's permission."

Dalton tried his best to keep his face stoic but increasingly found it difficult. He'd thought he'd found an escape from this madness, a way out where he wouldn't have to deal with these bloodthirsty thugs for much longer, and now that hope evaporated. They would make this colony into a hellhole!

"That's great," he said all the same. He shifted, trying not to look too uncomfortable. "I should get going, check on the project."

"Keep working hard." The Tarantula smiled and swirled the liquid in his glass. "You produce results, I will see to it that you are rewarded."

Dalton nodded, acting as grateful as he could before turning to leave. He had to find a way to make sure the Spider Clan didn't join him on this new colony, if he were even chosen himself. How could he influence the administrators without anyone noticing? He shook his head. His grand plan to escape had left him more trapped.

24

CLOSER

PEOPLE FILLED the steps outside Antony's former residence. Poor Governor Talben had to be saddled with being thrown into the job on a moment's notice and an assembly vote confirmation, followed by an endless media circus. *That's what we sign up for as politicians,* Antony thought to himself with a chuckle.

"What's so funny?" Bethany asked.

They stayed hidden behind a makeshift stage backdrop, between the crowd and the entrance to the mansion itself. They could have chosen anywhere else in the world to hold this speech, but Antony felt comfortable here. Bethany suggested that he stay within his comfort zone as much as possible while making this speech. She always had good advice.

"Nothing, thinking about politics."

"It's either worth laughing at or worth crying about, hmm?" Bethany smiled at him.

"Sometimes both." Antony glanced at his watch. Three minutes until go-time. Senator Marsh arrived with an entourage of additional senators and aides who wanted to get in on the press coverage, and have photos of them behind Antony while he gave his speech. Some things never changed.

Antony offered his hand to the Senator, who clasped it in return.

"Mr. Lemkin," Senator Marsh said. "I haven't had a chance to congratulate you."

He referenced the vote that had passed a couple of hours ago, formally allowing the Ark Project to move forward. The reason they all gathered here for this historic speech. The president himself had signed the bill into law without delay. All of the bureaucratic hoops had been jumped through. Antony and Bethany had won, if this were their big cause. But someone else would do the job at the end of the day.

"Don't congratulate me," Antony said. He pointed over to Kiyomi DePino, who wore a bright red blouse with a white skirt that hung fitted around her hips, provocative and classy at the same time. "Congratulate her."

Senator Marsh adjusted his tie. "I may do that. Heiress to the DePino Industries empire, hmm? And not bad to look at, either."

Antony chuckled. "That's my client's daughter. Don't even think about it."

Senator Marsh grinned and stepped past Antony. He engaged Kiyomi in conversation within moments.

Bethany tapped Antony on the arm. "Men. And they think we can't overhear them."

Antony turned back to his wife. "I didn't say anything," he said, even though he sounded rather guilty stating it.

"That's because I trained you." Bethany said. She smoothed down Antony's lapel. Her soft fingers on his chest felt good, even with the layers of clothing between them. "You ready?"

Antony nodded.

"Showtime!" one of the production interns shouted, motioning for Antony to step forward.

He moved around the screen and saw the hundreds of cameras on him immediately. Calling this press conference had achieved a media speculation rivaling the first couple of days after his resignation announcement. He'd missed being in front of the press like this. Speeches came naturally to him, and at risk of inflating his ego, he looked good on the holos. This announcement would be simpler, already having support from the government, but it would act as a call to good people out there who might want to join in on DePino's project.

The podium stood at his normal height specifications, set perfectly with a glass of water and a datapad which held some of the points of his speech, though Antony had worked through the night memorizing it. A lifeline, in case of fumbling.

The senators, their aides, Kiyomi DePino, and Bethany took their places behind and beside Antony at the podium. The reporters in front muttered amongst themselves but quieted as Antony reached the podium.

"Good afternoon," Antony said. The various microphones from the camera drones positioned around them would pick up his speech fine. Even from that distance they could filter out any ambient noise. "I am pleased to announce that the senate has voted, and the president confirmed, that DePino Starliners Industries will be permitted to embark upon their mission to start a new colony, so distant that they will live completely separate from the rest of humanity.

"The journey will place the colonists in one hundred years of cold sleep at the highest FTL speeds that can be achieved under current technologies. This will ensure that the population of this new colony will be undisturbed and likewise will not disturb Federated Earth. They will live in peace, with the freedom to seek their own destinies.

"This vision was brought about by entrepreneur Fabio DePino and his daughter, Kiyomi DePino. They have already signed up some brilliant thinkers, scientists, engineers and motivated workers who will take this colony from a dream to reality. In a few months' time—"

A loud *crack* resounded, followed by a scream from the crowd.

A gunshot. Someone had fired a gun.

The world seemed to slow around Antony, or at least his own reactions did. The gunfire came from close by, making his ears ring from the ballistic boom. He felt like he'd been encapsulated in a bubble where all the shouting and sounds blended. At least two more shots rang out.

Police from the edge of the stage drew their guns, pointing out toward the crowd of reporters and onlookers.

Something hard collided with him. Antony tried to turn, but strong, masculine arms wrapped around him. He fell to the ground. Had the attacker gotten to him?

He managed to get a glimpse of a man in a dark suit and sunglasses as the one who'd grabbed him. Antony hit the ground a moment later, the back of his head smacking against the stage. That made him more disoriented than he had been. Pain shot through his skull.

The security guard yelled at him. "Stay down!"

It looked like he mouthed, but Antony could hardly hear.

Despite being held to the ground, Antony squirmed, trying to break out of the man's reach. He had to get backstage, no matter how much his head pounded. Danger surrounded them here. He tried to scramble, use his hands to push him up, but they slipped. A slick, wet substance spread across the stage.

People ran around the stage. Others yelled and screamed. The steps in front of the governor's mansion had descended into chaos.

Antony looked back. Blood. Blood had covered the stage. Had he hit his head that hard? He reached up into his hair. Though some of that blood had gotten into his hair, he didn't feel nearly as much as there would have been if it had originated there.

He looked behind where he'd been standing. There, a woman lay crumpled on the ground, blood pooled around her. Despite all of the pain and all of the chaos going around, Antony focused.

Bethany.

Oh, God, no. This couldn't be happening.

Two sets of hands pulled Antony backstage. "Is he injured?" someone asked. They tried to lift him, move him.

Antony shrugged his shoulders, trying to get them off of him. He moved all of his weight forward, releasing himself from their clutches, crawling toward Bethany. Her chest still rose and fell.

She coughed. Blood spurted from her lips.

"Bethany!" Antony screamed. Tears streaked down his face. Please, no. Anything else. Not this.

A hole in her blouse. Blood covered it. Antony tried to compress it with his hands. They hadn't considered that this speech could be dangerous. They should have outfitted her with Kevlar, something. He kissed her forehead. It felt cold. He could hardly think.

"Bethany, please..." he whispered.

"Antony?" Bethany asked.

Her voice sounded so weak, worse than when she'd come down so ill a couple years back on their winter vacation and had to huddle up under the blankets while the fever passed.

"I'm here. I love you, Bethany. I'm here. I won't leave you."

"Sir..." a voice came from behind him.

"NOT NOW!"

He caught the security guard stepping backward from his peripheral vision, but he stayed focused on Bethany. "Someone get an ambulance... a doctor!"

Bethany coughed again, and this time choked. She didn't stop.

Antony didn't know what to do. She couldn't breathe. He needed to do something. He tried to press on her lungs, but it did no good. Shaking her would make her worse, that much he did know. He looked up, vision blurred by the tears that he didn't have time for.

"Why isn't anyone doing anything?"

"Sir, there's nothing we can do. She's been hit straight in the chest."

"Get her a replacement heart. Something!"

Bethany continued choking, and then she stopped moving entirely. Her body fell limp against Antony's leg.

"No!" he screamed.

The security guards grabbed hold of him again. They lifted him up this time. Antony couldn't fight. He reached out for Bethany, able to touch her lifeless face one last time as security pulled him away. This couldn't be happening. This couldn't be real. Why would someone do this?

His head throbbed from when he'd been slammed against the

ground earlier. The pain swirled in the back of his head until it overwhelmed him. If he had been moving of his own volition, he would have fallen again, but another man carried him.

The security officer put him down onto a stretcher and the world started to spin around him.

"Bethany," he tried to say.

"Save your strength. You've got a head trauma," someone said.

He couldn't leave her. Not like this. He had to do something to fix it. He couldn't go on without her.

The world spun more, and then everything went dark.

25

A RETURN TO FULL BLOOM

EARTH, JUPITER, FL

KIYOMI COULDN'T BELIEVE what had happened. Even having been there in person, it seemed surreal. Someone had tried to assassinate Antony Lemkin because he gave a speech about her father's project. A person out there had such sick thoughts that they deemed it a righteous cause to brandish a gun, not even a phase pistol or similar modern invention that would wound cleanly, but an old projectile weapon that shot lead bullets. Barbaric.

"The gunman has been identified as one Carlos Trenton, a former Interplanetary Navy officer who fought in the Drenite War. Authorities have found his online blogs calling for the destruction of the Aryshans, rants that claimed 'either us or them. They will take over known space until we are slaves or wiped out.' Disturbing, to say the least, though matching with a lot of angry public sentiment," the news host said.

"I agree. He had written of the DePino colony project as a traitorous act against humanity that must not be allowed. Indeed, this echoes public opinion polls that showed a high disapproval rate for it

147

up until this incident," a woman with thick rimmed glasses said. A banner that read *Vanessa Tellerman, public policy consultant* displayed below her holoimage.

"We haven't had new poll since the shooting, to be clear," the host said.

"The real victims in this are, of course, the men and women in the armed services who have to see this tragedy."

Those were the real victims? Kiyomi scoffed. The real victims were the Lemkins, both of them. Antony Lemkin had completely lost it. He'd thrashed around, completely inconsolable, even going so far as to buck his head and slam on the hard concrete. He'd been lucky to come out unscathed save for a minor concussion.

Unscathed may have not been the right word. Kiyomi understood the ripping feeling across her soul when she had nearly lost her father. To lose someone that you'd been married to for decades, your partner both in work and in life—she couldn't even imagine how traumatic that would be.

"Holovid off," Kiyomi said, and the entertainment system shut down.

Her father stood at the door to their family room, a cane in one hand to maintain his balance. Though he could move about now, he still had a long way to go. "I don't know why you watch that media nonsense. You know how they get manipulated into their narratives. We've done it ourselves."

Kiyomi stood and moved over to him to give him a small hug. "Someone has to predict where they're going with these things so we can make sure our plans aren't impacted by them."

"I can't believe that Bethany took that bullet." Dad shook his head, a deep frown crossing his face. "I wish I could say I didn't know how it felt to lose someone like that."

"I miss Mom, too," Kiyomi said softly.

"It goes to show how short our time is here. That's why we have to work hard and get what we can accomplished."

Kiyomi stepped back from her father. He'd given this lecture before, whenever Kiyomi started to get down. Both of them had a propensity to lose themselves in thoughts, devolve into a mild depression. Those funks took a few days to shake off. She had to focus on work rather than letting thoughts of the past drag her down. It was a tough mindset trick to get going, because it required a ridiculous amount of willpower, but Kiyomi had been able to do it in the past. She would do it again here.

"I know. I hate to sound callous, but one good thing this gunman did for us was to keep the story off of the prisoners who are going to come along with the colony. Our slots are filling up faster than before. We're not losing people like I'd anticipated."

"Good," Dad said. "To the future. I may call Mr. Lemkin to console him at some point, but I'll give him a few days to process. He'll need a new purpose in his life, as well... I wonder..."

Through his vibrant eyes, Kiyomi saw the wheels spinning in her father's head. She thought about what that could mean but stopped herself. He would tell her when he had a plan formulated. She wouldn't be able to pry anything out of him until then.

"Government's out of the way, the ark is complete, cold storage units being installed," she said. "Beyond making sure the algorithms are correct for the human quotient of filling a successful colony, I think we're pretty much wrapped up. I won't be able to do plant or soil analysis until we arrive. Everything I have so far is based on speculation, and I'll have to do some genetic modifications, regardless, to make sure our imported plants thrive."

"Hmm," Dad said, sounding lost in thought. He moistened his bottom lip. "There is one thing we haven't done."

"What's that?"

"Name the planet."

Such a simple thing, a small thing at that, but it did hold importance, symbolically at least. They'd spent so much time considering the ark project and the journey element of this, which made sense given their starliner business, that they hadn't stopped to think of a name for their civilization.

"Earth Two?" Kiyomi asked, mostly kidding.

Dad rolled his eyes. "I don't believe you'll let it be named something so uninspiring. We could name it for a person."

"Bethany? Reiko?" Two women who had passed that they had thought about. It seemed sensible, and they were on Kiyomi's mind.

"Doesn't sound much like a planet, does it?"

"No, I suppose not." Kiyomi glanced to the window on the opposite side of the family room. Its automatic shading for the holotainment system faded into a regular ultraviolet protected translucence. The backyard focused in her view, with her greenhouse, her flowers growing up the side walls catching her eye. "Jasmine? Jungle Flame?"

Dad stepped into the room, past her, his cane clicking on the ground with each step. "I do like the idea of naming it something after your contributions. It adds a personal element, something to say this is a DePino project." He turned his head and smirked back at her. "I am allowed to have some ego, aren't I? Not too bad a sin?"

"DePino Starliners. DePino wine. DePino Construction. I think you're squarely beyond the point of no return and already sucked into that black hole, personally," Kiyomi teased.

"Hmm," Dad said, not missing a beat in his thought process. "What's the scientific name for your flowers again?"

"Ixora coccinea," Kiyomi said.

"Too complicated. I like Ixora though. How about that?"

The genus name, encompassing all sorts of jasmine flowers. The more she thought about it, the more the term sounded good to her. Ixora. A colony that would bloom like the most elegant flowers in the world, in the nicest of climates like her home in Florida. That seemed like a good omen.

"I like it," Kiyomi said.

"Excellent. It's settled then." Dad tapped his cane on the ground like proclaiming his judgment with a gavel. "Call up Jim Singhal. Let's see if he's made any progress with the architects in terms of the colony layouts."

Back to work, as always. It meant her father felt better, which made Kiyomi smile, even in the wake of tragedy.

26

THE TEST BEGINS

THE HORIZON above Toltair glowed like a halo. A crescent-shaped continent had modest cloud cover and the rich blues of the planet's oceans covered most of the world.

When Morgan had first looked up the DePino Shipyards, she had assumed that it would be in one of the vast skyscrapers in the business districts of Nuevo Ciudad. While they had offices there, this Evelyn Tellmann had hers in a platform that had the massive ark itself attached. That made meeting more inconvenient, but the DePino company responded to Morgan's query by saying they would cover any transportation from the surface to make sure she arrived there.

Her journey from the spaceport had subsequently been one of the better ones in her life. A valet ushered her through security into a private lounge with snacks and cocktails—the latter of which Morgan opted not to participate in—before riding in a spacious private shuttle that had near the most perfect gravitational dampeners Morgan had ever had the pleasure to *not* feel. Typical military surface-to-space transports allowed the pilot and passengers to feel the different pulls to ensure readiness and awareness in case of facing combat simultaneously to an ascent into the atmosphere.

Upon arrival, Morgan had been ushered to a private waiting room, a large one with several sofas that faced a ceiling-to-floor window to give the panoramic view of the planet below. Behind her, through several meters of metal frame, would be the giant, boxy ark that would make this expedition a reality.

The thought of the scope of what Morgan considered embarking upon stifled her breath. Anxiety welled up inside her, but with the techniques she learned from Dr. Resin over her last few appointments, Morgan could identify the feeling, and forcibly tell herself that she would not be stressed today. She had to maintain control over herself.

The anxiety dwindled until it echoed in her chest. For as much as Morgan had questioned these self-help willpower techniques when Dr. Resin first proposed them to her, the exercises worked. She couldn't say she felt well, not like before, but at least she could find herself at a neutral level where she could function. That would be important today.

If she intended on taking the job. The commitment wouldn't get any easier to stomach, no matter how much she weighed the pros and cons. But she had been willing to come all the way to this platform for a meeting. Morgan had spent enough time with psychologists to know that the mind gave clues to one's proclivities by subtle—or in this case not-so-subtle—actions.

"Ms. Ezra?" a voice asked.

With all of her thoughts on anxiety and where it came from, Morgan hadn't noticed someone approach her from the side. A woman in a dark, somewhat fitted suit stood before her. She had long red hair and a square chin, skin that looked slightly too young for her eyes—a person had to have gone through rejuvenation treatment to look as good as she did.

Morgan stood to greet her, her hand moving up toward a salute by habit, but she caught it early enough to extend it for a shake before it looked too out of place.

"Hi, yes, that's me." Her voice came out higher than usual, sounding discombobulated as she had felt a moment prior.

"I'm Evelyn Tellmann, but you can call me Evelyn. Would you prefer to stay here to chat or go to a more formal conference room?" Evelyn patted the back rest of the sofa as she spoke.

Morgan resumed her seat to answer the question, as if led from that small gesture from the other woman. "You can call me Morgan."

The woman took her own seat on a sofa perpendicular to Morgan's. She crossed her legs and folded her hands over her thigh. "Morgan. I read over your resume, and it looks like you're very well qualified."

Well qualified? She'd barely had any experience, in her own opinion. Like she had with so many conversations as of late, Morgan found herself at a loss for words. "Thanks."

Evelyn scrutinized her, eyes calculating. "Military must make for a pretty interesting experience. We understand that you've been put on indefinite medical leave, but policy states against sharing any details. Under ordinary circumstances, we would leave private issues to the individual, but this is not an ordinary circumstance. This is a life-long journey, there's no possibilities for replacements if there's something amiss."

Morgan wanted to recoil from the woman, but she held in place. She had to act with the experience the woman had credited her with. Combat trained. Job interview pressure had nothing on her.

"I understand. There's nothing physically wrong with me. I've had some traumatic stress, is all." No matter how she said it, she couldn't downplay her problems enough.

Evelyn didn't give any outward appearance of judgments. "You were on the Esare colony during the attack, is that right?"

Morgan nodded.

"From the media records I've been able to dig up from there, you acted valiantly. You worked on rescue efforts to save civilian citizens before you were given your discharge."

She'd been in the media? She couldn't recall that having happened, though there were plenty of people who had come and gone at those makeshift tents where the operation had been based. Morgan stood guard there, as she had been commanded to, so perhaps her name had circulated in some reports. She'd never bothered to do a search on herself. In some ways, it would have been the right thing to do to tell the truth—her involvement in rescue efforts had been limited—but this was an interview. Best foot forward.

"I did. My commander saw the signs of stress and relieved me."

"Do you think that a journey to a new world, Ixora as we're calling it now, wouldn't create similar stresses? Would you be up to the task?"

Morgan chewed on the inside of her lip. She didn't have enough faith in herself to hold down a new relationship with a nice man because the social pressures had proved too much. It did have one thing going for it.

"I'm hoping a new world, out in nature without..." Morgan waved her hand around for effect. "...all of this around us, will do me some good."

"All of this?" Evelyn asked.

"You know, terraforming, people everywhere you look, buildings, traffic—"

Evelyn laughed. "I definitely understand that one."

"I don't think it's a good environment to recover in, to be honest. This new planet, Ex—?"

"Ixora."

"Ixora. It might be what I need."

A couple of people, presumably DePino employees, entered the room and left through the other side. Evelyn watched them walk through, as if to make sure of their privacy, before returning her attention to Morgan.

"This is a new colony with no back up, as I've mentioned. We aren't going to have the capabilities to deal with experimenting for someone's psychological needs. It's going to be life or death out there. If a person goes rogue on the colony, you would be the authority, Ms. Ezra." The woman paused. "Morgan. We have to have confidence that you will be on top of your game and ready to go when you first set foot on dirt."

Would she be? Morgan glanced out the window once more. Transports made their way up and down from the surface, the ever-changing landscape of economy. It never stopped, it kept going, whether she were a part of it or not. Like Evelyn said, the colony would not keep going if its members had problems or checked out. There were no possible reinforcements. But what could happen in a population of a few thousand that could be worse than the Aryshans?

She met Evelyn's eyes again. "I've been through the worst that can happen. I can do it," she managed to say, and oddly enough, sounded confident in those words.

If anything, the challenge from Evelyn had invigorated her. She could feel real desire burning inside of her for the first time since before the Aryshan attack. Had she been missing challenge in her life? Had this prescription of rest and relaxation been more of a problem than a help to her? Morgan laughed to herself.

Evelyn watched her like a hawk the whole time. "What's amusing about that?"

"Thinking about some advice someone gave me once. It's nothing." Morgan waved Evelyn off. She gathered courage and looked her straight in the eye soon after. "I promise you I'll do the best job I'm able. I'm not one to quit, and if you look at the assignment where my commanders worried about me, I tried to continue to do my job, even through the pain. I'm not going to curl up into a ball and break down. This was forced upon me. It won't happen on the colony."

The woman stared at her, expressionless, for a long moment. "Your determination through my questioning is strong. We have some tests for your compatibility for the mission that will glean more than a simple conversation, however. I believe you've earned the right to at least take those."

"Written?" Morgan asked.

She presumed, like most jobs, an aptitude test of sorts would be administered to her. Though she hadn't run logic problems to drill herself, she could handle it.

Evelyn shook her head. "A bit more intensive than that. We have some new technology where it induces sleep in a candidate and then runs a series of psychological screening scenarios. It will accumulate more than a year's worth of personality data in under two hours. I'll need you to sign a waiver for the test, of course, as it can cause issues due to stress."

A sleeper test? Bizarre. Morgan didn't relish the idea of putting her subconscious brain under psychological stress, but if she wanted this assignment, she would have to prove herself, leaving her little option.

"Okay," she agreed.

Evelyn stood, smoothing down her skirt afterward. "Excellent. Follow me to the testing chamber."

27

AT WHAT PRICE FREEDOM

PRISON COLONY 33-X4D

PRISONERS CROWDED into the square as they had been during the original relocation announcement. They didn't have much to do outside of mealtime, laundry duty, or any of the numerous physical activities available at the colony. Other than the Spider Clan, who had taken it upon themselves to do real work. It's what allowed Dalton to study architecture in the first place. The situation held the major drawback of bored, aggressive people with tempers flaring at all times.

Dalton had to tread carefully through the square, even though guards lined the counseling office. He didn't want to be caught in a scrum that escalated before one of them could get to it. Nor did he want to end up in solitary confinement again.

He tried not to bump into anyone in the dense crowd, though he couldn't avoid all contact as everyone tried to crowd the holodisplay.

Coarse hands smacked down hard on his shoulders, nearly causing him to stumble.

Dalton turned around to see a grinning Tarantula. "Came at the same time, I see. We have similar instincts." He shooed Dalton forward. "Get going. You're close to the front of the line."

He faced the holodisplay, able to peek over another of the inmate's shoulders to see the long list of names. It went for several rows, by prisoner number. He'd nearly forgotten his own, instinctively looking for the word "Smarts" as he'd been called most of the time for the last several weeks. For such stupid nicknames, those simple descriptors were surprisingly effective. Here, he needed Prisoner #11375. He traced his finger in the air until he came down to the number.

His number had made the list. He'd be going on the expedition. His record must have been clear enough. They didn't say what the parameters would be, but Dalton imagined there would be a hold on violent criminals or those who had caused too many behavioral problems on the colony. Fortunately, his single solitary confinement incident didn't trigger any negative protocols.

"Ha! I'll be aboard." Another smack to Dalton's back.

Dalton tried not to cringe from how much it stung, before turning around. "You, too?"

Surprise dripped from Dalton's voice, despite his efforts to keep it in check. Didn't the security teams know of the Tarantula's proclivities toward murder?

Strobes flashed in the courtyard before the Tarantula could respond. A dropship appeared in the sky, heading for the landing pad away from the other courtyard. This couldn't be a call to round them all up to go already, could it?

The guards fired their pulse rifles into the air, too close to Dalton to be comfortable.

"Prisoners," a loud, authoritarian voice came from all of the speakers in the courtyard at once, "a body has been discovered, murdered and mutilated. You will return to your dormitories for immediate lockdown."

Dalton shot a knowing look back at the Tarantula.

The Tarantula smiled. "Relax, Smarts. You're always too tense. Makes some of the other guys jumpy."

Jumpy? He made the other guys jumpy? The concept almost made him laugh out loud, but Dalton knew better than to pick a fight, even about the most trivial of matters. He weaved his way away from the holodisplay and toward his assigned dormitory room. Their new building may have been framed, but it didn't provide enough shelter from the cold elements of the evenings at the colony to reside in yet. It may never, since they hadn't found a way to get a ventilation system from the guards yet, and with Dalton and apparently other members of the Spider Clan going on the expedition, his project might never be complete.

He parted ways with the Tarantula without another word. How could that psychotic killer be on the approved list? The Tarantula had some sway with some of the guards, which probably came with his authority of the Spider Clan. None of the prison staff would care to have riots or gang fights—they probably did the Tarantula favors in exchange for keeping his men quiet. Could such favors extend to this?

Prisoners filed into their respective buildings, and the pushing and shoving increased, as did tension. The message repeated over the colony's speakers several times, which didn't serve to increase order, but created a stronger air of agitation among the prisoners than usual.

Around the fifth repetition of the message, someone pushed into Dalton, which sent him stumbling forward into Ogre, the very ape of a man who'd gotten him into his recent mess in the first place. It'd been rather amazing he'd been kept apart from him for this long, especially with Dalton's interactions with the Spider Clan. It made him wonder if the Tarantula had arranged for them to be in different locations.

"You," Ogre said with a toothy grin. "I've heard you've been hanging around."

"I'm sorry for bumping into you. I was pushed," Dalton said, placing his hands up to signify his surrender. He didn't need to get into a fight today.

Ogre seemed to mull over Dalton's words, but he also had his jaw clenched so tight it would have taken a crowbar with a few strong men to pry it open. Not the type to reason with, he smacked his fist into his palm a couple of times.

Dalton wanted to step backward but didn't dare risk getting pinballed back into the crowd.

"You're in tight with the Tarantula now, eh?" Ogre asked.

A couple prisoners brushed past Dalton. He ignored them.

"That's right." He tried to sound confident.

Ogre frowned. "I'ma lay off you, cuz I don't want no trouble with him. You fuck up once though, you're a dead man."

Dalton's eyes couldn't help but go wide. *Read you loud and clear.* He didn't reply, but carefully stepped away from the man, heading toward his dormitory. Ogre didn't follow him, and didn't press. Dalton kept his head down all the same.

Hopefully, that violent psychopath wouldn't be on the list to head to the new colony. Dalton could only imagine what it would be like living with a limited amount of people, in a free environment, with that danger looming over his back.

Could he get a message to the counseling office, let them know the Spider Clan contained dozens of deranged killers? They shouldn't be allowed anywhere near some new colony. If he narced on them, he ran the risk of being disinvited himself, which would do him no good. Worse, if he were discovered, he might end up dangling by his entrails like the last man who crossed the Tarantula. The thought made him shiver.

He fell in line and hoped that he had made the right decision by applying for this journey.

The doors to the dormitory slammed closed behind him.

28

RAPID HOPE LOSS

EARTH, SAN FRANCISCO, CA

KIYOMI TAPPED the screen of her mobile as she waited in the lobby of the ritzy apartment building in downtown San Francisco. A guard stood behind a desk, watching as residents and guests came in and out, dressed in formal wear. He kept his eyes on Kiyomi, probably more because she stood there for far too long than because of her attractiveness.

She'd received news that the colony's prisoner manifest had been completed. It only had taken a few days. They hadn't disclosed how they'd weeded out their worst criminal offenders. Kiyomi had protested this fact, but her words fell on deaf ears, no matter how far up the chain she went. Antony Lemkin might have some contacts who would be willing to listen. She doubted she'd get many results. They had to take what lumps were given them to get this project into space and out of the jurisdiction of anyone from Earth. The less fighting she had to do meant less reason for Earth to impose any last-minute restrictions and make it hard on her.

But she also wanted to check in on the governor. Antony had been reclusive since the death of his wife. He'd been downright impossible to get ahold of. Both she and her father had called dozens of times, as had several other senators and local businessmen. She found out about their attempts only because they'd called her when they found themselves unable to get ahold of him.

Most had been business calls, but some were personal inquiries, making sure that Mr. Lemkin hadn't fallen so far into depression that he would hurt himself. Those, Kiyomi had more sympathy for, but she only had an answer that no one wished to hear—she had no idea as to the whereabouts of Mr. Lemkin.

A few days of phone calls, and Kiyomi found herself bothered. Mr. Lemkin had helped them out, been a friend of her family. If the DePinos stood for nothing else, they stood for loyalty, especially for those who helped her father with his wacky causes. She'd decided to take the forty-five minute flight to San Francisco to check in on him personally.

She also had a major ask of him. After much deliberation, she and her father determined they still didn't have an adequate person to lead the colony. They needed someone with extensive management experience, someone who could react quickly in a crisis. For all of the planning they had done to make sure of a success—and they had found a diverse complement of skills and professions for the colony— no one had bothered thinking of who would be Ixora's governor.

The lack of a leader hadn't been due to an oversight on their part. The reason no one had looked originally was, her father would have been the natural leader of the colony. While Kiyomi had agreed to go and be a chief agriculture developer and botany researcher, she didn't feel she had the experience to be governor. Her father had told her otherwise, citing how well she'd managed so many of the elements of the colony preparation, but Kiyomi wouldn't take that leap.

When they got around to making a short list of candidates, one name stood out above the rest as having both the experience and the integrity for this bold new human experience. Antony Lemkin, they had both agreed, would be the best option.

Despite his lack of answering his calls, despite his going into hiding, and despite not being certain of his location, Kiyomi found herself in the lobby of his apartment.

Tired of procrastinating, Kiyomi spoke with the guard, gave her identification, and told him that she wanted to visit with Mr. Lemkin on the top floor. She'd been registered as a past guest, so she had no problem getting through. He sent her along on her way and activated the elevator to reach that floor only, which in theory prevented other guests from having any stray wanderers. It provided safety for a big city, though Kiyomi still preferred to have a larger amount of space.

The brass-colored elevator doors opened for her, allowing her entrance into the marble-clad cab. Classic decadence at its finest. Soon, she found herself up in the hallway and in front of Antony Lemkin's door.

Her mobile chirped at her.

Kiyomi rolled her eyes without looking to see who rang. If she answered every call that came through, she'd never be off the stupid thing. And she already spent enough of her time on her mobile for several lifetimes.

Instead of answering, she knocked hard on the door. A door chime button hung to the side of the door, but it would send a more poignant message to have that loud, visceral banging sound that a knock created.

No one answered. Kiyomi waited.

Her mobile buzzed again.

Once more, she ignored the call and balled her hand into a fist, hammering the door three more times.

This time, the door cracked open. "Whoever it is I don't want to talk," said Antony Lemkin, his voice raspier than usual.

Kiyomi took a step backward in shock.

Stale air wafted from the apartment. Antony smelled as if he hadn't bathed in several days. He had a pleasant natural body odor, Kiyomi recalled from the few times she had been around him. His muskiness was attractive for a man of his age, but today's stench had a sickly scent to it, screaming of a man who didn't take care of himself.

His appearance matched the haggard scents. A white shirt that had stains on it and a couple of moth holes that betrayed its age, and loose fitting pajama pants that had seen better days, as well. He'd grown a short beard, but one that didn't trim on his cheeks or neck. His face had an oily quality to it, as did his hair, which curled in haphazard directions.

"You look like death," Kiyomi said, unable to do anything but react.

In response, she only saw something more disconcerting than before. His eyes. They invited the prospect of dying. This man needed help.

Kiyomi instantly regretted her words. She must have reminded him of mortality, of the loss of his wife. She didn't know Bethany well, but she had seen the woman standing at his side every time she flipped on the news in the past twenty years. That feeling must be so awful. She couldn't even imagine the hurt and emptiness that must be inside him.

Her mobile buzzed a third time.

"You should answer that," Antony said. His voice croaked, dry.

"I think whoever it is can wait," Kiyomi said, her concern for him and his safety growing by the moment. "Are you going to let me inside?"

Antony hesitated, then stepped away from the door, motioning her ahead.

She'd been to his apartment a few weeks before, but in the absence of Bethany, everything had fallen apart. Clothes piled everywhere, along with a few books, as if he'd never bothered to pick any of them up. The amount of dirty plates and leftover food on the coffee table in his living room proved even more disconcerting. How long had those been there?

"Don't you have someone to come in and help you clean?"

It wasn't the sort of question she'd ask just anyone. Her life held privilege that few could relate to, but Antony, with his high-profile positions over the years, had many of the same amenities.

Antony shut the door, passing her once inside, and slumped down into a well-worn spot on the couch. "I told the housekeepers to go away. I don't want to deal with people."

Healthy. Kiyomi circled around the couch, removing a sweater from a chair across from him before seating herself.

"Someone needs to clean here. Smells terrible. Probably the old food."

"You get used to it." He sounded annoyed. "Why are you here?"

There had to be a better way to ask him to join the program. She hadn't envisioned that he'd been in this bad of shape. Of course, she assumed he would need some help getting motivated again. But the man in front of her wasn't ready to even hold a conversation with anyone. All of her planned speech went out the window. Which reminded her...

"Mind if I open a window? Get some fresh air in here?"

Antony shrugged.

Kiyomi stood again and made her way over to the windows that overlooked the San Francisco skyline. These windows had been designed to be somewhat functional, to allow residents to enjoy the fresh air and sea breeze of the bay, but they had also been built for safety. A panel on the wall controlled the windows, allowing them to crack open from the top, so that no one getting too close could potentially fall out.

The fresh air swirled into the room, cool, crisp. Kiyomi had been taking short breaths before, not wanting to inhale whatever caused the smells in the room, but now she could breathe normally. She turned back to Antony.

"I wanted to check on you. No one's heard from you in several days. Someone had to make sure you're okay." *So you don't kill yourself,* she thought.

"I'm fine. Just want to be left alone." Those last words held bite, sending her a direct message.

Kiyomi didn't back down. She'd dealt with a stubborn and powerful man all her life. She met Antony's gaze head on. "I know you're having a tough time. I understand, trust me I do, but you need to snap out of it. I mean that as respectfully as I can."

Antony frowned, his age showing on his face as he'd done so, something new to this last week. He'd been so spry before. "I don't want to. I don't care anymore. I'm done."

She hadn't heard those kinds of words since her teenaged days. What else could she say to him? How could she console someone this far gone? Why didn't he have closer friends who came to do that?

"You're not done. You've got decades ahead of you. My father wouldn't have supported you unless he though you an honorable man who wanted to change the world, and had both the wits and the energy to accomplish real change."

"Your father was wrong. I accomplished nothing as governor. And after that, I've only lost. What's the point?" He turned away from her, leaning back into one of the couch pillows.

"The point is that we can create something lasting, a legacy beyond our short time here," Kiyomi said. She had to gamble and press the point. "Why waste a moment? We might not have another."

Antony flinched at those words as if she had struck him.

Kiyomi opened her mouth to speak, but paused when her mobile buzzed yet once more.

"Seriously, answer it or throw it out the window. I destroyed mine a couple of days ago. Too many people trying to call, offer their bull-shit condolences."

She didn't doubt him. No wonder her calls had been going straight to message. This time, she pulled her mobile out of her handbag.

The display read *Marcus*, and it showed that he'd been the one to call the last three times, as well.

Kiyomi hit the receive call button, which connected to her earpiece. "Marcus, I'm busy right now."

"Kiyomi! There you are." He sounded panicked.

"Is everything okay?"

"No. Nothing's okay. You need to get back here now. Where are you? I don't know what to do!" Marcus's voice sound hurried, scattered.

"Slow down, Marcus. Tell me what's going on." She looked to Antony, who watched her with detached interest.

"I don't know how to say this, Yomi. It's Fabio. I found him on the floor of his office. He wasn't breathing... he's..."

No. No! It couldn't be...

"He's dead."

29

DOORS SHUT AND OPENED

Earth, San Francisco, CA

Antony watched the blood drain from Kiyomi's face. Her knees wobbled, and she stumbled. He couldn't hear any of the words on the other side of the line, but he recognized the shock hitting her. He'd dealt with the same emotions in recent days.

He scrambled to his feet, the first time he'd moved with such speed since he rushed to Bethany, seeing her collapse on the stage behind him. If only he'd moved sooner. If only he'd been the one to take the bullet instead of her.

He hopped the coffee table like a hurdler and found himself at Kiyomi's side. She fell into his arms. Unsure of what to do, Antony held her closely.

Kiyomi buried her head nose-first into Antony's chest. Tears poured out of her eyes, soaking Antony's shirt. She moaned, the sound muffled by fabric. Those wounds were still fresh for him, and this overwhelming amount of emotion stabbed him right in the chest where he'd been hurt before.

How could the world be so cruel? Kiyomi and he had shared a

common purpose these last months, that purpose being spurred on through people they had both loved. Their situations had more similarity than they did differences. What cruel God would torture them like this, so close to something great?

The question lingered in his head as tears welled in his own eyes. His lids drooped from the weariness of days of crying and lack of sleep. It'd been decades since he'd bawled like he had—not even the loss of his own parents over the years gave him the heavy gut punch losing Bethany had.

He'd found the strength to handle the losses through Bethany.

Now, she couldn't help him. She wouldn't be coming back. How many times had he thought those very words this last week? What good did it do him? By the same token, he couldn't get the thought of her out of his head. The apartment still carried her scent, and though he held Kiyomi close, he noted a different floral aroma to her. Pleasant, but not Bethany.

Antony shook his head as Kiyomi continued to cry. If her love for her father could compare to what he felt for Bethany, it would be an hour before she'd become coherent again, perhaps more.

All he could do was wait, hold her, and be there for her. Though they hadn't been the closest prior to this, they did have the common bond of the project, through her father. He had probably sent her to his apartment this evening to talk about the project. But they had nothing more to discuss. The government had caved. After the shooting, not one of the greedy senators even came back with other demands. No one wanted the bad public relations of picking on Antony right after that had occurred, live for billions to see. They had won, though Antony had paid the price by losing everything.

Minutes passed as Antony waited. The thoughts of Bethany made his whole body numb. Pain didn't matter anymore. Nothing mattered, even this young woman pressed against him, clinging to him as if his mere presence would put a stopper into the flowing bottle of her own painful emotions.

Kiyomi sniffled and took a deep breath, then pulled back to look up at him. Her eyes were still moist, reddened from the crying. Her make-up trickled down her face as evidence of the tears that had already escaped her.

"I'm sorry. I don't usually do this," she said, wiping her face with her sleeve.

Antony lifted his head some, still holding onto her lithe form. "It's okay. I know exactly how you feel."

That feeling came from such a close point in time that it crept up inside of him again. He gritted his teeth, trying to push the feelings back down, but God it hurt. Bethany.

Kiyomi frowned at him. "That makes it worse. I shouldn't put you through this. I'm sorry." She pulled herself back, and Antony let her go freely. "I'll leave. I didn't mean to bother you."

He watched her stand from his crouched position, staying there himself, immobilized by that simultaneous pain and numbness that thinking of Bethany brought him. Her red hair, her silk skin—those memories all flowed back to him. He would never see or touch her again.

The apartment seemed like a prison cell. The white walls that had brought him the comfort of home before drove him to insanity now. The skyline, looking out over the San Francisco Bay, meant nothing to him. He didn't have anyone to share it with.

The furniture in the room seemed so old and stale. Hadn't Kiyomi mentioned that it had smelled foul in here when she entered? How embarrassing. He needed to get out of this place. Permanently.

His apartment no longer could be called home.

Kiyomi made good on her word, walking toward the door, her shoulders slumped and feet dragging, exactly like one would expect from someone in the amount of pain she must be feeling. Antony had been there for days, energy sapped from him. It made his week-long loss of purpose when he had stepped down from his governorship seem like happy days. If only he could return to that time, days where he'd taken Bethany for granted. She'd been there for him then, asking if he needed anything, and yet he had brushed her aside. To have those moments back, to spend time with her once again—he would give anything for that.

Antony righted himself, using his coffee table as leverage to get to his feet with a grunt. He had two alternatives for what he could do. He could kill himself—find some underground doctor to inject him with a lethal amount of drugs and make it look like an accident. He didn't want to jump off the Golden Gate Bridge or make any flamboyant display, or especially have the media covering his death in such a grandiose exhibition. It would make his sacrifice of the governorship look like a cry for desperation. It would be analyzed for years, and in all the wrong ways.

Caring about his legacy meant he didn't truly want to die. Caring meant he had accomplished something, and he had more to accomplish. The only way he'd attain a new goal worthy of his pursuit would be a change of scenery. His thoughts returned to getting out of this apartment for good.

"Ms. DePino," Antony said, voice scratchy and raw.

Standing in the doorway, she turned back to him with those bloodshot, shining eyes, a beauty in her own right, even with her streaking makeup, messed hair, and wrinkled clothes. She had a curious look on her face, but said nothing.

"You came here to talk about the project. I know you have to tend to your estate..." He winced at those words. They sounded so cold. "Deal with your loss, I mean. But I knew your father very well. Most of our relationship was business, but he treated his business like family, for lack of a better way of putting it. What I'm trying to say is..."

He took a deep breath. What was he trying to say? His mental faculty hadn't magically returned to full clarity after days of crying, zoning out, and hoping the world would disappear. The back of his head ached where his skull met his neck. He needed some painkillers.

"What I'm trying to say is, I still want to help with your project, and with your father gone, I want to offer my services."

"To manage the project?" Kiyomi asked. "He spent every waking hour working on this, even ones where the sane ones of us weren't awake. There's no way we would have met his time tables otherwise. I don't even know how someone could pick up that slack. I don't even think I could do it, as close to the project as I've been."

Antony maneuvered himself over to her, not nearly as close as before, though he had to admit he did feel a connection to her since holding her for such a long time. He'd been there for her in her time of need. From the look in her eyes, she noticed it, too. It made for awkward silence. Neither of them were ready to connect with others.

"No," Antony said. "Yes. I mean, I'm happy to try to help in the planning capacity as well. What I mean is that I think I can help with the project's future. I don't have anything here now. I don't want to be on Earth anymore, and, I know your father sought candidates to lead the colony. He hadn't asked me, but he'd alluded to it on more than one occasion. This sounds presumptuous, but if you haven't chosen anyone else, I would like to volunteer to govern your new colony."

Several more seconds of silence followed with Kiyomi watching him. Had he made an error? Perhaps he shouldn't have talked of her father's project during her difficult time. She hadn't even had time to process what had happened. Her mental state couldn't be much better than his on the day Bethany had died, and from what he'd seen of the footage, he had acted like a feral animal, out of control.

He hadn't even processed what he'd heard. His donor, his business associate, and more, his friend, had died. Fabio DePino would never call upon him for favors again. This offer of his had been a bad idea and it'd probably hurt the kind, hardworking woman across from him. He opened his mouth to apologize, but stopped.

Kiyomi laughed.

She laughed so hard that she tripped over herself and braced her arm against the entryway wall. The sound echoed through the living room, interweaved with a couple of sniffles as she had to catch her breath. Fresh tears formed on her face, and she wiped them with her hand.

Antony didn't know how to react and stopped trying to analyze the situation. He laughed with her. It felt good, even if he didn't understand the humor of the situation.

Their laughter continued for a time and then that awkwardness crept back into the occasion, freezing both of them. Antony realized how silly he must have looked. He hadn't showered or bothered to change his clothes in days. He could barely communicate, and here he tried to give a speech about how he should govern a new, free colony and a fresh civilization.

Kiyomi broke the tension with the smallest of smiles. "You know what's funny?"

"What's that?" Antony asked.

"I came here to propose that very thing to you. Daddy and I had talked it over, and really couldn't find anyone else we'd be comfortable with giving the job to. I can't do it, not yet at least, and we really didn't have anyone that senior at leadership signed up for the expedition. I was prepared to stay here until I could rope you into the idea."

For all of his fears, he hadn't considered the reason why she would take the time to make a personal trip. He chuckled to himself. "Well, you got that done." He paused. "Your father would be proud."

Kiyomi nodded. She turned to the side then, averting her eyes from him. "Thanks. I... still need to go. I'll be in touch. Don't screen my calls, okay?"

"Of course," Antony said, opening the door for her and grinning. "Once I get a new phone."

30

UNPREPARED

Morgan took cover behind a support column, checking her pulse pistol to ensure it still held its charge. Once satisfied, she surveyed the open room. The room was medium-sized, with office furniture and cubicles that extended into the distance. Civilians were scattered across the room, making her task all the more difficult.

A masked attacker in black body armor popped out from behind one of the cubicles. He held a weapon, firing several shots in Morgan's direction.

She used the column for what modest cover it provided. Two shots hit the drywall, and several more blasted past her into a nearby desk. The resulting impact made a crater in the desk, cracking the wood and sending papers flying everywhere.

The weapons fire stopped long enough for Morgan to peek around the other side. The attacker had to recharge his weapon. She wouldn't panic here. She couldn't afford to. Instead, she took aim, extending both arms outward, straight, holding the pistol steady in the proper firing position. Then she pulled the trigger, holding it down so that several energy pulses erupted from the end of her gun.

Unlike the undisciplined shots of her attacker, Morgan's pulses struck true. Three in the chest, one on the arm, and the final blew the head off her target. His body collapsed to the floor. Blood splattered. Morgan resumed her cover.

The civilians around her panicked, deciding to make a run for it. With so many fleeing, it would only give the attackers the idea that they could cause more panic, and perhaps use some of them as human shields or hostages. A nightmare for Morgan.

But how many attackers were left? Morgan had to figure out the answer quickly. She'd seen at least three, more than enough of a challenge for her and her lone gun to deal with. If they had come at her together, she would have really been in trouble.

As if they had sensed her thoughts, two masked men in the same black body armor appeared in her field of vision. One motioned to the civilians. The second attacker grabbed a woman by the hair and pulled her in front of him as a shield, like she'd been worried about. The woman's body effectively blocked any shot Morgan might have had.

The first attacker turned to Morgan's direction. "We have a hostage. If you don't want her killed, come out now. Hands up."

Morgan hesitated from her place behind the pole. Now what? Unlike her stint in the military, she had no one else to make decisions for her. Her heart pounded inside her chest. She'd never had to deal with situations like this.

The hostage-taker pulled on the woman's hair and placed his pulse pistol up to her chin. "We're not screwing around!"

"Drop your weapon," the first said.

What else could she do? She could take one of them down, but the second might kill the hostage. Was one hostage an acceptable loss at this juncture? She didn't want to make that call. If only she had someone else to help her out of this jam.

Morgan tossed her pulse pistol off to the side. It clanked on the floor, harmless, out of her reach. She stepped from behind the column, hands up in the air.

"You got me," she said.

The first attacker rushed toward her pulse pistol.

Morgan locked eyes with the woman who had her hair pulled. *Resist*, she tried to will to her. Would it work? Something had to break in this situation. If the woman would help, Morgan might be able to tackle the first attacker before he reached her pistol. Either way, she had to try.

Before she could ready herself to pounce, the world flickered around her and faded to black.

Morgan pulled the VR helmet off of her head. Several diodes remained connected to her neck and chest. "Why did you shut down the simulation?" she asked.

Evelyn stood over her, along with two men in lab coats who monitored computers and machinery at stations behind her.

"You gave up," Evelyn said.

"I hadn't, though." Morgan shifted. The connectors irritated her skin, though she wouldn't risk damaging their equipment. "I was getting ready for a surprise attack."

"Our estimation was that you had less than a five percent chance of success in any future actions," one of the lab scientists said.

"Still, a good showing. You passed the first three levels. This one was trickier to navigate without any backup, something you won't likely encounter on Ixora, as you'll have a team of security under your command. I'm curious, though, why didn't you shoot the attackers? Odds were that the threat of violence against that woman was a bluff. If she were killed, he wouldn't have a shield, and it would give you the advantage."

Morgan grimaced. The two lab technicians made their way over and with gloved hands and carefully removed the wiring and diodes attached to her, ensuring not to touch them together or do anything that would cause a grounding problem. The VR equipment had a major sensitivity to any outside environmental shake-ups. It made sense, as it provided hyper-realistic pictures to the point where it tricked her body into feeling her surroundings.

"I don't know," Morgan said.

"You do," Evelyn said, pacing the room. "Think."

Why did she hesitate?

"If we're going to be out on a colony with fewer than ten thousand inhabitants, we'll need everyone. We can't risk even a single civilian casualty. If I'd attacked, he might have shot, or I might have accidentally misfired on her when trying to hit him. I couldn't find a way to handle the situation cleanly. I thought if I appeared to give up, even for a second, it would throw them off balance. If the civilian resisted along with me when I made my next move, we might have come out of it without losing her."

"But the plan increased the odds of losing *you*. With your status and authority, not to mention your experience, that would be a detrimental loss to security. Frankly, you're not expendable, Ms. Ezra," Evelyn said.

Morgan considered. Not expendable. In the military, everyone could be an "acceptable loss", depending on the situation. She'd never even thought of the concept of wanting to keep herself out of danger to preserve some experience or title. If she'd been ordered into a dangerous situation, she would have gone to it without reservation. Not that patrolling a supply depot had been particularly dangerous, at least until the Aryshans arrived. Even then, her priority hadn't been flight, but it had been to help as best she could. She nodded.

Her agreement appeared to satisfy Evelyn. "It's a different way of thinking for you, I understand."

The diodes had been completely removed, and the technicians moved the equipment off to the side. Evelyn motioned for her to stand.

Morgan pushed herself out of the chair, which had her situated perpendicular to the floor. "That all for today?"

"That's going to be all, period. Events have transpired where we've been ordered to speed up the process of the launch—so congratulations, even without all of the testing I would have liked to have done, you've been accepted for the job. What they're thinking back at H.Q., I don't know," Evelyn said.

"Isn't the project already going forward at a, uh, difficult pace for the crews?"

"That's the understatement of the millennium. No one thinks DePino's timeframe for launch is realistic. Now they're expecting the command team to be here in less than a week's time, and they want to launch immediately upon arrival?" She exhaled, her frustration showing on her face. "My job is the same no matter what, I suppose. There is one thing I wanted to alert you to, before you spend your final days in this system relaxing to your heart's content."

"What's that?" Morgan tilted her head.

"There's a group of prisoners arriving tomorrow on a transport from Prison Colony 33-4XD. They're going to be going to the colony along with you."

Morgan's eyes went wide. "Isn't that the federal penal colony?"

Many of the Federated colonies had their own prison systems, but crimes against Earth required special treatment. These were the worst of the worst, from what Morgan understood. She'd had a job offering to provide security for that world before entering into the military. She could have had a great life with the hazard pay, but she'd been too scared to go through with the assignment.

"That's right. It's part of the conditions that the senate gave for the expedition. Apparently, they had a population control issue and they wanted to thin the crowds some." Evelyn shrugged. "They were supposed to have weeded out those with violent criminal pasts, but you know how these things go with the government."

Morgan tried to give a smile as if she understood, though from what she'd seen—with the military at least—the government functioned smoothly and efficiently. "I suppose I should meet these prisoners and let them know who's boss? It'll be like training new recruits in a way."

Evelyn laughed. "You won't have time, but I do want you to see what you're getting into."

"No time? Why not?"

"Because there's two thousand of them."

MEETINGS

Dalton sat on his cot, in a shared cell with someone he didn't know, another man wearing bright orange. He stared across to the cell that lined the balcony beyond, a forcefield sealing more prisoners inside their cells.

Yet more prisoners lined the main floor below, with the rows of cells going up for at least a dozen decks. In the boredom of the journey, Dalton had little else to do while they traveled other than count them. His cellmate, like many of the prisoners he'd met during his served time, didn't provide the best conversation.

The steel-plated floors clicked and echoed as someone walked by, one of the dozens of prison guards who patrolled the ship in their black body armor with riot shields and stun weapons. This one stopped in front of the cell, pausing to look down at a datapad, and then up at Dalton.

"Prisoner One-One-Three-Seven-Five?" he asked.

Dalton's cellmate moved forward, as if in some anticipation.

"When are we gonna get off this hell bucket? We're supposed to be going to a new world, open air."

Instead of engaging, Dalton waited. The guard looked down at his data pad again and then back to the cellmate. "You'll be sitting here awhile longer, prisoner. We're here for him."

The guard pointed to Dalton.

His cellmate gave Dalton the stink-eye, as if Dalton could control what the guard wanted with him. He couldn't be sure why they requested him, but if it meant getting out of this cell before tensions flared and a problem occurred, he'd happily oblige. Not as if he had a choice, anyway.

Dalton stood, stretching before walking to the space in front of the forcefield. The guard pointed his stunner toward the other prisoner and deactivated the electrical field. The air in front of Dalton went from a blank space, to a flicker of orange light and back again.

He stepped forward and the guard reset the forcefield before motioning him along.

"Do I get to be told where I'm going?" Dalton asked.

The guard kept the stunner trained on him now as he led him down the platform, using a fingerprint to get past a door labeled "restricted". It opened into a much smaller hallway than the big open area containing the herd of confused prisoners.

"The Ixora Project chief of security wants to meet with you," the guard said as they continued. He led Dalton down a corridor, which connected to an airlock, and opened to another corridor row. The ship must have docked, though with the inertial dampeners, unless the passengers had been made aware by some other means, they wouldn't have been able to feel it. It wouldn't matter to the prisoners one way or another.

After a five-minute walk through a much busier area, with professionals and maintenance workers moving about, the guard brought Dalton to a small conference room. It had no windows, the room on the interior of whatever ship he'd been brought to. The guard motioned for Dalton to seat himself, and then stepped back.

Dalton complied, waiting, painfully aware of the stunner trained on his head. The door opened behind him again and an athletic woman with long red hair and a green tracksuit circled around the table opposite of him. She had pretty features, but something about the way she carried herself screamed that she'd been broken somehow. Sadness hung around her like a yoke. Curious.

"Dalton Ward from Prison Colony 33-X4D?" the woman asked with curious, shining eyes.

"That's me." Dalton crossed his arms casually.

"I'm sure you're wondering why I brought you here." She glanced at the guard. "Did you tell him who I am?"

"I did, ma'am," the guard said.

The project chief of security nodded. "My name is Morgan Ezra, and we're about to be spending a lot of years together. I'll have my team, and you'll be one of two thousand prisoners that have been brought along on this expedition. I'm not going to lie to you, no one's comfortable with that, and I've been tasked with making sure you and the others don't step out of line."

She paused.

Dalton considered how he should play this situation. What did she want from him? They'd asked for him by prisoner number, but she had his name. He wasn't anyone special within the prison. He'd had very little record except for the fight he'd been into a few months ago. By all accounts, he had no notability whatsoever—except for his association with the Spider Clan. What had he been thinking, joining them?

The same thing that he had been thinking with joining this colony —survival.

"I'm sure you're wondering why I brought *you* here, in particular," Morgan continued, unfazed by his lack of reaction, or at least not showing any problem with it. "I've gone through records and saw that you not only had a business background prior to your incarceration, but you also spent more time in the prison colony's academic center and library than anyone else by significant margins."

Dalton chuckled, his arms dropping to his sides. "I didn't think anyone was tracking."

"There's a robust database of behavioral metrics for prisoners. We used a lot of the same systems back in the service to monitor our subordinates." Something about the way she spoke sounded uncomfortable.

She opened up to him. Giving him a bit of personal information, which she clearly didn't like doing, and probably without the understanding that Dalton could read people like they were an open book. It's how he appealed to the Spider Clan in the first place. They were a bit easier to navigate as brutes, but she had a different power dynamic with him. He was a prisoner, and she a guard. Though in an open world, in theory, he and the others would be given a new chance. A chief of security would then want to monitor any potential problems, and rightfully so. It clicked for Dalton.

"You're looking for a liaison between the prisoners and everyone else."

Morgan smiled. "You got me in one. It's not exactly what you think. I'm more looking for someone to be my eyes and ears, see if something's amiss and let me know before it causes a problem. With that many people..."

A mass uprising is what she'd be worried about, prisoners running wild. As if he could do anything about that if the situation came down to it. But still, it offered a position of power and responsibility, usefulness. Winning any negotiation depended on the level of usefulness one could offer. He didn't have a plan for what he wanted out of this expedition, other than to be out of prison, and most importantly survive for the long run. This offer could be very useful to him.

"I'd be happy to help," he said.

"Great," Morgan said, visibly relaxing. She'd been worried in approaching him—her eyes shifting so often betraying her insecurities. He had all the leverage in a situation where he should have very little.

The more he scrutinized the way she looked, her body language, the younger she seemed. Whoever gave her this role had put this woman in over her head. Something to remember about this colony for later. It made sense. What kind of people would volunteer to go on a one-way trip to some unknown world, fending for oneself, not knowing if that path meant death? Desperate people, like himself, like the prisoners who were being forced to. On an isolated world, he would have plenty of time to find out what caused her desperation. "The prisoners aren't the most organized bunch. We've been held in cells, several of us let out onto the bottom deck at a time for exercise. I don't even know half of the people on the ship. Back on the Prison Colony, there's so many people it splinters into groups and gangs. You're not going to be able to control them all through one person, if that's what you had in mind."

"I figured as much. Like I said, I'm more interested in someone who can keep their ear to the ground for what's going on."

Dalton nodded. This had been a fortuitous meeting. It could set him up on the colony in ways he hadn't considered. "Do you know much else about the project? When we're going to leave? I hadn't even realized we'd docked with another ship."

Morgan side-glanced at the guard, her posture tightening again. "That's not my place to say right now. I'm only the security chief once we arrive at the colony. I'm limited to planning."

She wouldn't overstep right now. This ship or facility had bigger authorities at work, wherever and whoever they were. He wouldn't be getting information from her to bring back to the prison. Sensible, though he had hoped the innocuous question would get past the inexperience he'd perceived in her.

Morgan motioned and the guard stepped forward. "Thank you, Mr. Ward. I look forward to working with you soon and will be in touch as soon as I am able."

Dalton stood, pushing the chair back behind him. His luck might be turning for the better, and he would have to figure out how to make the most of it. The other prisoners and he would have to be able to co-exist not just with each other, but with several thousand innocents on the colony, as well. So many of these people hadn't interacted with the outside world in a long time. They were used to the gangs and settling matters by violence. He felt for Morgan Ezra. Did she even realize how much work she had cut out for her?

He caught himself, mentally telling himself, *it's not your problem.* But it would be his problem. If something went wrong, it would be everyone's problem on a small colony. In many ways, he'd agreed to be the narc. Around the Spider Clan, such a position could be precarious. He wouldn't be able to afford any missteps. And with the Tarantula on the list of prisoner-colonists, his life hung on the line with every conversation.

DEPARTURES

DePino Transport Ship Flight 404 to Toltair

KIYOMI MADE her way through the bustling crowd in the DePino Gold Star Lounge, one of the many swanky modern tapas bars each of her company's larger space liners had, filled with dark, sleek couches, small round tables, and intimate lighting. Though the food offerings and wine selection made it a place worth a Gold Star membership for frequent travelers, what really gave it a "wow-factor" was the floor-to-ceiling view of the stars streaking by outside, as the transport's crystal drive had engaged and sent them into FTL a day ago.

Happy hour had begun, which meant a slightly reduced price on select items, which brought the bored crowd of the transport forth to some of the only places to socialize on the ship. The VR Holo rooms or the gym didn't quite have the same appeal. Kiyomi couldn't help but smile. Her father had come up with many of these amenities for the transport industry. When he'd started as an investor, most ships were bare bones, shells used for flights back and forth without much to offer customers. In the last couple of decades, this treatment had become fairly standard, especially for the higher-end paying customers.

Though she'd been planning for this day for a long time, she couldn't help but think about how fast the days had gone by. Grieving for her father made the days seem like years, but she didn't have time to wallow in her loss. She'd spent recent days working around the clock, finalizing the list of colonists, approving the planned colony designs, making sure the cold sleep units were in place on the ark. It had been too much for one person to manage. Even if there had been double the hours in the day, she wouldn't have been able to keep up with the demands of the launch.

Even the brief thought of her father made her gut wrench. She imagined him at his table, reading his morning news, while Marcus brought over a plate of eggs and Portuguese sausage. Those mornings had transpired so many times over her life, and they would never happen again. Dad had the sternest look when he read the news, eyebrows pinching in toward his forehead as he deliberated on it. Often times, it would be minutes before he even noticed her, but when he did, his eyes would light up, and he would smile. He had loved her as much, maybe more, than she had loved him.

She still loved him, but she'd also been prepared to never see her father again. Ever since his health problems began, Kiyomi had been aware that this would be a one-way journey, alone, without him. Those thoughts had kept her up late at night those first evenings when he stayed in the hospital, but she had resigned herself to it by the time he passed.

This would be one of her last chances to socialize with people who weren't going to the colony. But she found herself to be quiet and introspective. Why was she being so morose? She shook her head.

The bar had people squeezing in tightly, occupying stools in front of a reflective glass countertop with embedded soft blue lighting. Chic and modern, as space travel should be. Kiyomi found herself a spot about two thirds of the way down the bar, and she smiled at a man who sat at a stool next to where she stood.

He raised his drink to her with a return smile, then turned back to his colleague, the two already deep in discussion.

Kiyomi made eye contact with the bartender, who shuffled over to her. He wiped down the bar top with a rag. "What can I getcha?"

"House wine would be fine. White, please," Kiyomi said. "Worked on the starliner long?"

"Second year." The bartender grabbed a bottle and poured the liquid into a glass. "Long trips, but pays pretty decent."

"Glad to hear that."

The bartender's eyes widened as if he had only just recognized her, and processed her relation to the starliner. Kiyomi gave a smile, taking the wineglass stem between her fingers.

"Corporate charge account," she said, then turned. When she did, she almost ran into a suited man's chest, spilling a small amount of her wine on him.

The man stepped back, patting himself down with a frown. Kiyomi had been so preoccupied she had failed to recognize him at first. Jim Singhal. Of all the people she could have spilled on, this had to be the worst possibility.

"Jim, I'm sorry," Kiyomi said.

Jim motioned to the tender who tossed him a rag. He scrubbed down the front of his suit where Kiyomi had spilled.

"Looks like you at least owe me a drink for this mess," he said, a playful tone in his voice.

He'd called her a dozen times, and she hadn't returned his calls, which made her feel all the worse. As of late, Kiyomi's life had been all-consumed by the Ark Project. She'd long forgotten his intentions to join the colony. It had been so long since they shared lunch on the Florida beach, him making his intentions toward her clear. Kiyomi had meant to talk to her father about it, to let him know that in a colony of ten thousand people, that it would be awkward for her to be in such a position. The people of the colony would have to reproduce, which left limited options. Kiyomi couldn't bring herself to be interested in Jim, even if that meant her being celibate for the rest of her life. Judging from the glimmer in Jim's eyes, the feeling was not mutual, and he hadn't been deterred.

"I should get back to my quarters," Kiyomi said, her voice coming out more timid than usual. "I came to grab a glass. Need to do work." She hooked a thumb toward the door.

"Why don't you stay and chat awhile? It's been months," Jim said. He jutted his bottom lip out to pout. "C'mon," he said. He waved down the bartender. "Whiskey on the rocks for me."

As he moved past her, his other arm slipped around her waist. The move came across as casual.

It couldn't have turned Kiyomi off more. She dropped her shoulder and wiggled away from him, bumping into the man behind her.

The man turned to check the situation, leaving Kiyomi in her second awkward moment in as many minutes.

"I'm so sorry," she said.

"My friend's been clumsy tonight," Jim said to the other patron with a chuckle. "Don't worry. I'll pick up your tab on her behalf." He brushed past Kiyomi and leaned on the bar.

"It's fine," the other man said, turning back to his conversation.

Kiyomi tried to extricate herself from the conversation, backing away this time.

Jim swung his arm on the bar, grabbing his drink with ease before meeting her step-for-step.

"Where are we going?" Jim asked.

With his breath so close to her face, Kiyomi could tell he'd had a couple drinks already before coming here. No wonder his aggression showed.

"I told you, *I'm* going back to my quarters," Kiyomi said. Her voice came out hesitant, not because she had a secret desire to stay, but because the whole situation had flustered her.

"Great. I'll come with you," Jim said with a big smile across his face.

It made Kiyomi want to slap him.

"I don't think so," a voice came from behind her—familiar, male, strong.

Antony Lemkin stood dressed in a thin, baby-blue turtleneck. The color suited him, brought out his eyes.

"Antony, hi," she said, relieved.

"Everything okay here?" Antony raised a brow, eyes settling upon Jim like a hawk. The rest of the lounge seemed to fade into an unfocussed blur, conversations around them turning to background noise. The air held tension like Kiyomi hadn't felt in a long time.

"Yeah, fine. Me and the lady here were about to get going," Jim said. He raised his glass to Antony.

"That's not what it sounded like to me," Antony said. He stepped closer to Kiyomi, posture defensive.

"Well, you heard wrong. We got business. Why don't you go enjoy your night somewhere else, old man?" Jim asked. What could deter him at this point?

Jim didn't recognize Antony. He probably thought he dealt with some DePino employee. With Antony out of suit and in casual clothes, he had a bland presence. This everyman look had served him well in getting elected.

"Actually, I need to discuss some of the colony plans with *Governor* Lemkin," Kiyomi said, hoping her emphasis stuck in Jim's mind before his hostility turned into violence.

Jim considered, his smile all but disappearing into a thoughtful frown. He peered at Kiyomi, then huffed.

"There'll be a lot of time for this later. As much as we need," he said, words slurred. Whatever it took for his alcohol-hazed mind to convince itself to leave the situation. After his words, he hurried past both Antony and her, stomping toward the exit.

Antony laid a hand on her shoulder. Kiyomi reflexively tensed and backpedaled. He drew his hand back cautiously in response.

"Sorry," he said.

Kiyomi focused on him for the first time since he'd arrived. Her gaze met his. They connected. Kiyomi could sense their collective losses, their passion toward hard work, the mutual respect they had for each other. More? Their connection felt safe, the kind of safety that her father had provided her, but different. The stress of Dad's death and the colony preparations—it had all fallen to her, and she hadn't had anyone to share it with other than him. Antony had been there for her when she had first heard the news, when she had needed someone most. She appreciated him.

"No, I'm sorry," she murmured.

"Don't be," Antony said. He turned his attention over toward the lounge's entrance. "Is he someone coming on the expedition?"

"Yeah," Kiyomi said, following his glance past the crowd of people in the room. Until now, she hadn't conceived or thought of her own safety, or how without her father, she had such an empty world. Did she need rest?

Antony narrowed his eyes, business-like would be the only way she could describe it. "Can we get him off the list? The way he was hovering over you can't be healthy long-term."

"It's our expedition. We have final say of who comes and who goes. Other than the prisoners."

"The prisoners, right," Antony said. "We'll need all the able bodies we can get outside of them, in case there's an issue."

"We could always replace him? I mean there's not much time to do background checks once we arrive at Toltair, but I could input a new request into the system."

"Might not be a bad idea," Antony said. "I really don't think we want him coming with us. Something feels off about him."

"He'd never been that bad before. I think the alcohol had something to do with it." Kiyomi didn't know why she defended him. Perhaps she had been so used to spending time with Jim as the man who'd worked for her father. Thinking back, he'd made one too many jokes about her marrying him since she'd known him.

"Still," Antony said. He shook his head. "How's everything else going? Are we set to go?"

"Everything's on schedule. When we arrive, all we'll have to do is load everything in the ark, set the AI parameters to take us to Ixora, and hop into the cold sleep chambers."

"You say that as if it's an easy thing." Antony chuckled. "I know loading procedures on big ships for off-planet transport. I had to manage some of those through union strikes, war efforts, all sorts of crazy times. You're as familiar with the troubles, at least from listening to your dad, I'm sure."

Kiyomi recalled Dad on his comm, screaming at people on the other end when problems occurred—and they happened more often than not.

She shrugged. "All we can do is hope this one goes smoothly."

"Indeed," Antony said. "But I have enough experience with your father to trust in his plan. Have a good night, Ms. DePino. See you soon."

33

UNPREPARED

TWO ARMED GUARDS escorted Antony down the shipyards' office corridors. He'd been shown his quarters earlier, a pleasant accommodation saved for executives and VIPs. The room proved more spacious than the transport had been, which he didn't enjoy. The large room mired him with a deep sense of aloneness. It crippled him for a few hours, sending him falling into depression once again. He found he'd been unable to sleep in the quarters. No matter, as soon as the ark departed the station, he'd be cold sleeping for close to a hundred years.

Weeks ago, the prospect of cold sleep would have scared him. What would it have been like to have never seen Bethany again? He wouldn't want to risk severing their connection. Now, the universe had done it for him.

The news claimed the shooter's motivation had been some kind of revenge because of Antony's stepping down. The man had some life event where he lost his job and blamed it on instability caused by

Antony's action. Everything had ripple effects, and the mentally-ill took matters to extremes.

As he rounded the corner, he spotted Kiyomi DePino. Working with her had been a joy, he had to admit. Her brightness, dedication, loyalty, and ability to get things done reminded Antony of Bethany. Kiyomi had her own quirks, of course, with her obsession with plants and agriculture. Antony didn't have any intention of familiarizing himself with the finer points of botany, but he found merit in having someone along at a brand-new colony who could keep an eye on agriculture. Her skills would be paramount.

She flashed him a smile on her way past him and in through some conference room doors. The guard with Antony motioned him forward.

The room already had filled in with people, folks whose faces he only knew from short bios. An older Asian man with a pointed beard would be the environmental manager, Tom Lee. Across from him sat a woman with a rejuvenated face and intense eyes, leaned back in her chair, who looked like the chief physician they'd recruited, Dr. Laura Torba. Kiyomi shook hands and made small talk.

"Governor Antony Lemkin," a voice said, clear, strong, female and from the head of the table.

Antony turned his head that direction. "Hello, Miss...?"

"Evelyn Tellmann, station director. Welcome, Mr. Lemkin."

The assembled group halted their various conversations and applauded for him.

It'd been awhile since Antony had felt the rush of people excited to see him. As much as he liked the serving aspect of politics and getting things accomplished, he had to admit that part of the appeal for his former profession came from the adrenaline and rush from cheering crowds. The rallies, the speeches, the events—even the smallest ones in the district—it felt good to know that people cared about him.

This time proved no different. "Hello, everyone. This is officially the first meeting of the senior staff of the Ixora colony. From the reports I read last evening, advanced computer simulations with our current personnel and resources are completed, including the redundant situations, and all project that we have a high probability of success for a thriving colony."

"That's great news," Tom Lee said.

"It is," Kiyomi said, sliding into a chair close to Evelyn. "We'd been struggling with the percentage likelihood projections for a while, but the last rounds have been positive. Our most recent personnel acquisitions have done wonders for us."

"On that subject," Antony said, pacing over to the opposite side of Evelyn, where a lone empty chair rested at the end of the conference room. Instead of sitting, he leaned over the back of it. "We recently lost our head construction manager due to personnel conflicts. If anyone here knows of someone, we would be grateful."

Kiyomi and he had discussed the subject several times during their travels. Antony didn't have any knowledge of the personnel situations on Toltair, and the prospect of getting someone from the contractors unions back on Earth on this venture would require meetings, convincing, and more. He'd asked her if she had any employees on Toltair, or perhaps this station in charge of construction. No one in upper management had been without a family or looking to relocate. It'd left them stuck. At the very worst, they could possibly train someone with building or more manual labor experience, of whom they had plenty of people, to be more adept at the management side of the work.

A younger woman with long red hair and fair skin raised her hand. Antony didn't recognize her but nodded for her to speak.

"Hi. Morgan Ezra. I'm going to be security chief for the colony," the woman said.

"Pleased to meet you Ms. Ezra," Antony said.

"I spoke with one of the prisoners who are coming with us, and his background stated that he had done an extensive study of architecture and design. He seems a savvy individual, and—"

The woman paused as some of the members of the room grumbled at the sound of bringing a prisoner into leadership. Antony frowned as she slumped in her chair. It could be hard for those not used to public speaking to enter into positions of leadership for this reason.

"Let's hear her out," Antony said.

A glimmer of respect appeared in Morgan Ezra's eyes, something Antony had seen when he'd won over tepid voters in the past. "His name is Dalton Ward, a prisoner in for a white-collar crime with circumstances surrounding his trial where he may have been lumped in with the real culprits by mistake. He's charismatic and sharp. I think he'd do well in a position of management, and that would avoid having to get someone with specific requirements to the colony."

"That would be ideal," Kiyomi said. "Part of the reason we're rushing this mission is my father understood government could change its mind at any moment—impose restrictions, tell us we're no longer authorized to leave. The more we delay, the more we risk complications from bureaucracy."

Antony nodded. "I know better than most how annoying those can be."

People around the conference table laughed.

"Ms. Ezra, thank you for the suggestion. Kiyomi and I will interview him as soon as we can. I presume he's still aboard the prisoner transport that's docked with the station here?" He asked.

"Yes," Evelyn said. "We have a full security contingent monitoring them so there's no issues."

"Excellent," Antony said. "Now, I should get to meeting the rest of you. If you—"

Ear-piercing alarms cut him off, followed by flashing strobes in the corners. The gathered group of his future senior staff stood. Confusion filled the room. What could possibly be happening?

"Keep order. Single file. It's probably an error," Evelyn shouted over the repeating alarm sounds. "If we can't get out of a conference room in an orderly fashion you won't be able to run a colony effectively!"

Her words had an immediate impact, as the room came to a single line as she demanded. She would have been an effective leader to have in the colony. Everything about Evelyn had been well-planned and organized. One would have to have a skill set like that to run a shipyard as large as the one here on Toltair. Antony would have to talk to

Kiyomi about finding a way to recruit her before they left, though she probably already had tried.

The group filed into the hall, Antony one of the last to leave, as he figured it would look best to be motioning people out of the confined space with the alarm first, as governor of the future colony. Little gestures like that gave people the perception that he cared about them more than himself, which would come in handy during the hard times.

When he reached the hallway, he spotted Kiyomi chatting with Evelyn. The others followed markers toward the station's loading bays and life pods. Even if the alarm were a false one, out in space, people had to follow the precautions. There had been too many accidents on stations and ships. Station personnel treated these safety procedures like a holy book, and would not hesitate to jail or fine anyone who didn't comply.

"What's going on?" Kiyomi asked Evelyn.

The other woman placed a hand to her ear to dampen the alarm sounds.

"Uh huh," Evelyn said through her comm unit. "I'll be right there. No problem." She turned her attention back to Kiyomi. "Seems there is an actual issue. Ms. DePino, if you'd come with me to operations."

Antony looked between the women with him. He wanted to know what was going on as much as anyone else. "Ms. Ezra, I'm going to put you in charge of ensuring our personnel's safety and complying with station emergency regulations. I'll be heading with Ms. DePino and Ms. Tellmann."

"I think it'd be best if you remain with everyone else. This is a station internal matter," Evelyn warned with a side-glance at Kiyomi for confirmation.

Kiyomi waved for Evelyn to lead them. "Where I go, Mr. Lemkin goes. Let's head out."

Antony followed the two women while they left their new colony security chief behind. Ms. Ezra had the look of someone in over her head, but by her resumé and the suggestions she'd made, she should be able to handle this small emergency. If she couldn't, security would be a big issue at the colony.

Antony had dealt with more than enough evacuations and emergencies and kept calm. By contrast, the station personnel had tension, panic that came from a real crisis, not from a drill. Evelyn wouldn't have been able to pass this off as something routine.

They crossed several corridors and turned through a tunnel that created a connection point between opposite sides of the station. With the station's large size, being a ship repair facility, it required shuttle transportation through a tube. Evelyn led the way to a shuttle, and they entered along with several dozen other station personnel. The shuttle accelerated to high speeds, shooting across a transparent tunnel.

Several dozen ships, from small, personal luxury yachts to cruise liners, rested docked at different ports below. Bots and pressure-suited personnel worked on the ships. Machinery floated to their needed locations, transported via detachable thruster packs. One large ship stood out in all the scenery, something nearly ten times larger than the next biggest ship being worked on.

Kiyomi pointed to it. "That's our ark."

Antony stared at it in wonder. Such a massive ship spoke to the wonder of human achievement. He felt as if his body lightened, despite being in the gravity-plated shuttle that shot across the tube.

When they reached the center of the station, the shuttle slowed and fell into line with others into a roundabout section. Shuttles broke out from this area, shooting back into tubes that fed to different radiuses along the top of the station. Antony's shuttle turned into a tunnel across from where they had started their trip.

When they arrived, Antony's group waited for other passengers to depart before picking up their pace. After another minute's walk, Evelyn guided them through automatic doors that opened into the station's central operations.

The massive room held about two hundred employees, all in rows like an amphitheater. Each row had several people working at different computer terminals, with a private holodisplay unit in front of them. Each of their respective units had a low-sheen black encasement to it. The rows had steps with small walkaways in between groups of three workers. At the center of the room hung a giant holodisplay split between a map and the stars outside, with a view of Toltair's horizon off to the right. Nothing but stars and the darkness of space could be seen on that view. On the map, however, it had the station's location and a big red arrow that blinked and appeared to be heading straight toward the station.

"Status report," Evelyn said, approaching one of the workers on the first level.

The tech removed a headset which had a glass eyepiece, allowing for a user to perform tasks via eye movement. "Three ships entered the system and have not been responding to our comms. They jumped in at a distant orbit and are slowly approaching Toltair."

"Ships? Do you have configuration."

The tech nodded. "Yes, ma'am. They appear to be Aryshan warships."

Antony's eyes went wide. The Aryshans had come all the way to Toltair? The colony rested far enough within Earth's borders that they shouldn't have been here. He stared at the map. "Shipyards. This makes a prime target. Do you have military ships here under repair?"

"Two," Evelyn said. "This is mostly a civilian facility to service DePino Starliners, but with the War Effort Act passed three months ago, we are compelled to take in and assist Interplanetary Navy vessels if we can."

"What kind of shape are the military ships in?" Kiyomi asked.

The tech motioned on his holodisplay. Antony couldn't see anything from his position in front of the tech's workspace. "It says here that they only had a day or two more of work, most of which is cosmetic. Restocking, running diagnostics, that kind of thing."

"Do they have ship-to-ship weaponry?" Antony asked.

The tech shrugged. "I don't know. The IN doesn't give us specifics and we're not supposed to poke around. Camera blackouts near to where they're berthed."

"Could always ask them," Kiyomi said. "I think it'd be prudent that we launch those ships in defense of the station. I saw on the news what happened with the last major Aryshan offensive. We don't want that happening here."

"I'll try to reach them," the tech said.

Antony tried to consider all the possibilities. They had a lot of people on the station right now, waiting to get on the ark. If the Aryshans targeted the station, they'd be sitting ducks unless they could get the ark out of here. They had to prepare for that result. "I think it would be a good idea to get the prisoners from their transport in for cold sleep. I want them all situated and out of the way." Worse come to worst, they could keep the prisoners in cold sleep for a long time.

Kiyomi seemed to understand the plan. "I agree. Evelyn, can we facilitate that?"

Evelyn peered over the display of her tech, watching. "I don't think we have the personnel to spare. This is a real emergency situation, and we need to evacuate all non-critical personnel."

The tech pumped his fist triumphantly. "I got ahold of the military ships. They were on the same page. Prepped and ready to launch shortly."

"Grant them clearance," Evelyn said.

The tech tapped something at his station. "Done."

Antony considered how to get their ark ready for departure without the help of the station personnel. They had the ark's crew, didn't they? They weren't set to leave for another week or two at the earliest, but most of the personnel should have been on board the station by now. "How about our security team? They can guide the prisoners. May need one or two station personnel to help tell them where to go but that would be the best way to handle it."

"With all due respect," Evelyn said, "it may be best to head to escape pods."

Kiyomi shook her head adamantly at the suggestion. "No. If there's a problem, and we all know there's going to be one, the ark will go down with the station. If that happens, all my father's resources will have been sucked out of existence like a black hole. We can't do that, not with my father's legacy."

"Not to mention if the station does manage to survive the attack, Earth is bound to look at Toltair more closely. They'll delay the project in bureaucracy. They might even suspend the project indefinitely," Antony said. "Trust me, I know how the government operates."

Kiyomi cocked a brow. "We could always leave the prisoners here."

Antony shook his head. "We gave our word. As much as that's probably the best idea for the long run, I'm not leaving two thousand people here to get torched by the Aryshans. That wouldn't be right. Best plan for now is to get them into cold sleep as quickly as possible so we don't have to deal with them when we launch from here."

"Yeah," Kiyomi said as if she hadn't considered the unintended consequences. She turned her attention back to Evelyn. "Okay, let's do it."

Evelyn looked at them both like they were crazy. "It's your safety you're playing with. I'll give you one station member to help the transfer. The rest is up to you."

Kiyomi smiled. "Thanks, Evelyn. We should call Morgan Ezra and let her know we'll need her services right away."

"On it," said Antony. He removed his comm unit from his pocket and pulled up her frequency.

Morgan answered immediately. "Hello, Mr. Lemkin?"

"Ms. Ezra, listen to me. We're going to need you to assemble your team faster than we'd originally thought..."

34

AT THE GATES

"This is an emergency broadcast. All personnel are to vacate the facility. Please assemble peacefully and make your way to the fore of the ship. There, you will follow the orders of DePino security officers," a female voice came through the loudspeakers.

It marked the fifth time Dalton had heard the words, as they repeated approximately every two minutes. Bright strobes flashed in the open area pit of the vessel.

Dalton already stood in line with the other prisoners, filing through to the singular exit point that led to the station he'd been brought to when Morgan Ezra had recruited him for his services. How could he make in-roads with the other prisoners to be able to do his job? The other prisoners muttered about having to funnel into a bottleneck of a line, none of them particularly sociable.

The Tarantula appeared at Dalton's side. "Smarts, it's been awhile," he said. "Haven't seen you during the whole voyage. Thought you mighta pulled a fast one on the Spider Clan."

Dalton certainly wished that were true. If he could have managed to get away from the Spider Clan, he would have. The intention of him coming on the journey in the first place had been to distance himself from those crazies, lest they decide they should gut the traitor. With his new job as a liaison with security of the colony, he had to be even more careful.

"Nope, been holed up in my cell the same as the rest of you. I must have had different pit shifts for exercise."

The Tarantula seemed to accept that answer. "Where do you think they're taking us?"

"Search me." Dalton shrugged, continuing to move ahead at a slow rate.

"Hmm," the Tarantula said, scanning the crowd around him. "I'll find Beats and the others. We'll meet up soon."

"Got it."

The Tarantula disappeared back into the crowd, giving Dalton a moment of reprieve. He didn't particularly relish the thought of having to be in conversation with these crazies for the rest of his life. But what else could he do? He continued through the threshold and into a differently painted area with brighter lights. Those lights marked the connection between the ship and the station. As promised by the broadcast, security guards stood waiting, motioning with buttons and wrist lights for the prisoners to follow the path right, as the corridor cut into a "T". Dalton looked behind him, seeing that line of security guards, and behind them, several station personnel running across the deck as if for their lives.

Before he could get a moment to ascertain the situation, someone tugged at his shirt and ripped him out of line.

"Dalton Ward?" a security guard asked. Like the others, this one wore a helmet, holodisplay visor, and light body armor. Riot gear.

"Yeah?" Dalton asked, glancing around, hoping that no one noticed him chatting with security. He didn't see any of the Spider Clan usual suspects around.

"You're wanted. This way please." The security guard led Dalton back through the stream of prisoners moving one direction and brought him off past the security line down the hallway on the opposite side of the T section. They turned down another corridor, passing station personnel who filed in a similar manner to the others, quickly hooking into a small guest quarters room, complete with cot, desk, and holodisplay wall.

Morgan Ezra stood there waiting for him. "Mr. Ward, thank you for joining me." She looked frazzled, out of her element. The guard escorting Dalton stepped outside to give them privacy.

"Dalton's fine. What's going on here? The station's gone crazy."

Morgan bit her lip. "I don't want you to advertise this to the other prisoners, but Aryshans have come into the system. We suspect an attack is imminent."

"Lord," Dalton said under his breath. He'd calculated that he needed to get off the prison colony in order to survive, but he couldn't have anticipated that his life might end abruptly by doing so. "Does this mean they're bringing us to escape pods? Why not relaunch the prison ship?"

"Because the higher-ups want everyone aboard the ark for an immediate launch. They're bringing the prisoners to the cold sleep cells. I wanted you to be aware of that and to scout out any potential problems."

"I haven't talked to anyone since I boarded the ship. I don't know most of these people," Dalton said.

He didn't like the plan at all. Though he had very little knowledge of anything political, aliens coming to strike a system couldn't be a good thing. A quick launch meant the powers-that-be had worries that they wouldn't be able to launch otherwise.

"I know. Still, if you could do what you can to keep people from panicking, it will make my job easier. I don't have the best resources for getting everyone onto the ship and securing individuals into their cold sleep chambers. Not with this many prisoners, and not this fast. Maybe you could recruit some of the prisoners to help me?"

Dalton doubted very much that the Spider Clan would have any part in helping security

"I'll see what I can do," he said anyway. She wanted results and didn't have time for arguing. He'd been in that position before back when he ran his startup operations. These kinds of crises were the exact kind that led a company into big trouble, and then required sacrificial lambs for the legal system. It put him on edge, to say the least. "Anything else?"

"That's it for now," Morgan said. She weakly smiled at him, betraying her lack of confidence.

Some days, Dalton wished he weren't so good at reading people. "Okay." He turned back to the guard posted outside the door. "Let's go, then."

"I'll come with and lead you back. I need to head that direction anyway," Morgan said. She motioned for him to lead.

Dalton exited the quarters along with Morgan. The security guard took them around the line of prisoners via a much less crowded route toward the ark's docking point.

"What made you so desperate to take this gig?" Dalton asked along the way.

They couldn't make much small talk with sirens and alarms blaring in the background, but he needed to make in-roads with the colony's leadership as best he could.

Morgan grimaced at the question. "Been a rough couple of months. I needed a change of scenery."

"A permanent one?" Dalton raised a brow.

"I know what I'm doing." She sounded defensive.

Dalton decided to leave it there, as that line of questioning wouldn't lead to any help for him later. They arrived at the transit threshold to the ark ship. It looked much like any other freighter or transport that Dalton had seen, metallic floors and walls, faux-natural lighting to be easy on the eyes. This ship had been designed for a one-time use, one-way voyage where most of its inhabitants wouldn't be awake long enough to get tired of the bland scenery. No thought appeared to be spared for decoration or aesthetics at all. The walls weren't even finished with a coat of paint. The screws drilled into the metal sheets protruded from their joints. He hoped that the extra funds went into safety.

The prospect of going into cold sleep for a hundred years on a strange vessel scared him. It hadn't hit him until now, but being aboard made the situation much more visceral. Despite the roomy corridors of the ark, he couldn't help but feel claustrophobic.

Morgan took the lead then, pushing through the crowd of people and past the line, which so far held pretty well. Dalton passed the Spider Clan crew on the way toward the cold sleep chambers. They stared at him, with curious, beady eyes, the lot of them. He'd have to answer to them for security having rushed him through this line. He tried not to make eye contact with the Tarantula.

"Dalton," Morgan said, turning around at the most inopportune of times, saying his name directly within earshot of the others. "I need to go on ahead. You go ahead and take your place in line here. Thank you," she said. She nodded and left with her security guard in tow.

"What was that about?" Beats asked. "You makin' nice with some pretty girl from security? Why?"

"Because he's Smarts, that's why," the Tarantula said. "Good work, Smarts. An in... and in more ways than one, eh?" The Tarantula chuckled hard. "What'd she spill to ya?"

"We're leaving early. They're getting everyone into cold sleep now."

"What?" The Tarantula's eyes went wide. The others in the clan muttered behind him.

"You heard me."

"I don't like this at all," the Tarantula said. He glanced around the prisoner line. "We need to find out why and what they're doing. And I think we have a shot to get outta here. There's no guards anywhere in sight. What're we waiting for?"

Beats grunted agreement. The others muttered similarly.

"I don't know if this is such a good idea," Dalton said.

"Bah," the Tarantula said, waving him off. He stepped out of line and moved to the opposite side of the corridor, scanning up and down. He jogged to a point. "Beats, Ogre, get over here," he said.

Ogre? Dalton hadn't heard that name in a while. He turned back around and smashed his face right into the bigger man's chest.

Ogre looked down at him and growled. "You're askin' for it. Once we get to the colony, it's you and me, bub. You hear?"

Dalton did his best not to show any fear. Never show any fear with these types. He gave a wry smile. "Sounds delightful."

The two larger men did move over to where their boss stood, several others Dalton recognized from the Spider Clan following along. Dalton had to admit the Tarantula's findings made him curious.

The Tarantula pointed. "This is a maintenance hatch. Probably requires a tool as a pressure lock. Bet you five thousand colony credits that you two won't be able to pry it open with your bare hands."

"Five thousand colony credits?" Beats asked. "That's a lot."

Credits meant nothing. Dalton and the Tarantula didn't know what form of currency would be used on the colony, if any. A stupid bluff, but it did rile up the testosterone-addled giants all the same.

"Let's do it," Ogre said. He stretched his arms out, locking his fingers together, and cracked his knuckles.

Ogre took one side and Beats the other, each taking one of the grips of the hatch. The two men pulled as hard as they could, arm muscles bulging from the strain. Beats had a view veins popping out of his bicep. Some people found it to be good luck, but Dalton thought it disgusting, a sign that someone overworked their body. Both men grunted, pulling as hard as they could, faces turning bright red in the process. They looked like they were going to blow their tops.

"You can't do it," the Tarantula said with disappointment.

The men didn't give up. They pulled harder, their bodies shaking as they taxed themselves to the point of exhaustion.

The hatch seal finally gave way. A loud hissing noise came from inside as the two rooms met a pressure equilibrium.

Once open, the Tarantula scanned the inside. "Just like I thought, maintenance hatch. Ladder and everything. We can take control of this damn ship before anyone'll even notice."

Several other prisoners filed into the area, trying to get a glimpse of what was going on. At the same time, a pair of security guards rounded the corner. "Hey, what are you doing?" one shouted.

"Hurry!" The Tarantula said, making a windmill motion with his arm to get the attention of the Spider Clan. Beats and Ogre ducked down into the maintenance hatch, along with several other members of the clan.

Security called for reinforcements and ran toward Dalton and the Tarantula. Prisoners flooded toward the maintenance hatch, creating another bottleneck. Had there been this many members of the Spider Clan on the prison colony? Dalton never seemed to see more than a dozen together at once, though people in the clan had told him that their numbers measured well over a hundred. At least that many prisoners surrounded Dalton in the hallway. Rioting prisoners and security officers flanked him on either side.

The guards brandished shock sticks and began to club the prisoners closest to them. Screams of pain came from collapsing men. Without organization, the prisoners would be no match for the guards, but the prisoners could overwhelm them in numbers. Did they have the intelligence?

Dalton didn't want to stick around long enough to find out. The Tarantula had already disappeared through the maintenance hatch in the confusion. Though Dalton stood close to the hatch himself, several prisoners brushed passed him. The guards slammed their shock sticks into several more prisoners' stomachs, and yet more people collapsed to the ground.

No time to wait or consider. Dalton had to stop this insurrection, and for that, he'd have to reason with the Tarantula. The clan leader didn't have his knowledge of the looming alien assault. He'd acted too fast without listening, as Dalton should have planned for. As prisoners with no clearances, no codes, there would be no way they could gain control over the ship's systems. All it would accomplish was giving security a good chase, wasting everyone's time. People would get hurt or killed.

With a shake of his head, Dalton squeezed through the hatch, down into a small corridor which required him to duck. Other prisoners ran ahead. The maintenance corridor broke into different directions as the regular walkways did, following a similar pattern to the rooms they serviced. Dalton had no idea which way the Tarantula had gone, but he couldn't wait. Security would be behind and would soon be firing their pulse guns instead of beating crowds down with shock sticks.

Dalton hustled ahead. When he passed the next intersection, someone reached out and grabbed him by the collar. The grip caused him to stumble, but he regained his footing quickly. He clenched his fists and spun. Whoever grabbed him had better be ready for pain.

A grinning Tarantula greeted him. "You're funny, Smarts. Sometimes I doubt that we gave you a good name, if you think punching me will do you any good."

"Tarantula," Dalton said under his breath.

"Got me. There's prisoners running all over now. We have to find our way to somewhere that controls this ship so we can take over. We'll get set ourselves up a base on a world somewhere. I ain't going into cold sleep."

"There won't be any taking over," Dalton said. More cries of agony came from the maintenance shaft. "Let's keep moving, security is catching up."

The Tarantula frowned but moved down the corridor, picking up the pace. Most of the other prisoners seemed to be heading in a different direction, though several ran ahead of them on this path. "Won't? That's not a word I like to hear for my plans, Smarts. What did security want with you, anyway? You working for them?"

"No," Dalton lied without hesitation. "I don't know how to operate a ship, and I'm guessing none of the other prisoners do. Not only that, but there'll be security codes. There's no way we can hijack this thing."

"We can defend the ship systems, take hostages," the Tarantula said.

"To what end?" The Tarantula's relentless aggressiveness grated on Dalton's nerves. Dalton could be opportunistic. If there were a way to profit long term off of seizing the ship, he wouldn't find some moral reason against it. With aliens on the outside of the station and armed guards on the inside, the Tarantula's idea amounted to posturing, nothing else.

Beats came back down from one of the other intersections, followed by Ogre. "There you are," he said to the Tarantula. "Been lookin' all over for you."

"Been talkin' to Smarts. We gotta get out of here, though. Can't stay put for too long. You think there's some weapons storage somewhere on the ship?"

"If this ark is meant for ten thousand people to form a full-fledged colony upon landfall, we'll never find anything without a guide or a map," Dalton said.

"Guide. Always thinkin', Smarts," the Tarantula said. "We're gonna head back for the line of prisoners."

"What?" Dalton and the two large goons asked in unison.

"Trust me. We need to get a couple guards alone. Then we can—"

Pulse pistols fired from down the corridor. An escaping prisoner collapsed mid-run, skidding across the flooring in front of Dalton and the others. His mouth hung open, drooling from the lack of muscle control after the stun. "There's our guards. I'd suggest we get going."

Dalton wanted to shout for security, but with this many of the Spider Clan around, it would be too dangerous. Besides, if the prisoners somehow won, he didn't want to be known as the rat.

The Tarantula pressed himself against the wall perpendicular to the side where the shots originated. He motioned for the others to do the same. Dalton and the goons followed along, waiting for him.

A few moments later, footsteps came padding down the corridor. "You think there's more of them close by?" one voice said.

"Maybe. Can't have gone too far."

The guards passed into view, unaware of the ambush that awaited them. Before they could turn, the Tarantula sprang from his crouch, tackling one of the guards by the midsection. Both hit the floor hard. The second guard pointed his pulse pistol toward the Tarantula, who was now on top of his companion. On instinct, Ogre followed suit and tackled the second guard. The pulse pistol shot rang out, its energy dissipating against the wall across from Dalton and Beats.

The four men wrestled on the ground. Dalton moved to assist the Tarantula while Beats helped Ogre. The men in front of Dalton struggled over control of the gun, but Dalton had better leverage. He grabbed it by the barrel and used his full weight to fall backward, while the Tarantula kept the guard pinned down. The guard loosened his grip. Dalton had the weapon now.

He pointed it to the other group, as the guard there played a better keep-away than his companion had. He fired his gun on the floor, causing Dalton to hop to avoid the energy shooting too close to his direction for comfort. Beats moved in and stepped on the guard's wrist. It ground between Beats' foot and the metal floor, making an audible crack and then pop. The guard screamed in agony, dropping the gun.

"Smarts!" the Tarantula called.

While Dalton had been watching the other fight, the Tarantula had maneuvered the guard so that he faced Dalton, the Tarantula safely away from the line of fire.

Dalton got the clue immediately and raised the pulse pistol toward them, firing a shot into the guard's back. The guard convulsed, then fell to the ground, unconscious.

The other guard had stopped fighting, too focused on his own pain. Ogre took the grapple over and sat up on the man's stomach. He managed to push the guard's helmet off. Then he pounded at the man's face. Punch after punch, bruising and bloodying the guard.

"Lord," Dalton said. "Stop it, man! He's down. You're done. You don't gotta kill him."

Ogre looked back at Dalton, blood rage in his eyes. It reminded Dalton of his first fight with the man that had gotten him into this mess. The man was an animal. He should have never been allowed out on this colony excursion. He growled at Dalton.

The Tarantula patted Ogre on the shoulder and moved past him to pick up the second pulse gun. "Smarts is right. Let's not create problems in case something goes wrong. Now we got these weapons and a couple of hostages, we can go make some demands. Gotta send a spokesman." He considered with a frown. "Smarts, I think that's your job. They seem to like you."

Dalton already saw the pickle that outside forces put him into. If he didn't find a way out of this, he'd be squeezed right between security and the prisoners with both sides wanting him dead. He'd gone along with the Tarantula so far because it seemed better than being labeled a traitor and getting whacked. But at the end of the day, he wanted to put a stop to these prisoners' idiotic plans and help Morgan.

The actual people in charge had the right of it in this situation. They needed to get this ark going and people into cold sleep before they ended up as space dust. They could use information about the escaped prisoners to contain the situation. Dalton could end up a hero if he played his cards right. "Alright. I'll go talk to them. What do you want me to tell them?"

The Tarantula flashed his toothy grin. "Tell them this..."

IN MOTION

Kiyomi stood in the flitter as it descended from the upper management levels of the shipyards station. Through the front viewer, she caught a glimpse of the loading and unloading teams moving cargo from port to ship and vice versa. Sparks flew off of an engineer's tool as he welded additional hull plating onto the ark.

It provided a captivating sight. Kiyomi hadn't seen a shipyard in action for the last several years. She'd spent too much time studying for both her undergraduate and master's degrees. Her father had done plenty of traveling during that time, but she didn't go on those trips with him like she had when her family had been whole. The trip reminded her of riding in a similar flitter as a little girl, gripping onto her father's pant leg while he surveyed his work. He'd enjoyed the fruits of his labors, ever with a smile on his face. Even with as much wealth as he had, he liked to keep an eye on his work to make sure things got done right. Kiyomi hoped she inherited that trait.

Her heart sank in reminiscence of her father. She missed him so much. Seeing his project in its full glory hit her hard in the chest. She tried not to weep, show any weakness in front of already scared personnel who needed strong leadership from her. They needed her to guide them, needed faith that she would make clear and steady decisions. She couldn't break down.

The ark had tremendous beauty in a *form-follows-function* way. It didn't have the brightly colored paints of most DePino Starliners, nor did it have any of the chic retro-futuristic designs many of the wealthy had on their yachts these days. The ark had no viewing section for people to gaze out into the vastness of space from the comfort of a posh lounge. This ark had a boxy shape with a flat bottom, flanked by two compartmental wings. The bottom allowed for ease of landing so it could be used as a building while workers constructed the colony, or perhaps to be utilized for longer if they felt it would be necessary to keep its shell for future living accommodations.

The plan already involved using the ark's crystal drive as a power reactor plant for the colony. It was oversized to accommodate the secondary use, and carried the fuel to provide enough power for generations. The bottom sections provided for a stacked hydroponics system, rotating and cycling crops automatically so that it could maintain itself in perpetuity. That concept had been Kiyomi's originally, brought to life by the team of engineers that her father had hired from the agriculture industry back on earth, as they'd used the stacked fields agricultural method to accommodate Earth's large population.

With its simplicity and lack of frills, Kiyomi loved this ship. She had as much ownership of it as her father could have claimed. It brought her the kind of pride she'd remembered seeing him have when he launched a new starliner.

The flitter pulled into the rear cargo bay where drones and docking workers loaded giant crates and storage. Scores of scientists had determined what would be necessary for long-term human survival without any possibility of contact with home. It made sense to Kiyomi, and her father, the greatest genius she had ever known, had signed off on it. She hoped their calculations would prove enough. They would find out soon. Though a hundred years would pass in cold sleep, it would feel like not a day had gone by when they awoke on the other side.

Kiyomi activated her wrist comm and dialed the operations center. "Evelyn, status update on the Aryshans?"

"They're coming closer. Weapons are powered from our estimations. We've got about two-thirds of the station personnel evacuated. I hope that's enough. I hadn't heard of the Aryshans going after escape pods and civilian targets in the past, but if they do, we've got thousands of sitting ducks."

Kiyomi grimaced. "We'll see what we can do. What about the colonists? What's our current loading prospects?"

"We'd been able to get ninety percent of the colonists to the station before the crisis hit. Another few have trickled in, but we've had to stop incoming spacefaring traffic to the station with the enemy warships so close. I'm sorry to say that more than a few went with the station personnel into escape pods. You're not going to be leaving with all of your colonists."

They had close to bare minimums for long-term colony survival and an adequately diverse gene pool. The latter could be manipulated with medical processes. Much like her own genetic experiments with plants in her master program, medics could ensure that there wouldn't be a problem with inbred human specimens in the future. It didn't feel right having humans experimented on, but they would do what they had to in order to survive. Kiyomi worried more about the skillsets each of the colonists brought in the short-term. "I understand. Have you had a chance to run any simulations on what this does to our survival chances?"

"It drops them, but you still have a safe enough margin."

Kiyomi let out a breath. "What's the status with the alien ships? How much time do we have?"

"They're moving slowly, which is a good thing. They appear to be waiting for something. It's giving us the time to make sure we get as many people to safety as possible. The two Interplanetary Navy ships in the hangars are prepped to launch and will be moving to intercept shortly. I have no idea how our military ships stack against theirs. It's not my expertise, but I'm hoping that buys us at least a few hours."

"Me, too," Kiyomi said. "You know, Evelyn, with us short-staffed, we could really use someone of your competence on the colony."

Evelyn laughed. "They need me here as much."

"I don't know. I have a bad feeling about what's happening. I don't think anyone in this system is safe," Kiyomi said.

"You're trying to convince me to come with you."

"No! I wouldn't do that. I'm not that manipulative."

"Sure. Neither was your father. I'll be honest with you, I've been toying with the idea for months, not sure I'm ready to pack up and leave everything. It's not like I have family here, or much of a life outside of this job. Part of me wants to take you up on your offer. I've still got a couple hours to decide, and I'll let you know if it changes, okay?"

Her words brought a small smile to Kiyomi's face. She would feel more comfortable with Evelyn coming on the journey.

The flitter hatch opened. A ramp descended with a mechanical *whir*. One of the personnel on the outside cocked his head to try to get her attention.

"I gotta go, looks like I'm being presented with some cargo manifests. I'll check back soon."

"See you."

Kiyomi tapped her comm to end the call and jogged down the flitter ramp to meet the tech. He greeted her and handed her a datapad of information. "I wish we had some more time to confirm all of the supplies are making it aboard. The list looks right, but the plan was to have a visual inspection for a confirmation. Way it is, we won't know what we have until we reach Ixora."

"Not much we can do now." Kiyomi took the datapad and scanned over the manifest, but the file had hundreds of pages. She wouldn't even have time to thoroughly confirm. "I hope we have everything we need."

COMMAND

TOLTAIR ORBIT, THE ARK

ANTONY ASCENDED to the ark's bridge in the lift tube. Unlike the ships that Antony had been on in the past, which had the bridge atop and forward to give a view of the stars and scenery beyond, the ark had its command and control center buried in the middle of the ship. It made sense, since it would remain most protected compared to any other location, save for the main crystal reactor core.

The lift door opened, and, to his surprise, the bridge was no bigger than a small conference room. It had four stations, a small area to maneuver between them, and a wraparound holodisplay wall currently containing a panoramic view of the center of DePino Shipyards. The two military vessels moved toward the main bay doors, one after the other. Alarms sounded in the bay, preparing the crew and everyone inside for the giant doors opening and coming depressurization.

Only one other person graced the ark's bridge—a muscular man in his twenties with dark skin.

His eyes widened in recognition of Antony. "Sir!"

Before the man could scramble to his feet, Antony motioned for him to remain at ease. "This is the bridge, huh? I figured I should oversee the launch from wherever command would be. I also thought it'd be bigger."

"Efficiency, sir. As most of our trip is automated, and the ship is meant for only one outing before it's disassembled. Ms. Tellmann told me I'd be needed here for an emergency launch, so I came. All the systems check out so far." He patted his console. Then his eyes went wide again. "Oh! I forgot to introduce myself. My name is Rawle Tejada. I'm your primary flitter pilot for the colony, and back-up for the ark in case of any AI issues." He extended his hand.

Antony gave his hand a firm shake. The fellow had an excitable countenance, but any young person would in this situation. The excitement rubbed off on him to some degree, giving Antony an energized feeling he hadn't experienced since before he'd resigned his governorship. "Good to meet you, Rawle. Antony Lemkin. I'll be the governor."

"I know who you are. Voted for you twice." Rawle smiled and spun back toward his console. "Suppose we're waiting for orders now?"

"Waiting for everyone to get loaded onto the ship. We're on a tight deadline to get out of here before the Aryshans get too close," Antony said.

He glanced at one of the workstations and slid himself into one of the seats. The chair back conformed itself to the curvature of his spine. Smart-Posture chairs. He'd heard of those and always wanted one but never got around to buying himself one. An odd comfort for what would likely be little-used on the journey, but then, Mr. DePino had been eccentric and passionate about certain things. Antony shook his head. No time to reflect on the past. He motioned over the console, bringing up stats on the ship systems. Though he could call himself a quick learner, he had no experience in vessel operations. Most of the display looked like gibberish to him. "Do you know how to navigate the ship systems? Can you tell how many people are aboard, for instance?"

Rawle stood from his console to make his way over to Antony's. He leaned over from the side.

"Right here," he said, sliding his hands over the visual in a fluid motion.

Several different screens popped up then disappeared. He made a pinching motions with his fingers and a display of biosigns appeared.

From this view, Antony could see different forms all across the ship. Rawle had brought up only human forms, but there were options for the livestock and plant matter, as well. A robust sensor system. He'd seen similar when he toured military installations, but only from afar. Antony hadn't expected to have an up-close and personal experience with them. A cluster around the cold sleep chambers, several down some maintenance shafts that must have been sent by Evelyn for last minute checking of systems. A numerical readout of the ship's population displayed in the left corner. Eight thousand seven hundred. Less than ninety percent of the number of inhabitants that they should have had.

They would have to get everyone situated into cold sleep later. For now, security focused on getting the prisoners secured for the task. Getting them out of the way would make it easier on everyone. If it grated on his nerves to have so many convicts in close proximity— and it certainly did—the others must have been in a near panic. They'd been fortunate to have everyone proceeding in an orderly fashion so far. There had been something to Fabio DePino's computer models that had picked those with the calmest psychological profiles —at least of the applicants they had to choose from. Colony members had been screened for certain qualities, and presumably one of those qualities would be a predisposition against panicking in emergency situations. On a new world without backup, they would face emergencies sooner or later.

"Thanks," Antony said.

"No problem."

"You all ready to go? What's your background, if you don't mind my asking?"

Rawle nodded. "No problem at all, sir. I ain't never flown anything this big before, but I've been a DePino Starliner pilot for five years. They gave me my first job out of flight school and have been the best company to work for. They really care about their people. That's why I wanted to make sure I came with them. I believe in them." He frowned. "It's a shame about Mr. DePino."

"That it is," Antony said.

He felt like he should be in front of more people, giving a speech or getting to know some of his future colonists. Something to give them a semblance of calm. He fumbled with the controls to see if he could find the comm system access. It didn't appear as if one had been installed.

His wrist unit bleeped.

Antony answered the call, tying it into the console in front of him.

Evelyn's face appeared in front of him. "Mr. Lemkin," she said. "I have bad news. The captain of the lead military vessel sent an order back to us and to Toltair not to launch any more ships. They don't want any civilian vessels to impede their fight with the Aryshans."

"What?" Antony said. That news sent a jolt of horror through him. They would be trapped inside the station. If the Aryshans made it past the IN ships, they'd be sitting ducks, and they'd certainly get killed here. "We can't do that. Can you patch me through to him?"

"I can try," Evelyn said. She made a few motions on her end. "No response."

Antony fumed, feeling his face turn hot. He couldn't lose his cool here, not now. He didn't want Evelyn on their side. What were his options? He could launch anyway, despite it all. "What kind of defenses does this ship have?"

"Some really robust hull plating meant to repel asteroids," Evelyn said, sarcasm dripping from her voice.

"Great."

"Tell me about it."

"We'll hold for now," he said, aware that they were on an open line. "How many more people do we need to load onto the vessel?"

"We've got everyone who made it to the station aboard, except for one," Evelyn said. She glanced to the side, nodding to someone that Antony couldn't see.

"One? What's the hold up?"

Evelyn smiled back to the screen. "I needed to wrap things up here and make sure the rest of my team made it off the station safely."

"You're joining us?"

"I just decided. Hope it's the right call. I won't have time to get most of my personal effects aboard."

"We'll make you new ones when we reach Ixora. Honestly, I'm happy to have you aboard. You've done a great job with organizing everything. I'd have killed to have someone like you on staff in the governor's office," Antony said.

Evelyn laughed. "Government wouldn't shell out the perks to get someone like me."

"Get to the bridge as soon as you can. I want to talk offline."

He stared hard at her, hoping to communicate his intent on launching anyway, despite what some military bureaucrat might think. He hated their whole system, hated this war. Even though the Aryshans looked like the aggressors in this situation, he had no idea as to the reason for their aggression. There were always two sides to the story, and in war, often both sides being stupid.

"Understood," Evelyn said. Whether she truly understood, Antony had no idea. Her image disappeared from the display.

Rawle glanced back at Antony. "Planning on cutting and running anyway?"

"That's right, I am. You good with that?"

"I ain't ever planning on finding out how strong the Aryshan pulse cannons are," Rawle said.

"Me, either." Antony exhaled through his nose. "Any way to pull up the conflict on the main holodisplay?"

Rawle hit several commands. "Mm," he said, staring at his console. "Looks like I can get some station camera feed. I'm not sure how close of a view we can get."

"Do it."

The view changed. The rear of the earth warships glowed as their thrusters exhausted radiation. He could barely make out the Aryshan vessels, little more than small metallic dots on the screen. How innocuous giant war machines looked from a distance. It didn't do anything to curb how frightening they were in reality.

TRAUMA

T<small>OLTAIR</small> O<small>RBIT</small>, T<small>HE</small> A<small>RK</small>

M<small>ORGAN CHASED</small> the escaped prisoners through the ship. Those idiots. What were they thinking? The Aryshans were out there, ready to attack, and she had to deal with firefights and wounded personnel. Her patience all but evaporated the moment she heard they attacked her guards.

She turned down a corridor and popped the maintenance hatch to find three prisoners crouched over like strange primates, shuffling down the ladder as fast as they could.

Without hesitation, Morgan fired three heavy stun-grade shots from her pulse gun. All of them struck true. The prisoners made gargling noises and cries of muffled pain before they crumpled at the bottom of the shaft unconscious.

"How many more do we have left?" Morgan asked one of her guards. She still hadn't gotten to know many of their names. She turned to one closest to her, a man with a few days' stubble on his face. "Officer...?" she prompted.

"John Roland. We still have more than forty on the loose. Our men have secured more than two thirds of the prisoners. What a pain."

"I know it." Morgan squeezed into the maintenance corridor, crouching into a ridiculous position to avoid hitting her head. The only way she would find them all would be to get down and dirty with them.

Moving through the corridor brought her a claustrophobic sense of confinement. This ship had no escape other than out through the station, and there she would find the destructive power of the Aryshans she remembered all too vividly. Memories of the Esare colony flooded into her head like a dam had broken. She remembered Dylan Wong, her friend, her co-pilot, as they tried to escape the relentless assault of Aryshan dropships firing on their military base.

It'd been awhile since she'd had her nightmares. Ever since making the decision to join the colony, Morgan had felt free, as if she could finally get rid of the weight that she'd dragged around since being dismissed from her guard duty. She had a purpose, a calling.

It may have been her anxiety, but the ship seemed to lurch around her. She stumbled into the corridor wall. Balancing on her feet became a difficult task. Morgan braced herself.

"Ma'am, are you okay?" John Roland asked, coming up from behind her. He had the sense about him to give her a decent berth. His footing held steady as he walked through, a bad sign for her mental state.

"I'm fine. Need to breathe," Morgan said.

She followed her own advice. Slowly, she inhaled through her nose, and exhaled through her mouth with similar calmness. "Repeat the exercise five times when you're feeling stressed," her psychologist had told her.

It didn't work. Wong's lifeless face held center in her mind's eye. She couldn't get rid of it. Soon, she'd watch more people die when the Aryshans attacked the ship. It had been a mistake for her to assume this position. She had to get out.

Morgan found herself stumbling through the maintenance corridor. John Roland followed her and kept with his persistent questions, but she could barely hear them. All the words sounded muddled.

She had to escape into a bigger area, somewhere she could have some space where it didn't feel like the walls closed in all around her. But it became harder to move. The ship went from rocking to spinning. She struggled to hold the bile down in her stomach.

A familiar figure rounded the corner. He wore a prisoner's jumpsuit, but he also had a kinder, more handsome face than the other prisoners. Dalton. She remembered his name through the swimming haze cluttering her mind. She couldn't let him see her out of control like this. How could she get herself back to normalcy?

Morgan leaned against the wall, still hunched over in an awkward position that crimped her neck. She grimaced.

"We should get you to a doctor or something," Roland said. He stood beside her, worry all over his face. He leveled his pulse gun at Dalton. "Hold it right there!"

Dalton stopped in his tracks. He had his own weapon in hand but held his hands up in surrender.

"I'm here to talk to Ms. Ezra," he said.

The floor plating kept spinning. Morgan wobbled, unsure if she could stand for much longer. She had to maintain her composure. She'd put so much effort into ensuring Dalton would be on her side.

"He's fine. Don't fire," she said.

Roland lowered his pulse gun.

"You look really sick," Dalton said, resuming his way toward her. He stopped again in front of her.

"I know it. She needs a medic."

"I don't need anything. I'll be fine in a moment. Give me space to breathe." Irritation couldn't help but project through her voice.

The two men stepped away from each other and sized each other up. Roland frowned. "Where'd you get that gun?"

"Off of another security guard," Dalton said.

Roland reddened, his clutch on his pulse gun tightening. "You took one of ours out? Morgan, we should bring him in."

Morgan still had to settle herself. At least the spins slowed to some degree. Her head pounded with each heartbeat, as if it shook her skull with each pulse. She had to think of something else and deal with her own scars later. They had a job to do.

"John, stand down. Whatever happened, he came to report to us."

Dalton nodded. "I was part of a group back in the prison colony. They call themselves the Spider Clan. It's an idiotic name, I know, but it inspired loyalty in a number of the nastier prisoners. These aren't your non-violent criminals who have escaped here," he said. "Their leader is a man who calls himself the Tarantula. I don't know his real name, but he started the escape. I don't know how many went with him, but a lot. They took down two of your security guards."

"We already don't have nearly enough staff," John Roland said.

"Nothing we can do about that now. So they're hiding in this maintenance hatch?"

"They were scattered when I last left them. A couple of the Tarantula's men are with him. With the Aryshans outside, I tried to plead with them to come back, but they wouldn't listen. The Tarantula seems to think he can take over the ship."

John Roland snorted.

"My reaction exactly," Dalton said. "But I think we all don't want a big battle between security and the prisoners at this juncture."

"I agree," Morgan said. "What do you propose?"

Before he could respond, Morgan's wrist comm chimed. She glanced at it, the holographic display compounding her headache. Why did it have to be so bright? Antony Lemkin's name appeared on the display.

"Governor?" she asked.

The sound came through on her wrist, no time for activating a privacy mode. "Ms. Ezra. We've received word that the Aryshans have overcome the Earth ships sent to intercept them. They'll be moving for the station soon. We have to undock, even if no one's ready. Our gravplates should be able to deal with most of the inertia, but it might get bumpy. Hopefully, you're close to having the prisoners secure."

Morgan glanced between the two men, who didn't say a word to interrupt. "Still need time on that, but I'll inform the rest of the guards."

"Thanks. I'll check back later." The comm link chirped to signal its closing.

"Not good," Dalton said.

"Agreed," John Roland said.

Morgan pushed herself back upright to her feet. The spins had subsided. She had no means by which to deal with her headache for now. "Okay. John, go with Dalton. I'm gonna have to trust that you can figure out the prisoner situation over there. I'll go get my team ready and see what we can do. I hope most of the other prisoners are in the pods by now."

Dalton motioned with his gun, and the two men made their way back down the corridor where Dalton came from. They disappeared around a bend after a time, jogging.

Morgan moved the opposite direction, back where she had come from. She still needed to get out of the cramped space if she were going to fully recover. Lost in her thoughts, she stepped carefully over the two prisoners she'd shot when she had first entered the shaft. The two bodies still lay crumpled on the ground, across each other. With such a heavy stun, they wouldn't wake for hours. One had his mouth open, spittle falling from the side of his mouth to the floor. Before she forgot to get them situated, Morgan tapped her wrist comm. "Chief Ezra to security officers. I need a couple strong arms down in the maintenance corridor to lift incapacitated prisoners and carry them to the cold sleep pods."

"Humphreys here. We'll get someone there right away."

"Thanks," Morgan said. She stepped over the bodies and then ducked back through the small hatch opening. The main corridors had been cleared of the long line of prisoners, leaving lonely walls with metal studs in every direction. Even the areas of the ship meant to be used by human personnel felt cold. The designers hadn't intended to live here, but to be in hibernation until they could get to their new world.

Morgan took a deep breath. Now what? The dozens of security

personnel would need someone to oversee them getting the prisoners into their pods, lest any more escape. She hustled toward cold sleep chamber one, where they'd been working before. They'd managed to get everyone inside in quick order. Even the large room appeared empty and devoid of people. Pods lined the space, connected with monitoring equipment as far as she could see. Several personnel stood around, lost expressions on their faces.

The group led by Humphreys moved past her, acknowledging her as they passed.

Even with everyone in cold sleep, were they safe? What if they Aryshans came after them? If they fired on the ship, they would be defenseless. Death in the darkness of space. How had she let Evelyn and the others talk her into coming on board? She could have taken an escape pod with the other station personnel.

And then what? She would still be a sitting target for the Aryshans. Even if she managed to get to the planet, she couldn't assure her own safety. Those dropships came for the people below as well as those up in space. Nuevo Ciudad, with all of its modern, tall structures would be leveled as sure as Vega City on Esare had been.

Morgan found herself leaning against the wall with her eyes closed. The sensation of being trapped hadn't been some irrational panic from her prior experiences. If anything, her past trauma provided an apt warning. Every last person on this ship would be dead soon, and no one wanted to admit it.

A CHANGE OF PLANS

Dalton led the guard down the corridor. He had been trigger happy at first, but the stern security officer John didn't seem that bad of a man after exchanging a few words. All in all, having the trust of Morgan Ezra had been a bonus. He wouldn't have an armed guard following him and ready to execute his own orders otherwise.

But he still needed a plan. The Tarantula was a rational being, as much as a ruthless killer could be. He listened when it suited him or when profit would come from it. It would be Dalton's job to convince him there wouldn't be much profit in his current plan, and more importantly, he would have to defer his authority to security.

Which would be difficult. As much as the Tarantula had some rationality—much more than the goons following him—he also could be as stubborn to move as a brick wall.

Dalton became so lost in thinking about his strategy in manipulating the Spider Clan's leader that he hadn't seen a leaking pipe. It made the floor slick. Dalton slid across the puddle on the floor, outstretching his arms for balance. He took several steps after the slide, slipping with each of those. He must have looked like a cartoon treadmilling in place until he finally caught his balance.

"Nice save," said the security guard from behind him. The other man carefully stepped around the puddle, using the pipes on the wall to sturdy himself.

"Something's leaking," Dalton said, looking back at several pipes that ran through this corridor. Each had a colored band on it every several meters. That would have made it so a maintenance worker knew which pipe he or she would have been repairing. He spotted a small leak coming from one of them with an orange band around it, right at a joint where it split in two different directions. "Wonder what caused it."

John shrugged, and then his eyes went wide. "Look out!"

Ogre bounded down the corridor, head first in the most ridiculous crouch. He headed full steam for Dalton.

Ogre lowered his shoulder into Dalton's gut. "You traitor! I knew you was working with security."

He followed with an uppercut to Dalton's chin, sending Dalton stumbling backward. His pulse gun flew out of his hands and clanged against one of the pipes before dropping to the floor.

Dalton's back foot slipped into the puddle before he caught himself.

"Listen, Ogre. It's not what it looks like," Dalton said.

"I ain't stupid," he said.

That's a debatable point, Dalton thought. He had to deescalate the situation quickly.

John pointed his pulse gun at them, but he hesitated. Dalton stood directly in the way of a clear shot of Ogre. He had to get to the side somehow, difficult in the small maintenance corridor.

Ogre delivered a hard blow to Dalton's stomach. "This is for gettin' me in solitary. For messin' with the Spider Clan. For everything. Yer dead!"

That punch sucked all the breath out of him. He couldn't help but bend forward in an attempt to catch his breath. No time for defense. No way to outsmart his opponent. He could go to the ground, but that would risk getting his teeth knocked out or his ribs broken if Security John didn't fire fast enough. He couldn't trust a low-level security guard to do anything right.

"Hold it!" A voice called from down the hall.

Ogre turned his head back, giving Dalton a moment of reprieve.

Dalton tried to get a glimpse around the bulky man in front of him, finding it difficult to see anything in this slim corridor. More red jumpsuits came into view. The Tarantula walked over, followed by Beats.

"What's going on? You fighting Smarts over there? Don't do that. We need him," the Tarantula said.

"Smarts is a rat traitor like I thought. He brought a security pal with him," Ogre said, pointing toward Dalton and John.

"I told you to let me explain," Dalton said.

He tried to sound calm, as if there were nothing wrong, despite the pain. He brought a hand to his chin. It stung, though it could have been worse. At least he still had his teeth.

"Hear him out," the Tarantula demanded, motioning for Ogre to move out of the way. It proved easier ordered than done, the big oaf of a man squeezing himself toward the side of the corridor to allow the Tarantula to see.

The Tarantula grinned at Dalton. "He got you good, huh?" He sounded as if he found it amusing. The amusement disappeared from his face immediately as he saw John. "Who's your pal?"

"John Roland. I work for Security Chief Ezra," John said.

He had about as quick a wit as Ogre or Beats, in Dalton's estimation. Who would announce themselves as security to hardened criminals who were angered by the sight of security? Better to remain silent.

Dalton didn't have time to teach the guy street smarts. "That's right. Here's the deal though. We're about to be under attack. It's much worse than we thought. Do you know who the Aryshans are?" Dalton asked.

"The silver aliens with the weird heads?" Beats asked, suddenly curious.

231

The Tarantula spared a glance back for Beats and then shrugged at Dalton.

"They're in the system, and they're gunning for the station and planet here. The reason they're rushing us onto the ship is because we're about to be under attack. They're trying to launch as quickly as possible so that we can get the hell out of here before they start firing on us. That means the full crew is aboard this ship, they're all at their stations, and there's no way we're going to find a way to gain control of it. You understand?"

"Could still take hostages," the Tarantula said.

His lower lip protruded as he thought, showing a dimple in the area above his chin.

"We're outnumbered ten thousand to... how many of us escaped? Twenty? Thirty?"

"I see what you're sayin'," the Tarantula said. "So what do you think? We go into the chambers and play docile like they want? What if they don't get out in time? We're stuck."

"We're stuck either way," Dalton said. "But that's why I talked to security. They wanted to let us know." He jutted a thumb back to point at John. "We can work together with them and make sure that we all make it safe. If we get to the colony, we'll be able to start fresh. That's why we're all here, to start fresh, remember?"

He couldn't wait to be beyond the confines of Earth. Even if he had managed to survive the prison and make it out, he would still have the convict tag all over his identification and profile. No company would never give him the same chance again. It would be a liability to have him as a spokesperson or even a salesman. In a lot of ways, the prison system only made things impossible to live the straight-and-narrow once released. Sure, some of the outer frontier colonies might have taken him in, but he would have been in the same spot as with this colony. Only this one wouldn't be maintaining Earth databases or setting up as one of their worlds. The Tarantula had to realize the same thing.

Ogre looked like he wanted to pound Dalton into dust, but when hadn't he? Beats stood back looking confused.

"Alright. What do you propose?" the Tarantula finally said, breaking the tension.

Dalton motioned. "Come on. Let's get back and work with them to get everyone else back together."

"I already was workin' on that," the Tarantula said. "Boys!" He called out behind him.

From the corridor to the right came at least fifteen men, lined up, all wearing red jumpsuits.

"While you were gone I figured it'd be best if we got together. Strength in numbers," the Tarantula said, grinning again.

Fortunately, his plan had worked. Otherwise it would have been a very bad day for both him and John. The guard who had his wrist smashed wouldn't be too happy to find out that Dalton and the prisoners had returned and with little or no consequences attached. Oh well. At least he'd been able to convince them out of their schemes.

It felt good to be listened to, and oddly enough, the Spider Clan had listened to him several times now. For whatever reason, the Tarantula trusted his instincts.

"Great. Follow me," Dalton said. "Let's get out of this back-pain central."

Beats laughed too loudly at the unfunny joke.

Dalton turned around, motioning to Security John, and they made their way back to being decent citizens again. Or so Dalton hoped.

39

HERDING

Toltair Orbit, The Ark

Kiyomi found herself in a crowded corridor, in between several of the giant cargo holds that had been built to house cold sleep chambers. As she didn't have any real ship experience, she determined it would be best to fall into line with the other colonists. This group would be her family in the coming years, and someone needed to get them herded so that they could depart safely.

A sea of people stood in gridlock around her, worse than New York air traffic at rush hour. With such limited time, the colonists hadn't been given any instructions other than to board the ark. Individual cold sleep pods had been programmed to specific designations, each requiring personal calibration, but few of the colonists had the directions for who would go where.

They had five cold sleep holds, each meant to hold two thousand people. One of those holds had been delegated to the prisoners, but that left the other four as possibilities as to where a person should go. If only they had been in alphabetical order, that would have been easier, but having to cram so much power and chemical distribution into four rooms, the engineers had arranged people by size, weight, and relative age in order to keep the four holds equally distributed. It left most of the colonists trying to guess where they were supposed to go.

Several of the colonists had been chosen to help facilitate. Kiyomi couldn't recall many of their names, even though she had spoken with them. Too many people to get to know in not enough time. In theory, the colonists should have lined up to ask after their name and which hold they should enter. The result was people crowding and pushing.

Someone bumped into Kiyomi from behind, nearly sending her into a bulkhead.

Kiyomi spun. "Okay!" she shouted at the top of her lungs. People close by turned their attentions to her but it didn't stop the bustling of the rest of the crowd. She breathed in deeply, pushing her lungs even harder. "I said *okay!*"

The room quieted, and she had everyone's attention.

"Most of you know me. I'm Kiyomi DePino, the head of this project. I know you all rushed into here, and I know you're all scared. I am, too. But we can't continue on like this. We need to get smart and organize if we're going to make it out of here." She took a long look around the crowd, meeting with the eyes of as many as she could, as her father had taught her to do when speaking in front of large audiences. "That means getting everyone safely into cold sleep for takeoff. There's only one way to do it. Volunteers, can you hold up your data pads?"

The volunteers raised their arms with datapads above their heads.

"These people are the ones who can help you determine which bay to go into for your cold sleep. In each bay, there will be another volunteer to direct you to your pod number. Let's all slow down and get ourselves lined up in an orderly fashion for the ones in the hall. Stay to the left side of the corridor—my left, that is. Allow traffic to move through on the right to get to the bays proper. Don't stop unless you're inside. We need your cooperation if we're going to get through this."

"If the Aryshans attack, won't we be completely helpless if we're in cold sleep?" someone shouted.

The question irritated Kiyomi, but she didn't miss a beat. Everyone had to remain calm. She couldn't spot the questioner through the crowd of people, but she turned to that general direction. "If the Aryshans attack, we're likely dead whether in cold sleep or not. That goes for those on the station and for escape pods as well. Our best shot of survival is to keep calm, follow my lead, and get ourselves ready for our new lives on the Ixora colony. If everyone is patient and gets into the pods, we'll be able to drop into FTL and get out of here."

It sounded simple, but no one, even those close around her, seemed happy about it. Kiyomi understood the sentiment. She didn't much want to be rushing into cold sleep either. Who knew if one would ever wake again? She wouldn't lie to them and tell them everything would be alright. No one could guarantee success.

Following her own advice, Kiyomi moved into the stream of people heading for different cargo bay rooms. She wished there were a ship comm for those who occupied the bridge to give an update to everyone on the status. Even in this giant ark, it felt like they were small, trapped in, and helpless. The Aryshans could have moved off or they could be right on top of everyone.

Fortunately, others followed her orders. She did her best to come across as confident in the speech, and it had paid off. The lines moved better now. Fewer people migrated in haphazard directions. They would get going soon and everyone would wake up at their new home, with their new lives. She wished all the fears inside her weren't holding down the pride she should have felt for achieving her father's dream.

40

BREAKING THE BONDS

TOLTAIR ORBIT, THE ARK

THE ARYSHANS HAD MADE short work of the Interplanetary Navy vessels. Their pulse cannon volleys ate right through the newly repaired ships' shields. These ships didn't have their full complement of missiles or defenses, and it showed. The aliens outmaneuvered them, out-fired them, and out-defended them. Damage mounted on the Earth vessels, and the Aryshans didn't look like they would be slowed for long. Was this how every battle went between the Earth fleets and the Aryshans? There might not be an Earth left if it continued this way.

"Doesn't look good," Rawle said from his station.

"No, it doesn't," Antony agreed.

They'd been watching the battle unfold for about fifteen minutes. At least the Earth ships had taken up a position to block the Aryshans from the station. They would have to maneuver around them to continue their assault.

One of the Earth ships twisted and rotated in a manner that didn't look at all like it moved under its own power. The Aryshans must have hit its crystal drive. It already had so many areas burnt and crumpled from the blasts. One down.

"They didn't buy us as much time as we would have hoped," Antony said. He paced the small room that had been called the bridge. The doors opened behind him.

Evelyn Tellmann stood at the door, dressed in her professional work clothes as she had been for the entire time that Antony had seen her, her chin up. "Mr. Lemkin, Mr. Tejada," she said to them and scooted over to an unobtrusive back corner of the room. "Took me awhile, but I finally made it aboard. I don't have many personal belongings—never been much of a materialist, so it wasn't difficult to determine what to bring."

"Is that all you had?" Antony asked. She didn't even carry a bag.

Evelyn chuckled. "No. I dropped my things on a hovercart down by the supplies compartment. No one is over there, thankfully. You should see how clustered the cold sleep chamber areas are."

"That bad?"

"Let's say I wouldn't like to be Ms. DePino right now." She inclined her head toward the screen. "How are our valiant defenders doing?"

"Not well," Rawle said from his station. "The Aryshans took a focus-fire tactic to take out one of the two ships. I doubt there's anyone alive on board anymore. The other won't last much longer, either, against three warships." He narrowed his eyes and pointed to the screen. "Wait a minute. Look!"

The out-of-control Earth ship spun slowly, much of its hull surface burnt to a crisp. If they zoomed in their view, they would be able to see between decks. It would also show human bodies floating in space. Antony didn't want the image in his mind.

The ship's exhaust changed from darkness signifying no life on the engines to a glowing blue and white. They'd come back online!

The vessel stopped spinning and moved toward the battle, completely ignored by the enemy. The three Aryshan warships had turned to focus fire on the other Earth ship.

"They're going to ram the Aryshans," Rawle said.

"How do you know?" Antony asked.

"See the way the pilot is shifting course? It's a slow movement because that's all you can do with a big ship in space like that, but they're pointing their fore directly at the center Aryshan ship. I bet they'll engage their crystal drive at any moment."

The ship launched, sudden and quick. It turned into a blur on the holodisplay. Before Antony could blink, it crashed into the Aryshan warship, a wave of kinetic energy blasting outward from the collision. They'd gone to FTL with a giant mass in front of them, exactly as standard guidelines warned against. A plume of dust, debris, and flames erupted from the Aryshan ship, then drove back inward to where the two ships met, imploding from the vacuum pressurization. Lights from both ships flickered off into darkness.

"One down," Rawle said.

Antony turned back to Evelyn. They'd wasted far too much time monitoring and watching a ship battle outside. Whether the remaining Earth ship won or lost, it didn't matter to the ark's survival. They needed to get out of the system, and quickly.

"Are you the last that we need to get aboard?"

Evelyn turned her attention to him. "Oh, yes. I believe so. I doubt anyone else could make it if they wanted to. The station's pretty much clear of everyone."

"Okay, then let's get ready for takeoff."

Rawle tapped several commands into his console. He shook his head several times. "It's no good, sir. The docking clamps are still engaged from the station."

"What?" Evelyn flung herself around the back console to see what Rawle had on his screen. "I told them to disengage." She leaned back over the console, inputting a comm frequency. The console made a pleasant chirping sound, connecting to the station's networks. It repeated that sound several times. "Damn. No one's answering."

"You did say everyone had evacuated the station." Antony frowned. "Is there any way to manually disengage the clamps?"

Evelyn moistened her lips. "No. Not that I can think of. The only way to do it would be from the station control." She glanced up at the viewscreen, which still had the battle between the remaining three ships raging on. "I could return there?"

"There's no time," Antony said. He motioned to the screen. "If the rest of this battle goes as quickly as it has so far, we need to get out of here before the Aryshans turn their pulse cannons to us."

"You won't have to wait for me to return. It's fine," Evelyn said. Her face carried a measure of pride on it, one in her work. The employees of DePino Shipyards were so dedicated to this family. Antony couldn't help but find it inspiring.

"No. We're already short colonists. I don't want to lose you. There has to be another option."

"Only thing I could think of would be to launch anyway," Rawle said. "But it might cause a lot of damage to the ship."

"I wouldn't recommend that," Evelyn said.

Antony rested an arm atop Rawle's console. "Where are the clamps? Is there any way to project what damage would occur?"

Rawle pulled up a holographic image of the ship's hull. "Four locations," he pointed to spots on the upper and bottom portions of the ark on either end. "If we could push forward I could squeeze out to only have two cause major damage, but the clamps would push through the hull on the upper and lower decks until I could swing the ship around. We'd lose pressurization in those areas."

"What systems are in those areas?"

With the extension of his fingers, Rawle zoomed in on the ship area. "Like most of the ship, storage, building supplies on the outside. It was designed that way so that if there were an issue on the perimeter, any people or vital ship systems would be protected by layers of metal."

"So, in theory, we could make it."

"In theory," Rawle said. "Like I said, I'm not sure how much damage the clamps would do."

Evelyn leaned over the opposite side of Rawle's console, three people crowded now in an area designed for one. The light of the holographic ship flickered across her face. "I really can't advise this. We didn't bring supplies for much more than would be absolutely necessary for a colony. If conditions at our destination aren't ideal, the loss of supplies could be detrimental to us."

On the main holodisplay, the two Aryshan ships barraged the final Earth vessel with their pulse cannons. Despite firing missiles in return, the ship broke apart into millions of splinters. Their last defender had been obliterated.

"If we stay here, we're going to be destroyed anyway. Do it, Rawle," Antony said. "No more time for debate."

Rawle flipped a switch on his console. The holographic form of the ark flickered off and different options appeared on the hard console. Rawle's fingers moved like lightning across them, speed and precision Antony had never seen before. His professional piloting skills proved invaluable.

"I'm going to switch the main display to the interior of the ship yards so we can see our progress," Evelyn said. She slid around to the rear console and made her adjustments.

The Aryshan ships disappeared and an image of the ark, from the perspective of station cameras, replaced them. Lights adorned the interior. The lines of smaller vehicles moving cargo and people between different ships had all stopped. The station's personnel had all evacuated. Fabio DePino had hired the best managers all around, and it had paid off. Evelyn would be a great asset for the colony.

"Can you zoom in some?" Antony asked. "I want to see the clamps."

Evelyn brought the view in closer. The clamps hung from long arms that protruded from the station walls. Four of them, as Rawle had stated. The clamps had giant, spring-loaded mechanisms that Antony had to believe operated off of a powered shock system. They conformed to the dimensions of the hull to be able to hold the ship with the most surface area.

"Ready to commence undocking, sir," Rawle said.

"Let's do it."

Rawle depressed an icon that appeared to move with his hand.

"Course engaged. Now all we can do is watch, while the AI figures out the best way to get through with the least amount of damage."

"How does it do that?" Antony asked.

"It's got sensors on the hull for the purpose of maneuvering. Also helps with tracking asteroid or space debris hits in case it causes a hull rupture."

"Makes sense."

The ship moved. Antony braced himself against a protruding countertop from the station across from Rawle, but he did not feel much rocking or rattling at all as he had expected. Shrapnel flew, metal colliding with metal. If there were any sound, it would have made the most horrific screeches.

Sparks continued to shoot from the ship's hull and grinding metal of the clasps. The ship tilted, its exhaust ports glowing. Then came the real struggle. The clamps couldn't conform far enough for the ship's movement, as their whole intention were to prevent a ship from moving. They tore through the upper decks despite the AI's best attempts to push the ship through in one piece. Debris floated away from the ark as smoke and dust clouded the impacted areas.

Whole swaths of metal peeled from the ship, larger than the flitter Antony had been on to get him aboard the ark. Antony couldn't help but wince at the sight.

"Section four-A through three-B have been depressurized," Evelyn said. She watched a graphicon a display in front of her. "Routing backup containment to sections behind. On the aft... we have less damage. Only one deck affected. New seals in place."

Antony let out a sigh of relief. "Good work, Rawle."

"It was all the AI, sir."

On the main display, the ark moved away. Debris floated toward the camera—crates, several trees from what would have been the fruit stock for the colony. Hopefully, nothing too detrimental had been lost. In front of the ship, a large opening to space outside. The circular gate held ajar, as it had been opened to allow the two Earth military vessels their exit. The ark would follow them. Lights blinked in quarter sections at the edges of the spherical opening, allowing the ship sensors to track exactly where to go.

The ark picked up speed and soon broke free of the station.

"We're on our way," Antony said.

Several months ago, he could never have imagined himself in a strange room like this, in essence commanding a giant ship, leading thousands of people as they reached for the stars. He couldn't help but smile. The image of the ark disappeared from the camera's view inside the station's feeds as they moved out of range. "Switch the monitor to our ship's cameras," Antony said.

"Aye, sir," Rawle said.

"How long until we can make the jump to FTL?" Antony asked.

Space in all its vastness covered the screen. The station and Toltair were behind them now. Thousands of little white lights, the stars of the Milky Way Galaxy, lay ahead of them.

"It's powering up," Rawle said. His voice changed to one of concern. "But sir, we have a problem."

"What's that?" Antony turned to Rawle.

Rawle tapped more commands then pointed back to the main holodisplay, which showed two claw-shaped, Aryshan warships. They tilted onto their side axes and headed straight for the ark. The warships were painted a strange blue-green, like a plant one would find on the bottom of the ocean.

"What are they doing? They're not firing," Evelyn said from her station.

Antony focused on the two images as the ships came closer. They wouldn't be able to safely launch into FTL with the ships at this range. It would risk destroying themselves along with the Aryshans.

It took a moment, but Antony spotted their plan. They maneuvered their ships to wrap around the two gaping holes in the ark. The claw shape allowed their vessels to latch onto others. The holes in the hull allowed the Aryshans an entry point onto the ark. "They're planning on boarding us." Now what would they do? As a civilian vessel, the ark had very little in the way of defenses. They didn't have the manpower to deal with trained combatants, especially of an alien species that were, by all accounts, stronger and faster than humans.

"Boarding? Why would they do that?" Evelyn asked.

"It doesn't make sense," Rawle said.

They were right. It didn't make sense. The Aryshans had shown only a pure path of destruction before, not an interest in occupying human territory. They felt humans had expanded too far into the galaxy, and they wanted to send a message to the humans to stay far away.

Antony tried to think from their perspective. What made this situation unique compared to the other battles Earth had faced? He snapped his fingers. "I think I understand. The ark is different. It doesn't look like any other human vessel they've seen. We had two of our own battlecruisers come out and defend us, and then we left the station with no announcement, nothing on traffic channels."

"They want information," Evelyn said.

"That's right." Antony nodded. "Can we contact them and tell them we're civilians? Communicate that our intentions are peaceful, if you can."

Rawle sent a comm signal, then waited. The Aryshan warships came closer still. The ark wouldn't be able to maneuver around them.

"No response, sir," Rawle said.

Antony frowned. All he'd learned of the Aryshans came from news reports. In all likelihood, they didn't have anyone who could speak a human language aboard. They had to have computers that could translate for them, though. Didn't they?

The ships pulled the ark into a gravimetric field. It acted like they were clamps themselves. The Ark stopped its forward momentum, despite the AI compensating to put power into the thrusters.

"I'm powering down engines so we don't burn them out," Rawle said. He input the commands to do so.

Two large tubes jutted out from the Aryshan ships at their center. Those tubes expanded and wrapped around the openings on each end of the ship, sealing into place. They could do little but watch from the bridge.

"Some of the decompressed deck sections have regained pressurization and airflow."

They wouldn't be able to find a diplomatic solution if the Aryshans wouldn't respond. Still, they had to find a way to handle the Aryshans, or at least hold them off until they formulated a better plan. Antony turned to Rawle.

"Pull up Morgan Ezra on the comm. She's former military. We're going to need her help and expertise."

41

FISH OUT OF WATER

Morgan had never led a combat situation before. The only thing she'd been able to do when the Aryshans attacked the last time had been to run away, get into a flitter, and try to escape. Her efforts had been unsuccessful. Now Governor Lemkin wanted her to protect the ship against boarding Aryshans? She would laugh, cry, and laugh all over again if she had time for a mental breakdown.

She'd signed up for this mission to get away from her trauma. A fresh start, fresh air, no possibility of ever running into alien invaders again. *Take a deep breath*, Morgan reminded herself. *In through the nose, out through the mouth. Deliberate. Slow.*

It didn't help. Her team of three security personnel returned, pushing a hovercart that had a crate filled with pulse weapons. She had to make some hard decisions, since they didn't have the personnel to split up and guard both entrances where the Aryshans would be penetrating. She set up her primary defense in the corridor around the corner from the cold sleep pod. It would be the most centralized location for mobility.

"Good work," Morgan said. "What's your name?"

"Trista. Trista Collins," the short and somewhat stockier woman said.

"Trista," Morgan repeated so she would remember. "We're going to pull all of security off of the cold sleep pods. Find anyone with weapon experience to report here and grab a pulse rifle. We'll need all the help we can get. Don't pull anyone else out of the pods, but if they're still waiting in line, draft them."

"Aye, aye, ma'am," Trista said. She snuck around the big crate atop the hovercart, and then jogged around the corner.

Several other security guards had gathered behind Morgan, who turned to acknowledge them. "The rest of you get going to the upper decks. We're going to make a stand across from the medical bay, which should be a good place to bottleneck the Aryshans and give us a fighting chance to defend ourselves."

Murmurs of agreement followed.

"Move it!" Morgan shouted.

She'd seen how basic training instructors had commanded their units, and tried to mimic their confident tone as best she could. In her guard duty, her management experience had been with personnel on an individual basis. Taking over a shift, ensuring her people stood in the right spot, filling out reports. She'd dealt with the occasional break-in by some unruly teenagers, and having to haul them off to the local authorities, but now she had the task of being the local authority.

She again tried her breathing exercises to calm herself as her team rushed toward the front line.

"Everything okay?" a voice said from behind her.

Morgan jumped, readying her weapon and pointing it squarely in the gut of a man who stood all too closely behind her.

Dalton Ward held his hands up in surrender, though he held a weapon. "Easy, there."

Morgan lowered her gun. "You shouldn't be sneaking up on someone like that, especially after my team's been hunting you down for the last few hours."

Behind Dalton stood several dozen more prisoners, all wearing their red jumpsuit garb. Some of them had guns.

Morgan's heart beat faster and she stepped backward, bumping into the hovercraft filled with yet more weapons. "Are you planning a mutiny?"

Dalton blinked, turned behind him, and then back to her. He laughed. "No, though I guess it looks pretty bad. I told the prisoners about the Aryshans. I stopped their little escape plan, and they're coming back to get into cold sleep."

John Roland pushed past some of the prisoners. He inclined his head toward Morgan to acknowledge her.

Morgan nodded to him.

"We decided ourselves," said one of the prisoners, another bald man who had the same traces of the spider tattoo on his skull as Dalton.

"Whatever they want to call it. The result is the same." Dalton shrugged. "Where do we go?"

Morgan considered. She could send them back into cold sleep or... "There's been a change in plans. Do your men know how to fight?"

Several of larger men behind Dalton snickered.

"I believe that's a yes," Dalton said.

"Okay, listen up." Morgan raised her voice to speak to the whole group. "The Aryshans are in position to board the ship. They're coming in from two locations on the top decks. I sent my security team to the aft side by the medical bay..." she paused, realizing specific locations on the ship probably meant nothing to the prisoners. They hadn't been here long enough to get their bearings or have any understanding of what rooms were where. She cleared her throat. "I don't have enough personnel to handle both entrance points. We don't know how many Aryshans will be coming, but they have two full warships attached to our hull. What I need you to do is handle the fore of the ship. I'm going to give Dalton Ward a map—"

Dalton cut her off. "She means me."

"Ah, Smarts!" one of them said as if in understanding.

"Whatever." Morgan shook her head. "John Roland here, the security guard you've met before, has a map of the schematics that will lead the way of how to get to their invasion point. I'm going to trust all of you because I've got no choice—*we've* got no choice—if we're going to survive this. We have to fend the Aryshans off so we can find a way to get into FTL and get out of here. It's our only shot."

She pointed to the hovercart and crate behind her. "This is our weapons cache. I see some of you are armed already. The rest of you will need to grab pulse pistols and follow Mr. Ward. Got it?"

The prisoners grumbled and muttered to that speech, but none seemed unwilling to fight. Everyone's survival depended on their cooperation. And who had any love lost of the Aryshans? In many ways, Morgan couldn't wait to gun some of those bastards down, even if she were deathly afraid of the situation at the same time.

Dalton lowered his voice to a whisper. "This is crazy. You can't trust these people as far as you can throw them."

"There's no choice," Morgan said.

"Alright, everyone. Let's get going," Dalton said. He nodded to Morgan and brushed past her toward the weapons crate, flinging the top open. It clanged against the metal wall behind him. He tossed his pulse pistol to one of the other prisoners. The others fell into line as he began to disburse more.

She wished that Dalton would have had some courtesy to let her by before the horde of prisoners went for the weapons. Handing them weapons in close proximity made her nervous. Pushing her way through the group of large, muscular men, she squeezed past Dalton, unable to help but press against him as she moved.

"Why, hello there," Dalton said in a teasing tone, though he continued to reach into the bin and hand out weapons.

"Gross," Morgan said as she moved past him.

"Hey, I haven't seen a woman in over a year, cut me some slack!" His words echoed down the corridor.

Men could be so disgusting, and prisoners had to be the worst of them, though truth be told, she found Dalton to be fit and attractive. But with the Aryshans coming, she had more important things to focus on.

The path to the place she and her team would make their stand took her a couple of minutes to traverse. Using the lift would be out of the question, with the possibility of weapons' fire taking out any mechanical systems. She had to climb a service ladder up several decks to meet her team. She slung her pulse rifle around her back, tightening its strap over her chest.

When she arrived, her team had already taken their positions. Several of her security personnel were down on knees, empty crate boxes piled in front of them with their pulse rifles pointed toward a sealed metal hatch across from them. Others lined the edges of the hall, taking cover in doorways and around corners. They had the best set-up they possibly could hope for in this situation, but she still had no idea how many Aryshans would be breaking through.

Morgan took her own position at the rear, catching Trista's eye. The internal hatch and doorway had become the barrier point for air pressure. They were several meters inside the ship, so whatever had happened outside to penetrate the hull had caused a lot of damage.

Before she could think of anything to say to her team, a crack formed in the door. It hissed as air pressure equalized between her place and the other side.

"Is the hull breaking down?" Trista asked.

Morgan focused on the small crack at the top left of the doorway. Sparks flickered from it, first a trickle of them, and then it came out like fireworks. The metal around the crack seemed to melt away as a line about ten centimeters thick formed on it. That line grew, expanding down the height of the hatch. Smoke and melted metal covered any glimpse to the other side.

"They've got a laser cutter to push through the emergency stop," one of her men said. "They're coming through."

The cut line of metal grew horizontally. Morgan flipped her pulse rifle around from her back, adding slack to the strap so she could move it into position to face the door. The others readied their rifles. "Hold steady," Morgan said, not wanting to waste fire on unnecessary shots. She had the feeling they would need every last pulse blast they could get.

The line drew up another side and then horizontal back the other direction, enough to make a hole for two or three people to come through at a time. Morgan hadn't seen Aryshans in person, only their drop ships, but from what she'd understood from holovids, they were about the same height as humans. They appeared strikingly similar, excepting their silver and gold skin colors and a crown feature around their skull that protected their heads. Internally, their version of blood coursed through passageways in their bones. Morgan had heard of their physiology in a science class in college, and the strange image had stuck with her. It didn't matter. A pulse weapon's full discharge would singe and vaporize them as well as it would any other flesh being.

The laser cutter on the other side stopped, a rectangular shape sizzled, forming what looked to be a door. Metal melted, dripping to the floor in a hot, red, molten form. Smoke filled the corridor.

The door blasted open with the force of an explosion.

In the confusion, dozens of Aryshans rushed forward, firing weapons toward her people. They had been better trained than Morgan's group. A real military, not some volunteer makeshift security force meant to police a small colony world. Several of her team fell from the initial burst.

"Fire all weapons! Now!" Morgan shouted.

Her team returned fire. The first line of security had lost too many men in that opening volley. Morgan and the remaining others fell back.

The Aryshans pushed forward.

42

DON'T MESS WITH THE SPIDER CLAN

DALTON CHARGED down a corridor that seemed like it would never end. The doors were labeled for ease of finding the various areas of the ship, but he had no time to stop to find his relative position. The security guard, John Roland, sped ahead of him, using his wrist comm to display a small schematic of the ship to lead them to the proper location.

Having been trapped inside a prison transport ship for far too long, Dalton found himself becoming winded. Running like this shouldn't have impacted him, but the only exercise opportunities he had down in the pit of that vessel had been involving weight lifting, and Dalton had stayed away so he wouldn't interfere with any of the other prisoners who might want to harm him.

"How much farther?" Dalton asked between gasps for air, as Security John kept moving.

"How out of shape are you, Smarts? Shriveling up like an old man?" the Tarantula mocked him. He laughed, not even breathing hard from the exercise.

Dalton ignored the taunt as Security John slowed his pace. They'd reached an intersection.

Security John checked the device on his wrist. "Almost there. We'll need to head left down this—"

Pulse blasts sputtered from the corridor to their left. They must have been pretty close to the Aryshans already.

The shots caused Security John to stumble backward. He dropped to a knee and then pushed himself right again, bracing with his back to a wall. "They're not supposed to be this far inside. We need to make our stand at least fifty meters away. There's too many exit points here toward the rest of the ship."

"We gotta stop them then," Dalton said. He turned back to his group of prisoners, about forty of them in all—he hadn't had time to do a full count. "Aryshans up ahead."

"Let's go break some bones," Ogre said to Beats.

"Finally," Beats agreed.

The Tarantula stepped forward, peeking his head around the corridor. A couple of blasts came his direction, and he stumbled backward. Dalton caught him.

"We need to be careful," Dalton said.

"I wouldn't rush into hand-to-hand combat with them," the Tarantula said. "I did some reading on Aryshans. They're supposed to be stronger and faster than us. Try to shoot 'em clean."

"We're going to need to do something to push them back," Security John said. "We're supposed to make our stand at a cut off, so they can't escape further into the ship."

Pulse fire continued from Aryshans' position. A couple struck the wall opposite where Dalton and the others stood, scorching the metal.

"We have to do something. We can't stand here forever."

The Tarantula turned back toward the other prisoners. "Spider Clan. The time has come to press forward. We've suppressed our rage for a long time. Forward! Strike the aliens!"

He made a whirling motion with his arm, calling his men to him.

The prisoners rushed forward at his words. Dalton and Security

John looked at each other, amazed at the loyalty these men displayed toward the Tarantula. They were willing to die for him!

Their will came to fruition. The first group to circle around into the line of sight of the Aryshans died as they were gunned down. Pulses flew from both sides. Groans of pain came from down the hall. At least they'd hit some of their targets.

Dalton kept cover in the corner. He maneuvered his gun around it and fired blindly toward the Aryshans. Several more cries of pain sounded. More of the prisoners fell—like flies being swatted as they rounded the corner. "This isn't working. This rate we'll run out of men."

"We can always get more from the pods," the Tarantula said.

"Not in time." Security John crouched, taking a position to point his gun around Dalton. "The Aryshans still have the positions in the doorways covered. We're sitting ducks when we go around."

"Can we sneak behind them?" Dalton asked.

Security John shook his head. "No, this is the only entry point we have that we can count on as still being pressurized. A lot of the hull was torn up when we left the shipyards."

"Grenades would be helpful," the Tarantula said. "Did they bring any aboard?"

Dalton had always wondered about the Tarantula's background. He had leadership qualities to him, a way of getting men to fear him that he hadn't seen from anyone else on the prison colony. He also had the ability to make snap decisions, like trusting Dalton. The Tarantula also had some tactical knowledge. Who had the man been in his prior life?

"We don't have more weaponry," Security John said.

He and fired a couple more shots down the corridor. Other prisoners had seen how the first wave fell, and stood back, hesitating.

"You could always wire the power packs from one of the guns to explode," the Tarantula suggested. "Hard to throw straight, but it can do a lot of damage."

Dalton raised an inquisitive brow.

"I fought in the Drenite war. Infantry," the Tarantula said, as if sensing Dalton's thoughts.

"I'd wondered," Dalton said. "How do we do it?"

The Tarantula slid against the wall, seating himself with his knees up, feet planted on the ground. He picked apart the top of his rifle, getting into the glowing power pack, back toward the stock of the rifle.

"Wish I had some tools," he muttered, digging his pinky finger into the hole beyond the power pack. He produced some wires. "It's really simple. Little trick we learned for desperate situations."

He glanced up, noting Dalton and the others watching him.

"Don't stare at me, keep the suppression fire going," he said.

Security John turned back around and crouched. Ogre moved to a place above him. Both continued their fire. Dalton swung around, seeing that Aryshans were rushing toward them. He shot one at point-blank range. The Aryshan blew backward from the force. His neck went limp and sideways when he hit the ground, lifeless eyes rolling back toward the top of his head.

"Almost done. Just need to dig positive and negative charged wires into the pack core here. It bypasses the switch, which is what the trigger activates, and creates an energy loop until it overloads."

"Better hurry. They're about to charge us again," Dalton said.

A group of Aryshans pushed their way forward. They had their weapons faced forward, firing continuously, not allowing the humans any space to get their weapons pointed around a corner. They reached the opening where Dalton and the others had set up, and turned toward them.

Ogre leapt toward the Aryshans with surprising speed, hands outstretched like some kind of ferocious animal, pouncing on the lead attacker. The sudden aggressiveness caught them off guard, giving time for Beats to follow Ogre's example and tackle another one. The move pushed the alien into several others, knocking them over like bowling pins.

A fist fight ensued between the larger men and the stronger Aryshans.

The aliens moved with incredible speed. Their fists punched as blurred flurries across the prisoner's faces, and then torsos. The Aryshans pushed Ogre and Beats off of them in mere moments, and the two prisoners collapsed to the ground. They then fell victim to several kicks from hard-toed Aryshan military boots. Bones *cracked*. Beats and Ogre both screamed in pain, a sound Dalton never had expected to hear from them.

"We gotta get them out of there," Security John said.

He dove toward them, valiantly grabbing Ogre by the ankles. He tugged backward, showing surprising strength, as Ogre must have weighed close to a hundred twenty kilograms. The Aryshans got in more attacks while Ogre tried to cover his skull with his hands.

Dalton motioned for a couple of prisoners to join Security John in helping the larger men. The Aryshans pointed their weapons toward Dalton and his team.

"Fall back!" Dalton shouted.

"I'm done!" the Tarantula cried.

He stood and chucked his rifle against the back wall, which clanked off of it and then fell to the floor at the feet of the group of Aryshans.

Pulse weapons fired. Security John and the prisoners dragged Beats and Ogre, managing to evade the fire as they retreated. Dalton took off running down the hallway. He pointed his pulse rifle back over his shoulder and fired. The Aryshans' return fire came all too close to blowing off his ear.

Even though the Aryshans had the upper hand, the prisoners had been successful in slowing the Aryshans down. It would be up to the ark's leaders to come up with a plan to end the siege.

"John, where's the next point where we can get cover?" Dalton asked. When no one responded, he paused in a doorway, peeking around its frame to look behind him.

The Tarantula and several of the prisoners ran past him. More shots came from the Aryshans. The men who had been bringing Ogre and Beats away from the Aryshans convulsed and fell, including Security John. The security guard reached out toward Dalton as if trying to be pulled ahead, but his eyes rolled back in his skull. He fell limp.

His flesh smoked, leaving a burnt, nasty smell in the hallway. The bastards got him, their man with the map of the ship.

"John!" Dalton called to him.

The Tarantula's rifle overloaded, creating an explosion too big for the corridor. The Aryshans standing at the intersection went up in flames, shouting and cursing in their language. The blast blew a hole in the back wall, opening up into some section with several tanks. Water gushed from the broken tanks in front of the blast, dampening some of the flames nearby, but filling the corridor with smoke.

The others took the opportunity to run. Dalton waited, and saw that the blast had managed to hold off the Aryshan advance as intended. The Tarantula had done a good job. Dalton wouldn't underestimate that man in the future.

Instead of running, Dalton moved forward and crouched by Security John.

"John. You still with us?" He asked. He flipped the body over.

John's head drooped to the side. No question that he no longer remained among the living.

But that's not what Dalton went back for. He grabbed the comm device from Security John's wrist and planted it on the back of his hand. He would have access to the maps and the comm channels Morgan and the others used to communicate.

A figure moved in the smoke, and Dalton raised his pulse rifle.

The sound of a pulse charge came from the figure shrouded in smoke. Dalton dodged, slamming hard to the wall to his side. Then he fired his own rifle into the smoky haze. An Aryshan dropped to his knees, his face showing through the smoke. Dalton fired another pulse at the closer range, blowing off the alien's head.

He had to regroup with the others. Dalton scrambled to his feet and ran back down the corridor.

PANIC AT THE SLEEP PODS

THE SECOND COLD sleep chamber had turned into mass panic. Unfortunately, the comm lines being used to broadcast between the security teams had been open through the entire Aryshan attack, messages blasting onto dozens of people's comm units.

The colonists had heard too much. They knew the Aryshans were aboard, and every effort Kiyomi had expended to calm them in the corridor had been for naught.

Matters had gotten worse since she had moved into the cargo bay proper. Two cold sleep units had been overturned in the commotion, crashing to the ground. Chemicals spilled on the floor. Half of the colonists had already entered their pods, but the other half had become frenzied. It looked like a riot in the bay.

Kiyomi had to deal with this mess on her own. The few people she trusted the most on this mission were all busy elsewhere.

"I'm making a run for it!" a man shouted. He nearly mowed her over, charging through her toward the exit.

Kiyomi took an elbow to the chest and stumbled backward. Didn't people have some common courtesy for others? "There's nowhere to go. The ark is meant for a single, one-way trip. We don't have escape pods!" Kiyomi shouted, but to no avail. He had already departed into the corridor.

"Looks like you could use some help," someone else said.

Kiyomi turned to find a young man in his twenties. He wore a gray, short sleeved shirt highlighting his impressive biceps.

"Name's Tyler Morales. I'm part of the infrastructure team."

She would have taken the time to linger on his fine physique if she hadn't been utterly flustered by this situation. Her nerves were more a mess than when she had to present her master's thesis in botany. At least then, she could dive into books and spend hours with her plants in her greenhouse.

"I could use some help, Tyler," she said. "I'm not sure what to do, though. People are panicking."

"Talk to them. Calm them," Tyler said.

"I tried it already. I can't even get their attention now!"

Tyler grinned. "I can help." He brought both his pinky fingers to his lips and then blew hard.

Kiyomi attempted to motion him to stop. She'd already yelled at these colonists in the corridor, before the word passed down that they were under attack. Could mere words satiate the panic now? They had every right to be afraid. Never in her wildest imagination could she have imagined that Aryshans would board this vessel.

Tyler ignored her motioning. He made the loudest whistling noise Kiyomi had ever heard. It bounced off the metallic walls, echoing.

The colonists stopped panicking and stopped running. They all turned to the direction of the whistle, hundreds of eyes on Kiyomi and her new friend. She repositioned herself toward the entrance, a nice focal point, even if several stacked cold sleep pods were in the way. The slats between them offered some viewing room at least.

Now she had to figure out what to say—again. Out in the corridor, she'd been able to use a few words to get everyone to listen. This would be different. Lives were held in the balance and people were scared.

"Everyone," Kiyomi said, trying to project as loudly as she could, trying to draw out the word to buy herself some time. "I told you before. We need your cooperation. If we stay ordered, they won't be able to—"

"Look out!" someone shouted. Dozens of colonists pointed toward her. "Look behind you," someone else said.

The crowd's focus disappeared in that instant. The colonists fled in different directions, crashing into one another in haphazard disorder.

Kiyomi turned around, jarred by the people cutting off her speech. Why had someone interrupted? She'd been so close to creating order again. Her eyes widened.

Three Aryshans in full combat armor had entered the bay. Even though they had a similar build to her human friends, their alien features were unmistakable. Their skin had a silver hue to it, devoid of life, as if a corpse. Dead men walking with beady eyes focused on her. They didn't wear helmets, but instead had a strange ridge line around their foreheads, like a crown. She had seen images of Aryshans on the news, but in person they instilled her with pure fear. Kiyomi backpedaled into Tyler. He grabbed her by the arms to hold her steady.

"Tu cala enchin!" One of the Aryshans commanded.

The three of them held their weapons up toward Kiyomi and the others.

"I don't know what that means," Kiyomi said. She turned her head back. "Does anyone speak Aryshan?"

No answer came from behind her.

"Tu cala enchin!" the Aryshan soldier repeated. He sounded impatient.

Kiyomi tiptoed forward. She moved with slow steps. She held her palms up to them, to show that she had no weapon. "I can't speak your language, but we can work this out. We are civilians. There's nothing here for you. I promise."

The lead Aryshan, or at least the one in the center that she presumed had the lead, appraised her. He seemed to sniff the air. Kiyomi didn't want to liken them to animals, but she couldn't help but think they looked like wolves hungry for prey. The alien looked down at her hands and then back up. The other two Aryshans readied their weapons.

The lead Aryshan jabbed his gun forward. A loud *crack* sounded. Before she could even react, she'd been knocked to the floor, her mouth open, as it would have hurt far too much to close it.

Her jaw hung limp. The Aryshan had smashed the butt of his gun right into her face. God it hurt. Blood trickled from her mouth, dripping red onto the cold, metallic floor. She stared at the ground, seeing the boots of the Aryshan soldiers.

Tyler jumped forward to defend her. He grappled with the Aryshan for the gun. The other colonists still in the room followed his lead, pushing forward and overwhelming the other two Aryshans. They trampled the soldiers. Even as they fell, the Aryshans managed to fire their weapons. Bodies *thudded* as they hit the floor beside her.

The Aryshans were the next to fall. They howled in pain as colonists trampled them. Bones cracked. So much violence.

Tyler managed to pry the weapon out of the lead Aryshan's hands, but the Aryshan punched him in the face. Kiyomi moved toward the weapon on the floor. She reached for it, but drew her hand backward as the Aryshan stumbled toward her, nearly crushing her hands under his feet.

Tyler didn't fare well in his hand-to-hand battle against the Aryshan. The Aryshan jabbed him in the chin. A crack sounded, reminding her of the pain in her jaw. It flared and swelled, making her whole face tense.

The Aryshan pelted Tyler multiple times. Tyler dropped to his knees. The Aryshan delivered one solid blow to his face, one that cracked his skull, the blow causing a fist-shaped dent in Tyler's head.

Despite the pain in her jaw, Kiyomi screamed. She couldn't believe the terrible violence in front of her.

Tyler collapsed, dead.

The Aryshan searched for his weapon, still on the floor in front of Kiyomi. He bent over to reach for it.

Move, Kiyomi willed herself. She had to protect the colonists, to stop this madness. No one else could help her. No one else stood close enough to the Aryshan to do anything. She grabbed the weapon, unsure of how to use it. She didn't have time to try to figure out the alien trigger.

She smacked the Aryshan across the face with the butt of the gun and scrambled backward in a crab-walk, the kind she recalled doing in physical education classes as a kid.

She still held the gun in her hand. She had to figure out how it worked. A surge of static electricity pricked her finger, causing her to recoil from it.

The Aryshan dove toward her.

Kiyomi squeezed on the sides of the weapon, sliding her finger forward.

A wave of pulse energy blasted from the gun. She'd done it. The Aryshan, hit at point blank range, exploded. His insides splattered everywhere, including all over Kiyomi. She wanted to vomit, hastily wiping the gooey substance away from her face.

Before she could get to her feet and see how the other colonists were doing behind her, another squad of Aryshans blocked the doorway. One of them shouted at her. She couldn't understand the language, but his tone made his meaning unmistakable: *drop the weapon.*

44

UNDER PRESSURE

Toltair Orbit, The Ark

"It's no good," Rawle said, his face perplexed as he stared at his monitor. "The Aryshans are effectively countering the ship's thrust with their own, holding us to motionless in space. I'm going to cut engines."

"Do so. We don't want to strain our crystal drive," Antony said.

He watched the monitor, which displayed the ark's hull and the giant, claw-shaped ships attached to it.

What could they do? They wouldn't be able to fend off the military forces on those ships. At last report, things weren't going well for security. They had at least twenty casualties, which only further depleted their already dangerously low numbers of personnel they would need when they arrived on the colony.

He would have to worry about the colony later. They had to survive this first. "Any luck in hailing the Aryshan ships?"

Evelyn shook her head. "No response still."

She didn't look up from her display, hard at work, her intense focus creating a crease beside each brow above her nose.

Antony paced in the center walkway between the stations. The confined space hindered his thinking. He shouldn't have been thinking about his thinking process. Why did his mind wander at the most inopportune times? Bethany used to tell him that it had been part of his genius. He would have felt a lot better if she stood at one of these consoles with him. She calmed him and got him out of jams hundreds of times. He'd never been in a high-pressure situation without her.

Pressure. That gave him an idea. He turned and slapped his hands on Evelyn's station.

She raised her eyes to meet his. "You look like someone far too excited given our current situation."

"That's because I have an idea to get us out of it," Antony said. "Remember earlier how we shut off compartments because they dropped in air pressure? The vacuum of space sucked out all of the debris and air that came from those gaping holes, right?"

"Yes," Evelyn said. "But I don't think any of those items would help us even if we had access to them."

"It's not the cargo we lost. It's the pressure. What if we could create, through our environmental systems, a pressure system that would force the Aryshan ships to break off from us, or at least to detach us from their tubes?"

"Huh." Evelyn typed faster than Antony had ever seen anyone else type before in his life. "I don't know how strong our systems are, but I think I could program the environmental AI to do something to accomplish your goal. We'd have to make sure we don't damage our own internal air distribution system, so we'll have a limited amount we can push."

"How long do you think it'll take you to program it?"

"Give me a few minutes." Evelyn leaned so she could catch Rawle's attention. "Can you work on a stopgap, somewhere close down the line and seal off a portion of the ship where it wouldn't impact our people? If we can get that done in tandem, it would help significantly."

"Sure," Rawle said. "I'm pretty familiar with the ship layout, so we can utilize some of our safety features." He zoomed in on his schematic, placing a finger over one area. "There's a damper here which we could close easily."

"We'll have to make sure to get our people out of that section. I'll start making calls." He could feel hope rising in his chest, an energy he didn't have before. They might get out of this after all.

"Great idea," Rawle said.

"Thanks. We'll have to see if it works."

"I hate to be a Negative Nancy," Evelyn said. "But we don't even know how many Aryshans we still have aboard the ship. If they've already overrun us, this plan may be for naught."

Her point dampened some of Antony's excitement. They had to hope their team could handle the onslaught of Aryshan soldiers. He paced toward the locked metal door keeping him and the others inside this bridge safe from being overrun.

Antony took a deep breath and exhaled again. "We can't worry about what we can't control. We can only do what we can to ensure our people have the best odds of victory.

Silence fell across the bridge. Rawle and Evelyn remained hard at work, and Antony didn't want to interrupt them. He slid into a chair at the back of the remaining two stations, opening a comm line to the security chief, Morgan Ezra.

Morgan answered. The sounds of repeated pulse gun fire came through the other side. "Morgan here. I'm a bit busy... crap. Retreat!" She breathed heavily. Boots clanked and something made scuffling sounds on the other end.

"I know you're busy, but I might be able to help. We've got a plan over here. Listen up," Antony said.

45

SURVIVING

Toltair Orbit, The Ark

THE PLAN SOUNDED good to Morgan. Whoever came up with it would have her undying thanks if she could keep herself alive past this next wave of Aryshan soldiers. She'd already struggled to keep her team alive. At least ten had died, maybe more. Once they got to the colony, she might not have anyone to be chief of anymore. She couldn't let negative thoughts overwhelm her.

Lemkin would be able to put a stop to the Aryshans pouring through the hatch. She had to stay positive. The only better news she could have heard would be if someone could discover a neurotoxin to neutralize all of these Aryshans. Any scientist capable of coming up with anything of the sort would have been in cold sleep by this point. And, unlike in the holovids, magical solutions didn't pop up out of thin air in the middle of a crisis. Scientific discoveries could take weeks, months, or even years.

She didn't have time for her imagination. Her task would lie fifteen meters ahead of her. The Aryshans had to be pushed back. It would have protruding edges all the way around, and a rubber strip on the floor which marked an emergency pressure door. And then the bridge officers could work their magic with the ship systems.

Morgan hadn't seen too much combat, but she had keen awareness of the cardinal rule that no plan survived engagement. It would be her job to make sure her people gave this plan the maximum possible amount of time for impact.

Shots fired from down the corridor. Her people returned fire. Morgan stood out of the range of crossfire. She used her security access to open a door leading to a large room of crates labeled "plumbing fittings". It reassured her to know that the future colony would have working flush toilets.

"Security, regroup!" she shouted.

How many of her team were within vocal range, she had no idea. At least five remained with her.

Those in front kept firing, crouching to reduce the possibility they'd be hit. They backed toward the door while the others from behind her regrouped with them. Morgan counted twelve in all.

"Alright. We have new orders from the governor. We need to make a push forward and drive the Aryshans back toward the sector we vacated."

"We haven't been able to get any traction so far. They're killing more of us than we are them," said a wiry woman Morgan recognized as Sasha Lim from her dossiers.

"I'm aware, but this might be the only way to save the ship."

"At the cost of our lives?"

Morgan frowned. These people had signed up for security duty, thinking that it would be basic police work. On a colony of ten thousand, there wouldn't be much crime to deal with, a pretty easy life. In fact, they had a disproportionate amount of security for such a small population, to account for the prisoners.

They needed more than security, however. A real military contingent would be able to handle this situation so much better.

"We'll die anyway if we aren't the ones to make the sacrifice," Morgan said.

"Easy for you to say."

Morgan dropped her gun and grabbed Sasha by the shirt, pulling the woman eye to eye with her.

"Listen. This is life or death, I'm not sure if you're aware. I've dealt with these Aryshans. They have no mercy. They *will* kill each and every one of us without a spare thought. I don't have the time to deal with back-talk. Do you understand?"

Sasha's eyes shifted to fear by the time Morgan finished her speech. "Yes... yes ma'am," she said quietly.

Morgan pushed her back, releasing her shirt. "Good. As I said, there's no choice. We have to act quickly and decisively, because if we don't, they'll be back to overrunning us.

"We're going to charge in. They won't expect us all to be going full-bore ahead and screaming like madmen after we've been so cautious and retreating this entire time. It might throw them off guard and give us the break we need. Got it?"

The others mumbled agreement.

"Good," Morgan said. "Now let's go!"

The two guarding the doorway stood from their crouching, rushing forward.

"For the ark!" they shouted.

A silly battle cry, but the others seemed to feed off of it, their energy increasing to the point where Morgan could feel it herself.

"For the ark!" The others shouted after them.

Morgan bent down to pick up her pulse rifle and jogged after her team. She wanted to be at the front of the pack to show some leadership, but she had to keep her relative position to her people. If something went wrong, they would be looking to her to regroup and formulate yet another plan. But how many more chances would they have left?

The first several guards fired their weapons haphazardly, no longer concerned by consuming too much energy. Toward the end of the corridor, an Aryshan popped from the cover of a doorway. The alien took a blast as soon as it reared its ugly face.

The security personnel arrived at the main Aryshan line. The aliens had piled a few cargo containers in front of them to use as a barricade. Two of Morgan's team fell immediately from the concealed fire. And then two more dropped. They were down to eight people.

The Aryshan line still lingered in front of the pressure door. Morgan could see it with her own eyes. If only they could manage to push the group back somehow.

Her team hesitated at the deaths, slowing to take cover behind the turn in the corridor.

"Keep moving forward," Morgan commanded.

Both sides exchanged more fire. The human shots blasted away at the cargo crates, blowing one of them into bits. The Aryshan behind fell victim to the next blasts. He didn't fall fast enough to be unable to return fire, however. His shot hit a security guard square in the face.

With the cargo crate down, it revealed at least twenty Aryshans behind that makeshift barricade. There were too many of them. It didn't matter. They couldn't stop now. The ship depended on this assault.

"Forward!" Morgan shouted and she pushed herself out of the cover and forward. Her team ran ahead, hollering and shouting. The sudden surge confused the Aryshans, who took hits from a barrage of pulse weapons' fire. Pulse energy lit the hallway into smoldering chaos. The remaining crates caught flame.

The aliens fell back.

Morgan tapped her wrist comm frantically. "If you're gonna seal them off, do it now!"

She stopped in her tracks, dropping her weapon and grabbing one of her team member's shirts to keep him from moving past the seal's threshold.

Before Morgan could blink, a large metal pressure door slid down from the ceiling. It met the floor with a *crack*.

Sasha approached the door, pressing her hand against it.

"We won?" she asked, sounding unsure.

With so many casualties, it didn't feel like a victory. If Antony's plan didn't work as he promised, it would amount to a small delay before the Aryshans broke back through with their laser tool.

"We'll see," Morgan said. "Let's prepare for the worst. See if you can find anyone who ran down to another section and have them regroup with us here."

She glanced back at her team. Haggard faces, bloodshot eyes, and frazzled hair. Blood splattered their uniforms. What could she say to them? She had to act like a leader and inspire her troops.

"You did well. Let's hope that's the last of it."

46

UNLIKELY HEROES

"That's what the governor told me," Dalton said.

He did his best to make eye contact with each and every one of the other prisoners. Those connections held the most importance. These weren't the type of people who would be predisposed toward helping the cause. He hoped he had instilled how crucial this plan would be to their own survival.

The Tarantula frowned. Dalton had gained respect for him after watching him fight these last hours. The prisoners followed his orders without question. He had characteristics of true leadership, despite his criminal tendencies.

"What about Ogre and Beats?" he asked.

The two larger men had fallen to the Aryshan attacks beyond the proposed threshold where Antony and the others would seal off the ship and work their pressure scheme. They'd been beaten within an inch of their life, and Dalton didn't even know if they'd managed to survive. The Aryshan hand-to-hand attacks had been brutal. They broke bones without breaking a sweat, and the two men had been kicked in the head multiple times. Odds of them still being alive were astronomically low.

"There's nothing we can do about them now. They knew what they were getting into."

Had they though? The other prisoners didn't appear to buy his explanation. Judging from their sour expressions, it made them more uncomfortable. Dalton didn't have a lot of time to convince them to keep fighting.

"We're out of time. We have to kick those alien bastards out of here." He tried to sound strong, like a man worth following.

Silence lingered in reply, as if the others waited for the Tarantula to make his decision.

Finally, the Tarantula nodded. "Let's do it," he said.

Dalton motioned them all forward. He would have to take charge, show them his bravery. He swaggered down the corridor to where the Aryshans had last been seen. If all went well, the blast from the overloading pulse rifle had removed most of their opposition. He inclined his head toward the Tarantula.

"Hey, do you think you could rig up a couple more pulse rifles to overload like that?"

The Tarantula lifted a single finger and two of the other prisoners came forward, holding their weapons out. "I had Speedy and No-Tooth fix up two of them already. Pull the trigger, and they'll start the overload."

Dalton found out why the prisoner had been named "No-Tooth" when the man smiled. His mouth looked emptier than space.

"We'll need them," Dalton said. "I'll let you guys know when to fire. Let's go."

He continued down the corridor. There would be no one to shield him from Aryshan fire this time. His palms sweat, and Dalton realized he had been gripping his pulse rifle far too tightly. Nerves did no good in this situation. He had to be strong.

A lone Aryshan came into view. Dalton pulled his trigger.

The Aryshan's eyes went wide as the blast sounded. He dove in an opening on the opposite side of the corridor.

272

Dalton rushed forward as fast as he could. The alien would have the advantage of cover, where Dalton would be exposed.

When the Aryshan showed his head again, the Tarantula shot true. The alien's head exploded with its gooey blood splattering on the floor.

"Damn," Dalton said.

"I miss this shit," the Tarantula said, coming up beside him.

He pointed his gun into the room where the Aryshan had dove into. The alien's body lay on the floor, but he had no backup nearby. The room had a few cots, some cleaning supplies, nothing of interest.

"Let's keep moving," Dalton said. "The pressure doors should be up ahead and to the left."

They kept moving forward. Before they reached the corner, the Tarantula flung his arm out to stop Dalton's progress. When Dalton had stopped, he brought a finger to his lips and then pointed to his ear.

Dalton listened. Footsteps. Talking in an alien language.

The Tarantula looked back to the others and motioned to them. He held out his hand expectantly. Speedy delivered him his weapons. The Tarantula took it and pulled the trigger, his eyes glinting as they often did when he inflicted pain.

The rifle buzzed as it came closer to overload. Mouthing a count to three, the Tarantula chucked the rifle around the corner. It banked off of a wall and disappeared out of Dalton's sight.

Aryshans shouted.

He expected to hear an explosion tearing the Aryshans apart as they had the last time they'd flung the rigged rifle at them. A moment later, the rifle spun right back to them. The Aryshans had pushed it back. The pulse rifle spun a couple of times and then stopped in place, less than a meter from Dalton.

"Run!" The Tarantula shouted.

He took off faster than the other prisoners could react, shoving No-Teeth out of the way. Dalton moved after him. The explosion would come at any moment. He jumped, diving for a safer place.

The rifle overloaded and rocked the corridor. The floor plates shook. Dalton could feel the heat behind him. No-Teeth had jumped and crashed atop Dalton. A wave of hot energy blasted their direction, but No-Teeth's body served as a shield for Dalton. The prisoner atop him let out a guttural howl in Dalton's ear.

Dalton pushed the man off of him, seeing that his fellow prisoner had his shirt and the skin off of his back burned off. "Aw, hell. That looks terrible."

No-Teeth writhed on the floor, curling himself up into a fetal ball.

Dalton pushed himself to his feet, gently touching the man's shoulder. Before he could try to assist No-Teeth, Aryshans bounded around the corner. No-Teeth's modified rifle lingered within reach. Dalton quickly pulled the trigger, and then bee-lined down the hall away from the Aryshans, leaving the overloading rifle in place.

Pulse shots fired after him. One of the other prisoners took the brunt of the blasts. Dalton didn't hesitate to use the convulsing man as a shield before spinning back into the room with the cots. The Tarantula had hustled further down the hallway, and he returned fire toward the Aryshans.

Dalton tapped his wrist comm. He brought it close to his face. "If anyone's listening, drop that pressure door now!"

Another explosion sound rocked the hallway, shaking the beds inside the room. Dalton braced himself against the wall. If the Aryshans made it through, he might be able to hide and catch them by surprise. He held still for several moments.

No footsteps came down the corridor. No one passed the door's threshold. Could it be the explosion had taken out the Aryshans as he'd intended?

Dalton peeked his head into the corridor. Body parts littered the corridor, along with broken and melted metal from the walls. The sight disgusted him.

With no apparent sign of danger, Dalton stepped fully into the hallway. He spotted other prisoners who had run down the hall. The Tarantula stood among them.

"No-Teeth," he said.

"Yeah," Dalton said with regret

"We're losing too many of our clan. We should have never agreed to come to the colony," the Tarantula said.

"Maybe so." Dalton frowned. "But we're here now, nothing we can do about that. It looks like the bridge got the pressure door closed. We should go meet up with the others."

47

THE PLEASURE OF PAIN

Toltair Orbit, The Ark

Kiyomi froze in place. She didn't know what to do or how to react. If she let go of her weapon, the squad of six Aryshans in front of her would likely gun her down anyway. She could possibly take out one or two of them before she did. Would that help? The loss of life would be too high.

She had no willingness to become a martyr and die for this group of colonists. This trip had been a venture to start a new legacy for herself, for her father, one where the DePino name lasted on a new world *without* endless war. If she had stayed behind, she could have had that as a scientist, as a business leader of DePino Industries, but she had come here. She couldn't give up the dream.

Kiyomi couldn't get words out in return. Her jaw hurt far too badly. She made a slow movement to lower her gun, crouching to set it down in front of her. Then, she placed her hands up in surrender.

The Aryshans moved forward, one in particular looking her over and searching her. He pointed to his dead companion on the ground and then said some words that didn't sound friendly. The Aryshan met her eyes, staring at her with cold, black orbs. He seemed soulless.

"Where... the hidden weapon?" The Aryshan asked.

Kiyomi blinked. He spoke to her in English, though his accent came across so thick she could hardly make out the words.

"I don't know anything about any weapon," Kiyomi said. Her heart raced. Did the Aryshans believe they had some kind of secret weapon on this ship? With the ark's unique design and the protection, Kiyomi could understand why they would board and be searching for something unique here. "This is a civilian ship. I promise!"

"*Kiyek*," the Aryshan said, drawing back his weapon as if it were a baseball bat. He swung at her head.

Before she could react, the blow hit her across the back of the skull. Kiyomi fell, unable to steady herself. She felt sick immediately. Intense pain flared in her, worse than the hit to her jaw before. She struggled to breathe as the world around her turned into a haze. The thick, metallic boots of the Aryshans seemed to spin in front of her. She'd definitely suffered a concussion. It would be dangerous to fall unconscious, but she was so, so tired. Her head throbbed.

Shouting came from outside the cargo bay. The colonists mumbled to each other. Anxiety grew within her. Kiyomi couldn't look up. She could hardly focus. Unable to contain it any longer, she vomited onto the floor. *Oh, God...*

Shots fired. The world around her swirled.

"Doctor," she tried to mutter, though no sound came from her lips.

Screaming and yelling enveloped her, echoed in her ears. The Aryshans moved away from her. Something had distracted them.

Kiyomi struggled to lift her head.

Pulse fire erupted in her field of vision. One Aryshan went down, and then a second. The one who had hit her fell, his head landing in Kiyomi's vomit. He faced upward, mumbling. And then he stopped moving.

Kiyomi couldn't help but feel terrible for him. What an awful way to die. The spinning stopped her from doing much else other than keeping in place. Breathing took tremendous effort.

The other Aryshans put up a valiant effort, trying to use the cargo bay doors as cover and make a final stand. They were well trained, but they lacked in numbers. Several brave colonists grappled with the Aryshans, pulling their arms back, forcing them to drop their weapons as they brawled.

Men in red jumpsuits flooded into the room. They had no mercy for the remaining Aryshans. They came up to point-blank range and shot the Aryshans dead, one by one.

One of the men crouched by her, trying to pick her up.

"No," Kiyomi said, barely able to speak. Her head pounded. She didn't want to be moved.

A voice came through the wrist comm on the man crouched in front of her. "The hatches are sealed. How are you doing down there?"

She recognized the voice. Antony Lemkin. Warmth filled her. Safety. It would be all right.

"We've cleared out all of the aliens we could find and made it to the cold sleep chambers. Got someone here who appears to be a bit injured," the man said. He frowned as he looked beside her. "We have one casualty at least, male."

"Is Kiyomi DePino down there?" Antony asked.

"I'm not sure who that is," the man said.

"Me," Kiyomi said as best she could. "Antony..."

"I think I found her. She's in need of medical attention. You get back to running the ship, and we'll figure out the rest. Dalton out." He tapped his wrist comm to end the call. He took Kiyomi by the arm, gentle with his touch. "Can you stand?"

The spinning slowed. Her head still throbbed. Each heartbeat seemed to bring fresh pain to her, as if the blood pumping through her cried out as it moved. It took everything in her to push herself to her feet. When she did manage to stand, she wobbled, embarrassingly having to hold onto this Dalton to keep herself upright. "Thanks."

"Don't thank me yet. We'll have to find a doctor, and I hope we have medical supplies aboard this boat," Dalton said.

They would. If she could speak beyond a word or two through the pain in her jaw, she would have directed him to them. But they'd accomplished the impossible. Even with the pain, the death, the destruction that others caused in the way—Antony would take care of them. They would reach their new world.

48

SNAP, CRACKLE, POP

ANTONY LEANED over the front of Evelyn's station, trying to peer at the display. The display showed both of the pressure doors.

"They're sealed. Time to push the pressure," Evelyn said.

He hoped this gambit would work.

Evelyn's display had a bar which showed steadily increasing pressure numbers. They didn't want to push too hard, too fast and break the environmental system, but they also needed to raise the levels fast enough for the differential to pop the other vessels off of them.

The pressure reached about seven kilograms per centimeter, double that of standard human tolerances. It could take double or even triple the amount to complete the task. All the excess air pressure would dissipate into space. If this worked.

The bridge quieted to nothing but their air system.

"Thirteen kilos per centimeter," Evelyn said. The glow of the light from the display reflected on her face as she sat hunched over it. "Anyone who wasn't dead before has to be now."

"If it doesn't work, we can go invade *their* ships afterward," Rawle said.

"We have numbers, but they've got more weapons and better training. It wouldn't be a good idea," Antony said.

His security team and the prisoners had to be exhausted from fighting by now. But how many Aryshans remained on the ship? They must have had most of their planned invasion force inside the ark, which meant Antony's plan would have killed a fair number of them. Deaths he'd wanted to avoid by stepping down as governor. Could he ever get away from war?

Evelyn sat up straighter, her eyes widening. "It's working. Look."

She pointed to the main holodisplay, which had its cameras turned in a split-screen view of the points where the Aryshan ships had extended their thin connecting tubes to attach to the ark.

It didn't go as he'd pictured, but it did work. He'd figured the tubes would pop off in a clean motion, like the cork from a champagne bottle. Instead, the tubes burst, like balloons popping, expelling all of the air.

But it didn't matter. It worked!

The environmental system went into overdrive trying to keep the pressure high amidst meeting full vacuum. Air ducts rattled, barely able to contain the force being pushed through. The controls blinked and sounded a warning, sensors only capable of seeing this change in pressure as a bad thing. The system power draw went into redline.

"Dammit!" Evelyn said.

She hurried to adjust the settings, tapping onto her console to cut off the vents. The pressure dampers closed, sealing the impacted sections of the ship. Large plates of metal would protect the rest of the inhabitants of the ark.

"Look!" Rawle said, calling Antony's attention to the display screen.

The Aryshan ships, without their attached tubes, floated off to the side and away. One tilted awkwardly, scraping into the ark, but fended off by the anti-magnetic repulsion that its hull field created to avoid asteroids. They were free.

Rawle clapped at the view. Evelyn followed, and Antony couldn't help but do the same. If they couldn't cheer on their own work, who would for them? No one else had any clue what went on here.

Evelyn slumped into her chair. "Wow. I need a drink."

Antony laughed. "Tell me about it. That was more stressful than watching the polls come in on election night," he said, stepping toward the big display, standing tall, victorious. It felt good, but they weren't done yet. "Punch it to FTL, Rawle. Don't let them get a chance to recover and shoot at us."

Rawle completed his commands. The air deadened, and the lights dimmed as the engines drew power from the crystal drive.

The ark jumped. With the artificial gravity, Antony couldn't feel a thing in reality, even though he swore he felt a small tug forward. Funny how the human brain made up some sensations. The screen showed a blur around the hull. The Aryshans were history. They wouldn't be able to catch up with the ark.

Antony smiled, seeing Rawle had held up his hand. He clasped it with a firm grip.

"We did it." He repeated the motion with Evelyn. "I can't believe it."

"Same," Evelyn said. "Now if you don't mind, I'd like to go find Ms. DePino and assist."

"We all should," Antony agreed. "Nothing left to do here. We'll have a few of our engineers check over the systems and then get everyone—including ourselves— into cold sleep. I'll see you in a hundred years, give or take?"

EPILOGUE

IXORA COLONY

THE FULL SIDEWALL of the ark descended onto the surface of Ixora, Antony watching with baited breath.

It had been designed to act as a giant ramp, over three stories tall and the length of four full cargo holds. It would be enough to get their large machinery equipment down to the surface, with a truck and crane to pull the large crystal drive unit out of the engine compartment for use as the colony's power plant.

The sky on Ixora didn't have the familiar blue hue of Earth, but instead the atmosphere had a pink hue, with a darker orange horizon. It made for an interesting view, a reddish tint coloring everything from the grass to the mountain ranges on the horizon. There would be fewer seasons here, less variation, much like the equator on Earth, but the cooler bands to the north and south on Ixora would remain permanently frozen. The ice caps comprised a third of the planet.

Three moons circled overhead, two above them now, bright in the face of the redder sunlight which gave them more definition than Luna.

The ark had set down on a peninsula, the shape of a miniature Italy, but with enough area to allow several cities across it, as well as plenty of room for building and exploration. The water supply nearby made the area suitable for habitation, and a flat clearing would make it easy for them to build. They still had a lot of analysis to do with tidal situations, weather patterns and the like, but from what they'd observed so far, the center of this peninsula would work for an initial colony.

"The soil is pretty high in nitrogen," Kiyomi said.

She sounded elated, standing and overlooking the open plain in front of them where they would make their home.

Antony turned to look at her. She glowed in the strange, Ixoran light. It gave her an exotic quality which he found beautiful. He didn't want to think those thoughts, or feel those feelings, trying to push them firmly down into the depths of his cold sleep-clouded head. It probably played tricks on his whole physiology, which may have explained his sudden interest in Kiyomi. He shook his head.

"No, it's not high in nitrogen?" Kiyomi asked, quirking a brow.

"Sorry, lost in my own thoughts," Antony confessed. "I'm not sure what that means, but I assume it's good."

"Very good. It means most of our crops should be able to adjust without much modification," Kiyomi said.

She gazed off into the distance, pride swelling in her face. Her eyes seemed to moisten. It must have been quite an accomplishment for her, fulfilling her family's vision, more than it meant to the rest of the crew.

Another woman, Morgan Ezra, arrived at the end of the ramp, along with several members of her security team.

"Sir," she said to Antony.

"Antony is fine."

"Old habits," Morgan said. Her face flushed, growing even redder in the pink light. "My team's ready to set up an electrified force field around the ark. It'll operate off of solar power, and we can move it any time we need to push the colony boundaries out. I've got a couple members of my team willing to scope out the wildlife and catalogue them with drone biosensors. We should have an idea of what lives here close to the colony site in the next couple days. Then we'll be able to send out scouting teams."

"You make it sound so militaristic. This is a bold new world for us." Antony motioned outward.

He took in a deep breath. The atmosphere here had a slight sulfuric smell, one that didn't make it feel like taking a breath of fresh air. Before they'd landed, they'd been assured by the science team the atmosphere would be breathable, but the aroma would be something they'd have to get used to.

"We've come this far to get away from the hectic pace of Earth. Let's have some fun," Kiyomi said.

Despite Kiyomi's optimism, they had to make sure they established their food sources sooner rather than later. The animals would need to be able to live and reproduce. So many variables, so many things to go wrong.

But those were problems to solve later. For now, he had a place where he could direct without having to deal with the logistics of a four-hundred-year-old bureaucracy, its military, and its various governmental branches. Thinking about Earth brought him a headache. He had to show the way. He put on a smile, the kind that he'd used for glad-handing at political events in the past. *Smile for the cameras.*

"Shall we take our first steps on the planet?" Antony asked.

Several colonists had gathered at the ramp's opening. They had taken a vote among the senior staff of the colony, determining Antony and Kiyomi should be the first to set foot on the planet. Next would be the various chiefs of staff, and then the others.

One of the prisoners approached him. He didn't seem as intimidating as Antony would have pictured a hardened criminal. One wouldn't have thought him to be much of a brute given his physique, save for the shaved head and a strange spider tattoo.

Preconceived judgements wouldn't help anyone. These people

deserved a fresh start as much as any of the other colonists. Antony extended his hand.

"Antony Lemkin," he said.

"Governor, yeah? I liked what you were doing back home. Back on Earth, rather. I'm Dalton Ward." He took Antony's hand, a bit firmer than was comfortable.

Antony didn't flinch. These types responded to straight-forward confidence. "That's right. This is home now."

He turned, as he would have plenty of time to socialize with everyone on the colony later. He offered his arm to Kiyomi. She linked her dainty arm with his, her fingers curling around his bicep.

"Ready?" Kiyomi asked at a near whisper.

Holovid cameras from behind would be on them. This would be a moment for Ixoran history books, and that made it all the more exciting. How would future generations look back at this moment? Would they remember him and Kiyomi as heroes? Would school children watch this moment in perpetuity, as he had grown up watching Neil Armstrong stepping onto the moon, or Brian N. Meier breaking dirt on the first terraformed colony in the Novus system? Or would they be remembered at all?

No, he wouldn't allow negative thinking. They had this ark, and better plans than any migration endeavor in human history. Nothing in this universe could stop them.

Antony descended the ramp with Kiyomi, unable to think any further except for making sure he planted each foot firmly in front of the other. He felt lighter than air, which in some ways he should have, since Ixora had approximately ninety-five percent of the gravity of Earth. Not enough to make much a difference in living, except to make him happier when he would step on a scale.

They reached the end of the ramp and paused. The red grass flattened where the ramp met the Ixoran surface, but stood about at about three decimeters beyond the ramp. Kiyomi turned her head toward him. Her dark brown eyes sparkled, reflecting the sunlight. Antony's smile changed from one for the cameras to something genuine. His heart filled with joy for the first time he could remember since Bethany's passing. He gave a knowing wink to Kiyomi.

Together, they took one small step.

NEXT IN THE SERIES...

The Aryshan War rages on in The Stars Entwined! Read about the war from the front lines, as Earth sends a spy into the heart of the Aryshan Empire!

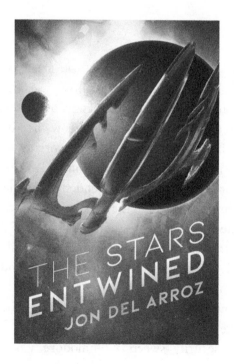

Join Jon's mailing list for updates on new releases.

AN EXCERPT FROM THE STARS
ENTWINED

AN ASSIGNMENT LIKE THIS COULD MAKE OR BREAK A CAREER. THOSE were rarities in Internal Affairs, with most cases dealing with petty theft, embezzlement, or matters requiring a few interviews and some paperwork to settle. Lieutenant Sean Barrows had been good at that job, keeping his head down and getting his work done. He'd never had such a high-profile case as his investigation on Palmer Station.

The transport shuttle hatch descended onto the station's flight deck. Its passengers crowded the exit, bottlenecking through the hatch to exit one at a time. Sean stood at the back of the line, ducking under the short hatch frame to accommodate his six feet in height. The line paused. Up ahead, security ran individual body scans on each passenger present.

"What's going on?" Sean asked a station security guard who walked along the line of travelers.

"Heightened security sweep. Commodore V'bosh's orders," the guard said.

That didn't give him too much new information. His assignment had been to interview Captain Jemile Grayson, someone from the fleet proper who had been investigating recent attacks in this sector of space. "I'm from INIA," Sean said to the guard, craning his neck to see the line of people extending in front of him. At this rate, it would take him hours to get through. "Any way I could bypass this?"

"Ident crystal please," the guard said, holding out his hand.

Sean reached into the pocket of his gray uniform and produced the crystal. The guard took it, stepping away to place the crystal in a scanner. He reviewed the information and called someone on a comm unit. Several moments later, he stepped forward. "You've been authorized. The commodore would like you to go directly to the scene of the latest incident. If you'd follow me, sir?"

Sean nodded. Though he had been hoping for a brief introduction to Captain Grayson, and an evening of settling in to adjust to local station time, it did appear as if some new emergency had created the need for additional security at the shuttle bay. Station personnel seemed tense, acting more formal than in his usual first encounters.

The guard led the way, and Sean followed without a word. They took a liftcar through several of the station's sections that led to a series of apartment quarters. The corridor they entered had been cordoned off, guards standing at the entrance. Those guards scanned Sean's escort's ident crystal before letting them pass.

They moved down the corridor until they reached an open door. Several members of station security swept the room with various equipment. Captain Grayson stood at the entryway, dressed in an Interplanetary Navy gray uniform, with a rank patch over his right breast pocket that signaled his captaincy. He looked exactly like his dossier: an aged face with dark skin, along with salt and pepper hair and beard. He had his hands on his hips, and he tapped the toe of his boot on the floor. "Any idea how long this is going to be?" he asked the men inside. "This is going to slow down the investigation another day or two at this rate."

The guard with Sean cleared his throat, stood at attention, and then saluted Captain Grayson. "Sir," he said.

Sean saluted as well, even though protocol from Internal Affairs technically kept him outside of the chain of command. It was better to be polite, especially to someone of such an advanced rank.

Captain Grayson turned, his face tight and lips clamped together.

He gave them a once-over. "At ease," he said. "What's going on? Did Commodore V'bosh send you to escort me to new quarters? I already told the last group, I'm not going without my belongings."

"No, sir," the guard said. "We have a visitor here from IA, Lieutenant Sean Barrows." He motioned toward Sean.

Grayson's glare was so strong it could have cut through the station hull. "I'm sorry you traveled all this way. At this point, you're probably not needed."

Sean tried to remain impassive. It wasn't unusual for the subject of his investigations to be hostile to him. After all, it was their career on the line. But information from someone like Grayson was as useful as anyone else. It would be best to keep a cordial relationship if he could manage it. That required de-escalation. "Why's that?" Sean asked in as polite a tone as possible.

Grayson pointed to the scene in front of him. "You see station forensics in there?"

"Yes," Sean said.

"I heard a strange beeping sound coming from the air vents in my quarters about an hour ago. Thankfully, I have sensitive hearing. It turns out it was a timed explosive device," Grayson said. "They keep scanning the room to make sure there's not another one, but I need my space." He raised the volume of his voice with the end of that statement, as if to be sure the men inside heard his frustration.

Sean watched the crew do their work. They covered every nook and cranny of the room, going through drawers, files, and everything. He could see why Grayson must have been frustrated with such an invasion of his privacy. By the same token, they couldn't risk another problem.

He had been ordered to look into Grayson's work in the sector. A few weeks had gone by, and there'd been little progress in confirming an increase in Aryshan activity in this area. More than that, a series of strange incidents had occurred around Grayson. The Senate back on Earth requested that IA get involved in bringing further evidence that the Aryshans were becoming aggressive and to monitor Captain

Grayson's work thus far. His report could determine far more than just the fate of this captain's career.

"I see you have your hands full here," Sean said, trying to be careful with what he said. "Has security made any headway as to who may have planted the explosive?"

Grayson grumbled and shook his head. "Not yet. They've been hovering in my quarters for hours."

"I see," Sean said. There was the possibility that Grayson planted it himself, but that seemed unlikely. Despite the coincidental nature of the recent incidents occurring around Grayson, he wasn't truly suspected of any wrongdoing beyond mismanagement of a case. That, and he had been accused of a propensity to lash out at his subordinates in inappropriate ways. Sean could see how there might be some truth to that.

"But you can bet it's the Aryshans," Grayson said.

There was something Sean could use. He quirked a brow at the Captain. "Why do you say that?"

Grayson took a couple of paces away from the door. His steps were hurried, his eyes cast to the floor. Concern filled his face. "I'm sure you've heard a great deal about the trader ship that disappeared inside Aryshan space. They were last seen on the scanners by my ship on a routine border patrol. We couldn't keep that one out of the media when it was so public."

"Yes, sir," Sean said. The incident had been one he'd studied on the transport flight over to the station. What he'd found interesting was that after the ship had disappeared, communications with the Aryshans had ground to a halt. Almost nothing had come across the border from them. Even the usual merchant channels had slowed compared to normal. "Then, there was the other incident, which occurred while you patrolled this sector, correct?"

Grayson frowned. "The disappearance of the *Hong Kong*. I was on station at the time, though it was during night cycle hours. Alarms went crazy throughout this place. I've never seen so many people rushing into the hallways in various stages of undress. By the time I reached main ops, the ship was long gone."

"Did they see which way it went?" Sean asked, somewhat jokingly. He wanted to alleviate some of Grayson's stress.

Grayson gave him a look like he was an idiot child. "Space doesn't work that way, Lieutenant. You have to realize, when a ship engages their crystal drive to go into FTL, it sends out energy patterns in several directions with little to no dissipation since there's no friction in the vacuum. Not only that but when your options are in three dimensions, it makes tracking routes much more difficult. Little details like that are why I suggested to the commodore against bringing out life-long dirtside personnel for investigations. Spatial experience matters."

Sean didn't want to argue that he had past experience on ships, stations, and planets with dome structures. His last assignment had been on Mars, but it wasn't relevant to the discussion. "What you say doesn't implicate Aryshans. Any number of groups could find value in one of our battleships. I know the outer colonies and worlds are plagued by raiders."

Grayson gestured wildly to his quarters. "An explosive was planted here, Lieutenant. I've been investigating the Aryshan involvement. It's not a coincidence." He took a deep breath to collect himself. "Have you heard of pirates operating this close to Aryshan space? Come now, Lieutenant. It's obvious who would benefit most from having that kind of intelligence, and the Aryshans have grown odder and more xenophobic over the last several years. Now, they have all the specs on my ship."

Sean didn't know much about the geopolitical situations with the Aryshans, and though Captain Grayson was biased and hostile, he was inclined to take his word on the matter.

Before he could ask another question, the forensics investigators came to the door, holding their equipment in their hands. "We're all wrapped up here, Captain," one of the investigators said.

"About time," Grayson muttered. He stepped aside to allow the investigators to pass. Then he moved into his quarters' doorway and turned to Sean. "If you'll excuse me, Lieutenant. It's been a rough day, and I'd like to have a bit of peace and quiet so I can get back to work on this." His eyes softened. "One more thing, though. Commodore V'bosh has told me you have interest in a command track. Even when you're the captain, you're never in command. All of our orders come down from government bureaucrats, whether the civilian board of directors for Palmer Station or the Earth senate. If I were allowed some leeway to profile them, rattle a few Aryshan feathers, we wouldn't be sitting here, and these cases would be solved. But procedures and politics dictate everything. And so, we have to work together."

This was the first indication that Grayson perceived him as anything but an enemy. Some might describe his behavior as erratic, but Sean wasn't ready to put something like that down in a report. "I'll keep that in mind."

"Good day, Lieutenant, Ensign," Grayson said, inclining his head to the guard who had brought Sean there. He tapped his door control panel, and it slid shut a moment later.

Sean had almost forgotten the guard existed, with him having been so quiet in the conversation. He turned to the man. "You don't say much."

The guard smirked. "I know better than to interrupt a conversation with Captain Grayson, sir. Would you like me to escort you to guest quarters?"

"Please," Sean said. He followed the guard down the corridor once more. They stayed silent along the walk. All he could do was think about the immense amount of work ahead of him.

Continue reading The Stars Entwined here!